THE SOUND OF MANY WATERS

SEAN BLOOMFIELD

For Ever

"The many Indians from Florida we saw were archers, and,
being very tall and naked, at a distance they appeared
giants... They had heard of us and of how we cured
and of the miracles Our Lord worked through us."

- Álvar Núñez Cabeza de Vaca,
Spanish Conquistador (c.1490-1558)

ACKNOWLEDGEMENTS

First of all, I would like to thank *you* for taking the time to
read this book. To my wife, Lisa, I am blessed to have you;
this book would have been impossible without your help and
understanding while I locked myself away to write. To all the
fantastic teachers I had while growing up—thank you for your
encouragement. I also want to acknowledge Jerald Melanich for
his books about Florida's native peoples and Julian Granberry
for his Timucua language dictionary; these works offer amazing
insights into the lost tribes of Florida and the role of the Spanish
in the New World. Also, throughout this book you will find
drawings believed to have been done by Jacques le Moyne, a
French artist who accompanied an expedition to La Florida in
1564. The drawings provide a rare glimpse into Timucua daily
life. There are simply too many others to mention, so, to my
family and friends, know that you are invaluable to me—try as
I might, I could never create characters as unique as you.

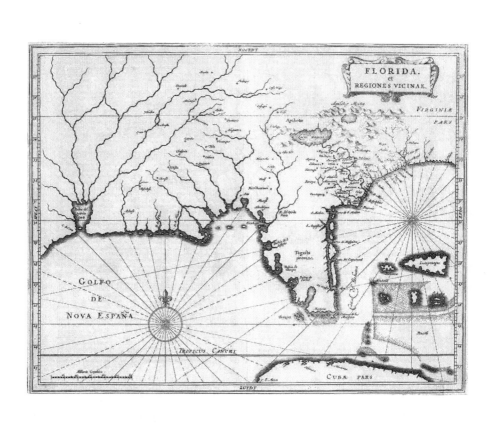

CHAPTER ONE

Death. It was familiar to Dominic, as certain as the changing tide, as mundane as a moonrise, and no less ordinary than the coming and going of a visitor.

Going where? He cared not.

As his father died — sprawled on the stone floor of a villa in northern Spain — he asked Dominic to hold his hand, but Dominic ignored him. The old man looked pathetic, Dominic thought, gazing into nothingness and drowning in air, like a fish thrown on deck.

"No quiero morir," were his father's last discernible words, which he said repeatedly. *I do not want to die.* The phrase gurgled out of his mouth with each exhale until it was nothing more than a soupy whimper. At midnight he began moaning and Dominic longed for the end so that he could finally put him in the ground and sell his belongings. He did not have to wait long; by morning, the old man was as stiff and crooked as a piece of driftwood. To Dominic's contentment, he was just as quiet, too.

The old man had passed, it seemed, while in the midst of trying to scream. His face held the look of a nightmare, and his gaping mouth was like the entrance to a dark cave, with rotten teeth for stalagmites and a fly darting around — a tiny bat. Dominic tried to close the old man's mouth but it sprang back open.

"Even now you cannot keep it shut," said Dominic.

1

Within a few years of arriving in *el Nuevo Mundo* — the New World — Dominic's loathing and indifference burgeoned while he ascended the military ranks. During his career, he rarely cried about anyone's passing, unless the feigning of sorrow might have somehow benefited him. It often did.

When natives raided the camp in El Salvador and killed the commander, Dominic stood beside his former superior's beautiful wife at the funeral mass and conjured up a believable fit of sobbing. Days later, Dominic held the commander's post, and, on several occasions, his widow as well.

The deaths that least affected him, though, were the ones he brought about himself. He could not even count the number of natives and Englishmen that had succumbed to his sword, the blade of which he lovingly sharpened and polished and caressed every night in the privacy of his quarters.

It was not until he killed his own son that he finally tasted the bitterness of grief.

The day had begun serenely enough, with a pink sky devoid of clouds and a gentle easterly breeze that barely wrinkled the surface of the Atlantic. Such a fine morning incited wariness in Dominic and caused him to contemplate the duality of nature; for there to be good weather in one place, he knew, there had to be foul weather somewhere else, but he never could have envisioned the raging behemoth of a cyclone that was thundering toward *La Florida*.

Juan, his son, woke late that morning, as he often did, and stumbled across the ship's uneven deck before relieving himself through a cannon hole.

Dominic watched Juan with disgust. "You've wasted the day in your bunk."

"It's still early, father," said Juan. "The sun has only just risen."

"A real man is always up *before* the sun."

"Yes, father. And perhaps one day I will be one."

Dominic's ship, the *Nuestra Señora de los Dolores* — Our Lady of Sorrows — sagged low in the Gulf Stream, her belly filled with silver ingots, gold doubloons and other treasures destined for Europe.

2

Already, the seven other galleons in the fleet had sailed a great distance ahead and out of sight. Dominic had insisted that he be the one to oversee the transport of the King's share, and so the other ships were not as bloated with riches as the *Señora de los Dolores* — or, as the other captains called her, *la Señora Gorda*. The Fat Lady.

Juan staggered to a cast-iron cauldron of steaming porridge that the galleymaster had prepared on deck, a manner of breakfast only possible in the calmest weather. With a ladle as long as his arm, Juan filled his bowl until it overflowed. He licked the sides of the ceramic to capture the surplus but winced when it burned his tongue.

Stupid boy, thought Dominic. You're as daft as your mother.

Juan slurped the porridge. Studying Juan's features, Dominic could understand why the other sailors mocked the boy. The dark skin, narrow eyes and flat nose clearly divulged the quarternative that sullied his genes, for Juan's mother — whom Dominic had sold into slavery — was a half-breed.

Dominic first noticed it eleven years before, when Juan was an emaciated infant who few thought would survive. As enamored with the new baby as he was disturbed by it, Dominic would lie beside Juan and watch him tremble in his sleep, hoping that the native might fade from Juan's appearance as he grew older. The opposite, however, took place, and as the years crept by, Juan looked more like his mother. There were days when Dominic considered leaving Juan at a remote port or enlisting him in an expedition bound for an uncharted jungle, but there was something within that prevented him from abandoning his son, some inexplicable instinct that contradicted Dominic's logic and, occasionally, infuriated him due to the nuisance of caring for a child in a savage land.

The first indication of an approaching threat was the birds. On most mornings, the terns and seagulls would leave their nighttime roosts and fly east over the open ocean where marauding tuna and dorado drove smaller fish to the water's surface. On this morning, however, the birds soared west toward land, clustered together in massive flocks that intermittently blotted out the sun. The sight troubled the sailors.

"You know what this means," said Pablo, the one-handed navigator whose white, windswept hair hung over his face like a foamy wave about to break.

Dominic, stoic, glanced at the birds. "Are you really so afraid of a little bad weather?"

"You know how eagerly these waters claim ships." Pablo squeezed a bead of his rosary between his fingers. "Do not pretend we're immune to God's wrath."

"Oh? And have we lost his favor?"

A gust of hot, humid wind flipped Pablo's hair back and caused the ship to lurch to one side. "I fear *you* have."

Red-hot anger rose in Dominic's neck. He had a sudden urge to mangle Pablo, but a faint howl drew both men to look east. In the distance, the water's surface changed from blue to gray as a wall of wind overtook it. Dominic and Pablo grabbed the ship's rail to brace themselves just as the barrage struck; the tremendous force of air caused the ship to list. Timbers groaned. Sails ripped. The cauldron of porridge overturned and sent a flood of hot, boiled oats across the deck; it surged over the feet of the sailors and spilled into the sea through the scuppers.

"Look now, captain!" Pablo screamed over the roar of wind. "You've offended God!"

His thoughts clouded by rage and fear, Dominic leaned back and struck Pablo across the face with a clenched fist. Pablo fell to the deck and slid to the opposite side of the galleon on a slimy bed of porridge. "Your sins are unforgiveable, captain!" he yelled. "Unforgiveable!"

The sky went black and the sea morphed into a churning clash of wind and water. The waves tossed the galleon around like porpoises playing with a baitfish. Fierce gusts piled globs of foam and seaweed onto the deck and Dominic watched in horror as a fish leapt from the ocean and was sucked up into the storm. When he felt the deck of the galleon undulate like a jellyfish, Dominic knew that his beloved *Señora* would not survive the storm. But there was one thing more valuable than the ship.

"Fill your pockets!" he screamed to the sailors, who stared at him with eyes full of terror. "Go below and gather all you can!"

4

"Papa?" Juan had planted himself beside Dominic as soon as the weather began to deteriorate.

"You, too, boy! As much as you can carry."

Hours later, Dominic woke on a deserted beach, surrounded by splintered shards of his ship and the bodies of his drowned crewmembers. He discovered Juan's body among them. The boy's pockets were filled with silver *reales* and his hands clenched gold doubloons. Weighed down by the coins and unable to swim, he had been sucked beneath the waves and spit onto shore, as if the ocean detested his metallic taste. The thing that troubled Dominic most was the serene smile on Juan's face. Death, it seemed, had finally brought him happiness, and he could not recall ever seeing Juan smile before.

CHAPTER TWO

Zane Fisher reached overboard and drove a steel gaff into the side of a 40-pound *mahi mahi*, pausing as the fish caught the water broadside with its wedge-shaped head. In one motion, Zane swung the mahi over the gunnel of his boat and into an open icebox, blood spattering all over the white deck. He slammed the lid of the icebox shut and lay on top of it. The fish — now incensed by the sting of the ice — thrashed inside so vehemently that it lifted the lid several inches despite the weight of Zane's 25-year-old body, like a caged beast trying to escape.

"He's still a bit green!" Zane yelled to his client, Miguel, referring not to the fish's emerald color but to the substantial amount of vigor left inside it. Miguel stood watching the spectacle from the safety of the bow, still holding the fishing rod.

"How the hell do you know it's a *he*?" said Miguel.

Zane was delighted that Miguel had finally engaged him in conversation. Best of all, he asked him a question he could answer. "It's simple really," said Zane. "The males, they've got square-shaped heads, and females' heads are curved. I guess human girls aren't the only ones with curves, right?"

Zane laughed at his own joke, hoping that the excitement of the moment would make Miguel more apt to laugh along with him. Miguel, however, did not even smile.

"I see," was all that he said.

The mahi continued to thrash inside the icebox, but with air flowing through its gills like slow poison, the veracity of its writhing diminished and Zane was able to latch the lid. He stood and wiped the blood off his face and listened to the fish's tail thump against insulated plastic.

What motivated the fish to continue fighting inside the icebox? Was it fear? Anger? Did it somehow know that it would never again stalk the quiet depths or glide on saline currents? Whatever the case, Zane wanted it to die soon. It saddened him to see anyone — or anything — suffer.

Only moments before, the fish had been prowling a deep expanse of ocean several miles off the coast of Palm Beach, basking in the balmy flow of the Gulf Stream. Its prey that day was flying fish and it had used a patch of sargassum seaweed as a shady cover, ambushing any school that passed. Like most local fishermen, Zane cherished sargassum. With tiny natural buoys scattered between its yellow leaves, sargassum was unique among seaweeds; it stayed afloat during its entire life cycle. It was a thriving ecosystem that existed solely on the tops of waves, a tangled oasis for countless creatures including baitfish, juvenile sea turtles, crustaceans, and the myriad predators that consumed them. Zane's heart had thumped with excitement when he spotted dozens of flying fish leaping frantically, bereft of their usual grace, from beneath a spread of sargassum.

"Get ready!" Zane said to Miguel as they approached. "Something's chasing that school of flying fish."

Miguel glanced toward the melee but showed no excitement about it, so Zane attempted a joke in hopes of drawing out a smile. "Or should I say a *flock* of flying fish?"

Miguel looked at Zane with a blank, almost irritated, stare. But the clatter of a strike ended the unpleasant moment, and Zane turned to see one of the trolling rods bowed over. Line peeled off the reel, causing it to sing out a high-pitched wail. The mahi at the other end of the line leapt from the water and shook its head in an attempt to throw the hook. Its body shimmered like molten metal in the afternoon sun. Zane was awestruck by the sight, but his mind quickly sprang to work.

"Grab that rod!" he shouted to Miguel. "Start reeling!"

Now in the icebox, the mahi was finally succumbing to the alien atmosphere of the world above water. Flopping turned to faint wiggling and soon all movement ceased. Zane lifted the lid. The skin of the fish — which had been vibrant and neon-green just moments before — was now a dull, silvery hue, and its eyes stared into oblivion. The beast was dead.

"Sweet fish, Miguel!" Zane's body still tingled with adrenaline. "Hold it up and I'll snap a picture."

Miguel glared at Zane. "I told you before. No photos."

In his four years as a charter fishing captain, Zane had never experienced such disinterest and animosity from a client before. What would normally be hailed as a trophy catch — a cause for celebratory high-fives and cold beers all around — seemed to mean nothing to Miguel, not even important enough to commemorate with a photograph. It was as if fishing was the last thing he wanted to be doing, and yet he had agreed to pay $500 for the trip. Miguel's dark face had carried that same look of indifference and melancholy throughout the day. None of the battles with fish — no matter how violent and thrilling — seemed to invigorate Miguel, nor had the sight of a sailfish vaulting from the ocean as if it were trying to fly. In fact, Miguel spent most of the day staring at the sky, even while fighting the mahi that now lay dead in the icebox.

To each his own, Zane thought. As long as I get paid.

Miguel glanced at his watch — a diamond-encrusted *Rolex* that flung veins of light across the deck whenever the sun hit it — and then looked at the screen of the boat's GPS system.

"This is where I want to fish next," he said, pointing to an area on the digital map that was about five miles north of their position.

"The bite's been more to the south," said Zane.

Miguel stared at Zane for an uncomfortable moment, so Zane tried to fill the silence with more words. "The Gulf Stream, you know, it comes really close to shore just south of here, and the fish—"

"I don't care," interrupted Miguel. "I hired you to take me fishing, and I'm telling you where I want to go. Take me there."

Zane looked away from Miguel's icy gaze. There was a disturbing air about the man, as if some vile thing lurked beneath his murky surface. Most fishermen lived by an unspoken code of respect and kindness while on the water, as if thankful for the mere opportunity to live a life connected to it. Boaters, for example, always waved when passing other boaters — a stark contrast to the hand gestures common on Florida's busy roadways — and anglers, for the most part, were courteous toward each other. With his terse, businesslike demeanor, however, Miguel was like no other fisherman Zane had ever met. Was he hiding something? Perhaps it was nothing more than a personality flaw, Zane finally told himself, or the product of a difficult life. And who was he to judge, anyway?

Zane forced a smile. "Maybe they'll be biting up north today, too. Let's give it a shot."

Miguel stared ahead. "Let's."

The center console fishing boat slid over the waves at over 40 miles per hour in the direction of Miguel's GPS coordinates. Zane glanced toward the shore as they cruised. Now five miles off the coast of Jupiter, Florida — his hometown since birth — he could see the Jupiter Lighthouse piercing the horizon, its hibiscus-red tower distinct against a dull summertime haze. Built in 1860 atop an Indian shell mound and taller than any of the condominiums and mansions that surrounded it, the lighthouse was a backdrop for some of Zane's most potent memories. The lamp at the top had been preserved and still swirled every night, casting an intense beam of white light across the entire town. It was like God's searchlight, Zane imagined, because it always found him in moments of intense happiness, danger or despair.

It shone down on him, for example, on the night of his 15th birthday when he invited his classmate and secret crush, Lucia, out in his canoe to fish for snook beneath the Loxahatchee River Bridge. He had been surprised and terrified when she said yes. With her heart-stopping smile, coconut brown skin, and eyes the color of shallow sea, Lucia had always intrigued him, but Zane was a shy boy who rarely found the courage to talk to girls.

That's why he asked her to go fishing; saying the word 'date' was impossible.

There was no wind that night. As Zane paddled the canoe across the glassy surface of the Loxahatchee, he glanced at Lucia. With her head tilted back to gaze at the night sky, she looked almost supernatural against the cosmos. Her shawl of hair, draped over her shoulders, was as black as the tannin-stained river below, and her skin was awash in starlight.

She's perfect, Zane thought, but what's a girl like her doing in my canoe?

"People shouldn't group the stars into constellations," said Lucia. "They're so much better when you look at them as a whole."

"I guess most people like order," said Zane.

"Like Miss Harper."

Zane laughed. Miss Harper, the neurotic school librarian, was known to throw books at students who talked too loud during study hours. She chucked a book at Zane once, but he was in no position to complain—Miss Harper's weapon that day was merely *The Old Man and the Sea* in paperback. An exceptionally defiant girl, it was rumored, once took *War and Peace* to the head.

They soon reached the bridge and Zane dropped a cinder-block anchor overboard to keep the canoe in place. He picked up a fishing rod and was about to cast the line when he noticed that Lucia was no longer staring at the universe. She was looking at him.

"Hi," said Zane. He flushed. Couldn't he have said something more interesting?

Lucia smiled. "Hi," she said, and then she leaned forward and pressed her mango-flavored lips to his. Zane had never kissed a girl before, and he could not imagine there being any feeling closer to bliss, not even catching a 1,000-pound blue marlin or winning first place in a fishing tournament. He closed his eyes and felt the warm glow of God's searchlight envelope him.

Zane and Miguel both heard the drone of the airplane at the same time. They were approaching the location where Miguel had demanded to go, so Zane slowed the boat to idle speed.

As he had done several times that day, Miguel peered up at the approaching aircraft—this one a single-engine seaplane—and studied it with squinted eyes.

"Here we go," said Miguel. He waved to the plane with broad sweeps of arms.

"What are you doing?" asked Zane.

Miguel turned. Zane's heart sank when he saw the .45 revolver aimed at his face. "I shouldn't expect a problem from you, should I, captain?"

"No, sir." Zane shook his head.

"Glad to hear it. If you do everything I tell you, then maybe you won't end up as shark food tonight. Am I clear?"

Zane trembled. "Yes, sir." Was this really happening? It felt like a nightmare, albeit a vivid one.

Miguel turned back toward the plane which was now almost directly overhead and flying at an abnormally low altitude. He raised his arm with his fist clenched and then dropped it toward the water. A small door on the airplane flung open and a square object fell out. It tumbled end over end and struck the ocean fifty yards away, sending a plume of white water into the air.

"Get us over there," said Miguel. "Quickly!"

Zane gunned the engines and brought the boat alongside the object, which now bobbed on the ocean's surface. It looked like a large pillow wrapped in cellophane. Everything suddenly made sense. Zane could see that the object was a bale—a common way for drug runners to deliver their products to the United States, strong enough to survive an impact but light enough to float. It was probably filled with cocaine, Zane guessed, cultivated by modern-day slaves in the highlands of Latin America, and then put on the plane for delivery. Miguel was likely the middleman in charge of collecting the bale, dividing the drugs into saleable units, and distributing them among a network of dealers in South Florida. It would then be divided further, sold through various underground channels, and, ultimately, complete its cycle after being consumed by a microcosm of society, everyone from the wealthy to the homeless. It was, as Zane knew well, the ultimate product.

Miguel leaned over the gunwale with a boathook in his hand. "Closer." When the bale came within reach, Miguel stuck the curved end of the boathook through a loop on the package and pulled it in. He grabbed the corner of the bale and strained to haul it over the side.

"Help me bring it in," said Miguel. Zane paused. Miguel was leaning over the side of the boat, focused on the bale. Here, right before Zane, was the perfect opportunity to push Miguel into the water and save himself.

"I said help me, dammit!" Miguel snarled.

Zane sighed, then leaned over and grabbed a corner of the bale. Violence had never come easily to him. Together they wrenched the bale into the boat.

"Seems awfully heavy for cocaine," said Zane.

"Who said it was coke?" Miguel gazed at the bale with eyes alight, as if he were looking at a beautiful woman. He ran his hand over the slick, wet plastic, and then he looked up at Zane with a crooked smile. "But if I tell you what it is, then I'll have to kill you, and unfortunately I still need your help."

That was the first time Miguel had smiled in front of Zane, but, to Zane's dismay, he had done it while delivering a death threat. Zane had only known this much fear a few times in his life. The first was when, at 13 years old, he had gone scuba diving with his father, Skip, off the coast of Hobe Sound, north of Jupiter, on the opening day of lobster season. A tropical storm had recently skirted the coast and muddied the water, but bad visibility did not deter them. They were hoping to catch their limit of "bugs" — the local term for Caribbean spiny lobster — and after splashing into the ocean and scouring the reef for ten minutes they came upon several of them huddled beneath a coquina ledge.

Zane tried to snare the largest lobster of the group but it bolted away, leaving only a cloud of drifting sediment. Skip swam after it and disappeared into the murk. Zane held onto the ledge and waited, but after a few minutes Skip had not come back. Panic swelled inside him and he swam off to look for his father. He shined his diving flashlight in every direction as he searched along the edge of the reef, hopeful that Skip would see the beam cutting through the cloudy water. Instead, a shadow much larger than his father appeared; the commotion had attracted an 8-foot-long bull shark. Zane froze and sank toward the bottom.

As the shark approached, Zane could see its black, emotionless eye studying him. The mouth gaped enough to reveal the tips of its serrated teeth, and its gills flared out like window shutters in a gale. As the shark passed him and circled around, Zane noticed a coral cave to his side. He pulled himself into it. The shark glided by and vanished back into the haze.

Thank you, he thought, not quite sure who he was thanking.

While he waited to ensure that the shark did not return, something inside the cave caught his eye: a small, yellow thing partially concealed by sand. A streak of sunlight swept over the object and it glinted. Was it a lost fishing lure? Or some hardware from a boat? Zane closed his fingers around it and pulled it in; the regulator almost fell out of his mouth when he opened his hand. There against the familiar creases of his palm lay something quite unfamiliar: a Spanish doubloon made of solid gold. The designs on the coin were rudimentary but clear. On the front was the number 8 and what looked like an old sailing ship, and on the back was an etching of the Virgin Mary with twelve stars around her head. A phrase was engraved on the border: *Nuestra Señora de los Dolores.*

Zane shot to the surface like a torpedo, forgetting all about the shark and ignoring the safety rules of scuba such as ascending slowly. He found his father sitting on the edge of the boat, tapping his bare feet to vintage reggae and nursing on a sweaty bottle of *Kalik* beer. If Zane hadn't found something so wonderful, he would have been furious.

"There you are, kiddo," said Skip. "Get any bugs?"

Zane removed his dive mask. "No bugs."

"Sorry I didn't come back for you. But look what I got." Skip held up a large lobster by its antennae.

"Nice one, Dad. I got something, too." Zane held up the doubloon. Reflecting the midday sun, it looked like a ball of fire in his hand.

Skip dropped the lobster. "Holy crap," he muttered.

Upon returning home, Zane's mother, Samantha, urged Skip to sell the doubloon to pay for the breast augmentation surgery that she so desperately wanted. Zane, their only child, begged them not to sell it, but they did anyway, and within a month Samantha was shopping for larger bras. That Christmas, however, Zane woke to find the doubloon on a leather cord around his neck. Without telling Samantha, Skip had purchased the doubloon back from the collector and hired a jeweler to make a pendant of it, and then he put it around Zane's neck on Christmas Eve. How Skip acquired the money, Zane never knew. A few weeks later, Skip bought a new pickup truck, left Samantha, and moved in with a younger woman, a student at *Florida Atlantic University*.

"Why did you leave mom?" Zane asked him several years later.

Skip thought for a moment. "I was bored."

Even now as he stood captive by Miguel, Zane felt comfort knowing that the doubloon hung around his neck. It was his connection to something ancient, something eternal, and he often wondered about its origins. Sometimes he tried to envision who might have held it long ago.

Rubbing his fingers across it, he could feel the face of the Virgin Mary. His was a tangled faith: a concoction of his mother's agnosticism, his father's unbridled optimism, and his own intense love of nature. He believed in *something* but was not sure what. It—whatever *it* was—seemed as invisible as air, and yet just as essential.

Zane gazed at the bale on the deck of his boat, increasingly curious about what it contained. Although it was not uncommon for bales like this to wash up on the coast, he had never seen one before. He had, however, often wondered what he would do if he did. It was a frequent topic of conversation at waterfront bars with other captains and mates, usually spurred by a question like this:

"What if you were out fishing one day, no one else around, and you found a bale?"

Would he abide by the law and call the authorities, or would he stow it in the bilge and try to sell it? There was a darker time in Zane's life when he would have done the latter without hesitation, probably even keeping a small portion of its contents for his own enjoyment, but now he hoped he would do the right thing if ever faced with such a choice. An average bale of cocaine could fetch half a million dollars on the black market, casting a powerful temptation for fishermen, most of whom made barely enough money to live and who, on a daily basis, were surrounded by the glitz and excess of South Florida. Given that offshore anglers plied the coastal waters year-round, and due to the fact that white, floating objects could be spotted against the cobalt face of the Atlantic from miles away, it was no secret within the fishing community that wayward caches of drugs were sometimes picked up and secretly "disposed of." Captains even had a code name for bales: square groupers. For a man with weak morals and nagging debts, coming across one was like finding buried treasure.

But what was inside *this* bale? If not cocaine, then what? A list of other drugs flashed through Zane's mind: marijuana, heroin, meth, ecstasy. A searing memory descended upon him—his fingers on the soft fleshy part between Lucia's jawline and neck, and his ear so close to her mouth that he could hear the hollow stillness, like the sound of the sea in a shell.

Miguel opened the icebox. Inside, the mahi lay submerged in icy water that was stained red by its own blood, making it look as if the icebox was filled with tomato soup. He picked up the bale, groaning as he did so, and slid it into the icebox, pushing it down beneath the fish and the crimson slush until it could no longer be seen.

He turned to Zane. "How much fuel do you have?"

Zane looked at the gauge. The tank was nearly full. "Plenty."

"Enough to get to St. Augustine?"

"*St. Augustine?* But that's—"

"I know how far it is. Do we have enough fuel to get there?"

Zane sighed. "I think so."

CHAPTER THREE

Dominic woke to the sting of a carpenter ant chewing on the nape of his neck. Like a small but intense burn, the bite roused a memory of the day he branded a native girl in El Salvador after a soldier accused her of stealing bread. It was a lenient punishment, he thought. After all, natives suspected of lesser crimes were often executed, but she was young, beautiful, and — unbeknownst to anyone but her and Dominic — several months pregnant.

When he overheard murmurs of disappointment from two soldiers who had expected to see blood, Dominic convinced them that a lesser sentence was justified because the girl was only half native. It was well-known and obvious that she had been fathered by a Spanish missionary priest whose vow of celibacy apparently excluded indigenous women.

"You stole two loaves," Dominic said during the makeshift trial. He sat in a large chair towering over her while she kneeled, her eyes at boot level. He realized that he did not know her name and wondered if she even had one.

"I do not steal," she said in a soft, dovelike voice.

"You stole, and God's law dictates that justice must be carried out."

"The priests tell us that your god's law is to forgive."

"You will be forgiven. First, however, you will do your penance, and you will be marked as a thief, because that is what you are."

Dominic had stuck the tip of his sword into a pile of hot coals and now that it glowed red he pressed the side of it against her neck. Her skin smoldered and the smell of it reminded Dominic of a roasted piglet. She did not scream or whimper like he had expected. Instead, she gazed into his eyes with a look of deep sorrow. Everyone knew that natives were forbidden to look directly at the Spanish. To the surprise of his soldiers, however, Dominic did not reprimand the girl, nor did he intensify her punishment. He simply dropped his sword and told her to leave.

The next day, it was discovered that the soldier who accused her had been the one stealing bread, but Dominic felt no remorse about branding the girl. He was still infuriated that she had let herself get pregnant during one of their furtive trysts in the jungle. He was certain it happened on the night they heard the jaguars fighting. Dominic had held the girl in the darkness until the snarling waned and the nocturnal insects resumed their evening chant. Then, without knowing why, he kissed a salty tear off her cheek.

There were hundreds of ants on his body now. They bit his underarms, his face, the backs of his knees, even his groin. Dominic could do nothing to stop them; his wrists and ankles were bound and his eyes were so full of soil that he could not open them. He heard a voice say several words in a language he had never heard before but he could not tell if the voice came from near or far because his ears were clogged with saltwater.

"Who are you?" Dominic screamed. "Untie me!"

There was no response. The ants burrowed deeper into Dominic's clothes and it felt as if his body was being consumed by fire. He strained to free his arms and legs but they were tied too tightly. He writhed in the dirt to scrape off the ants but that only made them latch on harder. Where the hell was he and how had he gotten there? His mind was cloudy, but then all the memories of the day hit him as jarringly as a lightning bolt.

"Do not leave me, Juanito." Dominic cradled his son's body in his arms and ran his fingers through his black hair. Juan's hair was one of the only physical features that disclosed the presence of Dominic's genes. When dry it was dark and flowing like the top of a thunderstorm. When wet, however, it burst into wild and unruly curls, and it was curlier now than it ever had been. Dominic tried to smooth it down against Juan's skull but the winds of the hurricane—which screamed around him like a legion of frantic devils—lifted it back up. Drifts of sand surged down the beach with each gust and the oscillating bands of rain felt like barrages of little arrows on Dominic's skin. He looked up at the swirling clouds. They seemed close enough to touch.

"Do not take him from me," he pleaded.

He looked down again at Juan, hoping to see him start breathing again and open his beautiful eyes, like Lazarus rising from the dead. Nothing happened, though, and Dominic's despair transformed into rage. Had God abandoned him? After all his years of service for the Lord—after all the natives he had converted and Protestants he had slain—was God now forsaking him? It seemed contrary to the reward he was taught he would receive.

"I have spent my life doing your will," he said to the storm as if the storm were God. "Now, do *mine*."

He looked down again but saw no change. The serene crescent moon smile on Juan's face troubled him now more than ever. He pushed down the corners of Juan's mouth with his thumb and forefinger but he did it too forcefully and the smile became a frown. He left it like that, though, because it looked more like the Juan he knew.

"You stupid boy," said Dominic. "Why did you obey me?"

Dominic thought back on his time with Juan. The boy had always obeyed him, even when the task was clearly frivolous or dangerous, like the time he instructed Juan to walk into a native village as if he were part of the tribe in hopes of gathering intelligence about a brewing revolt. Unable to speak the native tongue, Juan was recognized as an intruder and taken captive, but an impromptu prisoner swap bought his freedom.

"You stupid, stupid boy. You cannot leave me now."

Dominic closed his eyes and gathered everything he had in his heart—all his rage, zeal, ambition and hatred—and begged God one last time for Juan to revive. "Hear me!" he bellowed.

The wind ebbed and a shaft of sunlight shone down on Juan. Was it a miracle? Had God decided to be reasonable? But then the beam broadened and the entire beach became saturated in sunlight. Dominic gazed up, squinting. He saw the clouds disintegrating and realized that the abrupt break in the storm was not the divine intervention he had pleaded for; it was merely the hurricane's eye—the placid, cloudless void in the center of the storm's vortex that brought with it an otherworldly silence and calm.

I renounce you, Dominic prayed. *Behold your enemy.*

He looked down the beach and saw Pablo's body partially buried in the sand, his rigid hand still clenching the rosary. Even now he wanted to crush Pablo's skull with his boot.

You've offended God, he heard Pablo say in his mind. *Your sins are unforgiveable.*

The sun glinted off one of the gold doubloons in Juan's hands, as if trying to remind Dominic of his transgressions. Fury ballooned inside him. He pried open Juan's fingers, scooped out the coins, threw them into the cascading surf, and fell upon the body so heavily that some of Juan's ribs cracked. Guttural sobs emerged from somewhere deep within Dominic—sounds he could not restrain and up to now was unaware his body could even produce. As he wept, the shadow of a person appeared beside his own. It grew larger and then the two shadows merged. He turned and saw what looked like a man in a dark robe silhouetted against the sun.

Dominic squinted. "Who are you?"

The man raised a short, thick oak branch and swung it down against the side of Dominic's head. Everything blurred and withered to black.

....

Dominic now felt certain the ants would kill him. They attacked his head, biting the insides of his nostrils and crawling into his ears. The lower part of his body had gone numb, his joints had swollen into horrid knobs, and a growing tension in his chest made it difficult to breathe. Once again he heard a voice but he could not discern any of the words. He could only tell that it was a male voice, one with the fragility of an elder.

"Help me," Dominic wheezed. "Help me or for God's sake kill me."

Two hands shoved him and he had the sensation of rolling down a hill. His body slapped into warm, glutinous liquid. Fully submerged, he twisted around, unsure of up from down, trying to find air with his face like an infant emerging from its mother. Dominic's body yearned to breathe but he knew that even one inhalation meant death. Perhaps drowning like his son was a fitting end, but he had no desire to meet a God he despised. He could hardly fight the urge to inhale but his anger drove him on for a few more seconds, and he felt the hands again. This time they fumbled across his body until they gripped his torso and dragged him up a muddy incline.

He inhaled deeply; the air tasted of charred oak, and when the hands released him, he heard the crackling of a fire and felt its warmth. As he lay there savoring every smoky breath, he realized that the ants were gone. Their scorching bites remained, though, like tiny embers that refused to expire. Then he heard bones creaking and a sigh, as if an old body had just sat beside him.

"Identify yourself," Dominic implored. "Why do you torture me?"

A long pause ensued, and then came a coarse voice. "*Purificación*."

The response startled Dominic — it was in his own language. "Purification? God damn you, I am a commander in the king's —"

"The ants opened you," interrupted the voice. "The waters cleansed you, and now the smoke is sealing you anew."

"You will be arrested for treason. Who are you? I demand that you —"

"I am a protector. Rest now. Rest in the smoke."

Who was this man who talked so strangely? Was he one of his crew members, exacting revenge for something that Dominic had done in the past? Impossible. They were all dead and he had even counted the bodies on the beach. None were missing. The man spoke in a dialect similar to his own but his accent and the words he used sounded foreign, like a person from another time. No one on the ship had spoken so, and the only Spanish settlement in *La Florida*—San Agustín—was several hundred miles to the north. Aside from natives, only a deserter or a madman would reside in such fetid wilderness.

"Why am I tied?" Dominic asked, but no answer came and the heat of the fire coaxed him into a light sleep. He dreamt of Juan, five years old and feeding monkeys at the jungle edge, and then of gold flecks glinting in a mine.

"Awake," said the voice, and Dominic did. His sinuses saturated with smoke and ash, he tried to determine how long he had been sleeping. His eyes were no longer swollen; he opened them. Everything was blurry but he could see the orange glow of the fire set against a brooding darkness.

"Please know that I was once as you are," said the voice, "covered in the filth of my past iniquities."

Dominic gazed into the darkness beyond the fire and his vision adjusted enough to see an old man with a long white beard sitting on a stump, his eyes sparkling in firelight. The old man laid a piece of oak on the fire; the flame leapt into the night and danced about like the tail of a riled rattlesnake, giving Dominic plenty of light with which to see. What he saw, however, shocked and confused him.

The old man wore nothing but a strip of deerskin around his thighs. Ornate tattoos covered his neck and face—black spirals that could have been patterns of snail shells, fern shoots, coiled snakes or whirlpools—and small shards of bone pierced his nose and ears. His frayed, tatty beard ended at a tendril just above his distended gut, and the explosion of white hair atop his head was as disheveled as a bird's nest. He looked absolutely feral.

"Just like you," the old man said, "I was a demon skulking beneath a man's skin."

Dominic scowled. "You know nothing of me."

"I can see that you are filled with rage. Your eyes tell me that much. And I know that you have killed many people. Wickedness exudes from you like a stench."

"Every execution was lawful."

"Whose law?"

"It was God's will."

"God wills only life."

"No, I have seen his other side. He delights in the death of the innocent."

"The boy?"

"My son."

"Your son is not dead. His journey continues, just not in this world."

"You are wrong. God in his wretchedness took him from me."

"You do not know God. God is good."

"Then untie me, and let me send you to him."

"It would not be so horrible, but my time is not yet. Soon, but not yet."

Dominic squinted, analyzing the old man's face. "What are you?" he asked.

"Pardon?"

"Native? Or Spaniard?"

"I am neither." The old man smiled, revealing black gums that mourned teeth. "And I am both."

His name was Francisco de la Mar, he said, and as a young Franciscan friar many years before, he was asked to serve as priest and confessor aboard Juan Ponce de Leon's exploratory voyage to La Florida. One night during their passage, Francisco drank too much wine, tried to urinate overboard, and fell into the sea. His absence was not discovered until daybreak. He was certain everyone presumed him dead and probably prayed mightily for the repose of his soul, but his tunic kept him afloat and he washed up alive somewhere on the coast of La Florida.

"The Book promises that whoever calls on the name of the Lord will be saved," said Francisco, leaning toward Dominic. "But I should have never called on him. It would have been far better for everyone had I gone to the Kingdom that day."

Francisco wandered the desolate beaches for several days until a hunting party of Calusa natives captured him. They beat him and spat on him and cut off one of his fingers for a taste, roasting it over a fire in front of him. To his dismay, they seemed to enjoy the flavor, and as he sat tied to a cabbage palm at the edge of their camp, he felt certain that they would consume the rest of him before dawn.

"That's when God sent an army of his angels to save me," he said to Dominic.

Francisco had seen them hiding in the trees before his captors did, fanning out noiselessly as they approached. They looked like men made of shadow save for the whites of their eyes which moved like fireflies in the darkness. Closer, closer, closer they came, and Francisco was soon more terrified of the apparent phantoms than he was of the hungry Calusa. Swiftly and with the grace of panthers they pounced. The five Calusa had little time to react and after a burst of spears and flesh they all lay dead on the ground.

Francisco tried to stay still, he said, but the three attackers turned toward him in unison, as if guided by some hidden sense. Covered in dried mud, they loomed tall and terrible. The largest of the three approached Francisco holding a blade fashioned from the lip of a conch shell. Francisco trembled and watched the blade move toward him, resigned to the fact that he was about to be sliced apart. To his surprise, however, the muddy native used the blade to slash the twine that bound him.

"He was my Saint Michael," said Francisco. "My archangel."

Despite his discomfort, Dominic lay there engrossed by Francisco's story. "Why?" he asked. "Why did they save you?"

Francisco peered into the dark forest. "To entrust in me a grave secret."

CHAPTER FOUR

"**I**'ve decided," said Zane. "I'm gonna ask her to marry me."

Skip chortled, but Zane remained resolute. The amusement drained from his father's face. "What, you're serious?"

"Serious."

"Dude. You're only —" Skip looked at his fingers as if to count them.

"Nineteen. And that's how old you were."

"Yeah, but she made me."

"What?"

"Nothing. I'm rambling."

Skip sat sucking rum and pineapple juice through a red cocktail straw that looked far too dainty for a man's mouth, but Zane had never known his father as someone who fretted about appearance. A faded T-shirt, flip-flops and baggy shorts comprised his daily uniform. When not shacking up with one of his many girlfriends, he enjoyed a carefree life aboard his houseboat. He spent most days idling at waterfront bars — sometimes playing Jimmy Buffett songs on his guitar to cover his bar tab — but if the waves were big, Zane could always find Skip longboarding, somehow keeping pace with the younger surfers and never declining an invitation to party with them afterward. In fact, many of Zane's own friends spent more time with Skip than he did; such was the burden of having a boyish father who had no misgivings about buying booze for minors and flirting with women as young as his own son.

Having never held a real job, Skip was always energized about some new business idea or money-making scheme. After ordering *Ricky Rogers' Roadmap to Radical Real Estate Riches* from an infomercial he saw one Tuesday morning at 2 AM, Skip made a small fortune flipping properties during Florida's housing boom, but he lost it all—and then some—when the market plunged. These days, most of the local bill collectors and loan sharks knew Skip Fisher by name. He stayed perpetually broke despite occasional and mysterious bursts of cash which he'd squander on lavish gifts for girlfriends, meals at gourmet eateries, and rounds of cocktails for everyone at his favorite bars—temporarily satiating himself, it seemed, with fleeting doses of his bygone prosperity and pomp.

Despite Skip's flaws, Zane cared about him and was secretly happy that his father had gone bust. There were no more luxury cars in which wet bathing suits were forbidden, no more haughty words like *dividend* and *amortization* being thrown about, and no more enthusing about foods that were encrusted with other foods or drizzled with reductions of any kind. Skip had returned to his freewheeling, cheeseburger-loving self, and Zane could not have been happier.

Perched on a barstool beside Skip, Zane now ran his fingers over a dripping glass of ice water packed with lemon wedges. He had requested his usual—water with lemons—and then sweetened it with a packet of cane sugar filched from the coffee tray. Despite the doctoring, the acidity of his improvised lemonade was nearly intolerable and he winced at each bitter sip. It was the only free drink available to him that had any flavor, the alternatives being tap water or plain tonic. His father always said that he would never trust a man who didn't drink, but Zane had not yet reached the legal age—not that Slick Rick, the bartender, would complain.

"Let me get this straight," Skip blurted after several minutes of awkward silence. "You're not even twenty years old, *not even twenty*, and you're ready to commit to the same vagina for the rest of your life?"

Zane thought for a moment. "Why, do different ones do different things?"

Skip laughed but stopped when he saw from the look on Zane's face that his son's question was entirely sarcastic. "You're too young to think you've found the right girl. Trust me, you've gotta look around first."

Zane literally looked around. The only woman within sight was Heather, a fixture at the *Lager-Head Lounge & Live Bait*. Three times his age, she always held a glass of Vodka-Cranberry and a menthol cigarette in the same hand as if they were one inseparable unit. Hers was the skin of someone who had spent a lifetime broiling in the tropical sun—hence the nickname everyone used behind her back, Leather Heather.

There was probably a time when Leather Heather was considered pretty, but the years had not been kind to her—or, perhaps more appropriately, she had not been kind to her years. Her breasts sagged low and swung like pendulums beneath her dress, most noticeably when she staggered to the bathroom or swayed beside the jukebox. She was the bane of bar conversation and the joke of Karaoke Night, for her voice had lost all semblance of femininity. It was now a gravelly rasp, and her laugh—a rapid-fire wheeze.

Leather Heather's favorite song, the one that always drew her to the dance floor, was George Thorogood's *One Bourbon, One Scotch, One Beer,* and she mouthed each word with all the theatrics of a stage actor as she tottered. For extra impact, she sometimes raised her glass over her head whenever the song mentioned a drink, which, of course, it did incessantly. She seemed to be locked in a perpetual party of her own imagining, and, whether she knew it or not, she was always the only person dancing.

"It don't bother me none," Zane once heard her say. "Just 'cause no one else likes to have fun, it sure as hell don't mean I cain't."

Only one part of Leather Heather seemed youthful, but frightfully so: her silken blonde hair looked as if it had been pilfered from a 20-year-old. It gleamed bright against her toasted skin, giving the impression that it was a wig, but no one knew for sure, except perhaps for the drunken fishermen she occasionally lured home.

"I don't want to look around, Dad."

Skip peered up at the dusty fish mounts that lined the walls around the bar. "I'm just sayin, Zane, it's a big sea out there, and there's plenty of fish in it. Enjoy your youth, kiddo. I sure wish I had."

"If you had, I wouldn't be here."

Skip nodded. "That's right, but if you really want to know the truth, now that you're old enough, well, I'll just say it. You can credit your existence to a keg party and some latex that sat in a hot car for too long. But that's life for ya, I guess."

Zane had always assumed himself the product of an accident and the catalyst for his parents' hurried wedding, but hearing it said by his own father helped him see the full tackiness of his creation, the inconvenience of his place in their lives. He turned and looked out the window, at the grove of masts in the marina where his fishing boat was moored, at the pelicans lazing on pilings splattered white by their own droppings, at the cumulonimbus storm clouds billowing on the horizon.

"Zane?" said Skip. But Zane did not want to reveal his tears.

"Zane!? That *is* your name, right?" Zane turned and saw Miguel glaring at him, his hair slicked back by the wind. It was a risky habit, but sometimes while driving his boat, the drone of the engines would lull Zane into a daydream or recollection. This had been a particularly emotional one, and he lowered his head to dry his eyes with his forearm while still holding the steering wheel.

"Get back to earth, boy," Miguel shouted. "We've got a problem."

"Problem?" Zane checked his course: still heading north. He checked the fuel gauge: half a tank.

"Can't this boat go any faster?" Miguel stomped and the fiberglass rumbled like an earthquake.

"We're at full speed. What's wrong?"

"That bastard squealed and now the Feds are onto us."

"What bastard?" Zane scanned the horizon. "There's no one out here but us."

"Oh yeah? Look here." Miguel pulled a handheld monitor out of his pocket. It was rigged with a thick antenna that pointed to the sky like an accusatory finger.

The small screen on the unit showed two green, flashing dots chasing each other at about an inch apart.

"This is us." Miguel pointed to the dot in the center. "And this is them, ten miles south and closing." He pointed to the other dot so forcefully that it made a permanent blotch on the LCD screen.

"But how—"

"GPS tracking device. Like they put on sea turtles. I slipped it into their bilge last night, just in case." Miguel had a subtle haughtiness in his words, obviously proud of his foresight.

"Then what do we do?"

"We get ready." Miguel rushed to the forward hatch and wrenched a duffel bag out of it. Zane had forgotten about the bag since they disembarked. He recalled how surprised he had been about its extreme weight when Miguel first boarded, and how Miguel insisted that Zane not try to help him with it. So, it was hardly a surprise to see Miguel now extract an automatic rifle from the bag and slam an ammunition clip into it. Zane had never seen such a large gun.

"What's with the cinderblocks in your front hatch?" asked Miguel.

Zane thought up a lie. "I'm making an artificial reef. To attract snapper."

"Is fishing all you care about?"

Zane did not answer.

"Anyway, here's the plan," said Miguel, holding the rifle across his chest. There was a sudden wildness in his eyes, as if the gun had transferred some of its ferocity into him, and his words spilled out with frenetic intensity as he laid out their strategy. Zane would drive while Miguel would hide behind the gunwale in wait. When the Feds came close enough, Zane would slow the boat and pretend to comply, and then Miguel would leap up and try to disable their outboard motors with a quick barrage of gun-fire, the prompt for Zane to throttle away at full speed. That was Plan A.

Plan B, on the other hand, would be implemented should the Feds approach with guns already drawn. Plan B terrified Zane. For that contingency, Miguel had placed his revolver barrel-down in a fishing rod holder behind Zane, with instructions for Zane to grab it and use it if a firefight ensued. "Aim for their chests," Miguel said. "Heads are too difficult out here with the waves."

Zane did not want the gun anywhere near him. "Aren't you afraid I might use it on *you*?"

"Not really. You already passed my test."

"Test?"

"Earlier, when I was getting the bale, I gave you a chance to push me over the side—but you were too much of a coward, which is good because I was ready to kill you if you tried. So the answer is no, captain, I'm not afraid of getting shot by a scared little boy. You wouldn't even get lined up before I'd stuff you so full of lead you'd sink straight to the bottom and be worth an extra twenty dollars if they ever found you."

Miguel was right. Zane was scared—so scared that his hands were trembling. His stomach wrung itself nauseous as he thought about the approaching threat. Both plans put Zane in far more danger than they did Miguel and he was certain that shooting a so-called "Fed," or anyone else, was out of the question. Was there any way out? Any precaution he could take? He couldn't think of anything. His hand found its way into his shirt and he kneaded the doubloon with more force than ever before.

He looked toward land. Buildings stretched on endlessly, packed together like headstones in an old cemetery. What would have normally been a gorgeous sunset now filled Zane with dread. The broad tongue of darkness that had emerged in the east now lapped away at the last puddle of daylight in the west, and, by instinct, Zane flicked the switch to turn on his boat's lights. The red and green navigation lights radiated on the bow while the white anchor light blazed on the stern, altogether illuminating the deck with a dizzying patchwork of color.

"Are you an idiot?" shouted Miguel, turning off the lights and smacking Zane in the back of the head. "You're as stupid as your father, aren't you?"

"Sorry, I just thought — " Zane touched his head where Miguel had struck him, and then he looked up with sudden surprise. "You know my dad?"

Miguel studied Zane for a moment. "We'll discuss that later."

Zane stood there perplexed. His father had innumerable acquaintances, some of them shadier than others, but he could not recall ever hearing of Miguel before. Skip was no saint, but he was no hard criminal, either, and certainly not someone who would ever knowingly consort with a drug smuggler. Then Zane remembered that Skip had begun calling him not long after they picked up the bale, so many times that Zane's cellular phone — safely enclosed in a Ziploc inside his shorts pocket, as usual — was nearly depleted of its battery power. Miguel had forbidden Zane to answer.

The succession of illumined hotels and condominiums — elaborate jack-o-lanterns adorning the coast for the last hundred miles — ended abruptly. Beyond them, as far as Zane could see, stretched a long dark shoreline blanketed by the silhouette of forest and a sprinkling of dim lights. The digital chart on Zane's GPS showed that they were approaching Cape Canaveral. The lights, he now realized, sat atop launch pads, some of which were still used to hurl rockets carrying satellites — including the ones that provided GPS — into orbit; others were relics left undisturbed since the Space Race, decaying ruins that now sat as lifeless as most of the men who once worked on them.

Gemini. Mercury. Apollo. The *Space Shuttle.* At one time all had punctured the stratosphere above the Cape but now they were things of history. Some had failed dramatically, and Canaveral shrimpers still occasionally dredged up barnacle-encrusted pieces of the *Challenger* in their trawls. The rockets and vehicles that retired unscathed, on the other hand, had become tourist attractions in museums and visitor centers, their defunct metal controls now burnished by countless greasy fingers, their framework always creaking as if they longed for the thrill of the countdown, the furious shudder of the ignition, and the cold serenity of outer space.

"Three miles," said Miguel after a quick glance at his tracking device. "And coming fast."

Even though they were several miles offshore, Zane could see a swath of breaking waves in their path. Globs of white water would materialize, peak rapidly, and then disappear. He realized that they were coming upon the Canaveral Shoals, an undersea peninsula of shallow sandbars that jutted out many miles from shore. Some parts of it were only a few feet deep and his chart had the word DANGER inked in red across the entire area. Experienced mariners knew that the shoals had caused countless wrecks throughout history. Most of the vessels were swallowed so completely by the shifting sands that traces of debris were rarely found.

"We should go around the shoals," said Zane. "We need to change course."

Miguel shook his head. "No way in hell. We'd use too much fuel."

"We could capsize."

"You really are gutless, aren't you? We go north and nothing else. Got it?"

Zane trembled. Behind them and before them peril was imminent. If by some miracle the authorities did not stop them, the sea surely would. He reached into his pocket and turned on his cellular phone, then snuck a peak at it. Both the low battery light and the voicemail indicator flashed. He yearned to pick it up and call his father, but he felt certain that Miguel was waiting for any excuse to kill him. He turned it off again and sealed the baggy.

As they reached the edge of the shoals, Zane felt a change in the sea. The waves were confused now; no longer traveling with the wind, they barreled in from every direction, slapping into each other and drubbing against the hull.

Zane watched the depth sounder readings fluctuate wildly. Twelve feet. Six feet. Ten feet. Four feet. He was trying to envision the immense humps and trenches of sand beneath the boat when a breaker came out of the darkness and reared up like a frothy warrior in front of him. It grabbed hold of the bow and lifted it into the air, but then, just as quickly, the wave lost its footing in a trench and collapsed. Zane let out a deep exhale as his boat cruised over its remains. He spent the next few minutes weaving in and out of the breakers while trying to maintain the same course.

"Here we go," Miguel said. He had taken his position stooped in the stern, cradling the rifle. He peered over the gunwale. Zane followed his gaze to see a dark thing bounding over the chop in their direction. Fear coursed through Zane's body like an injection. His breaths became short, his stomach tossed, and he wanted it all to end. But it would not end, for the boat was nearly upon them.

"Stop your vessel," a voice boomed across the sea through a bullhorn.

"Do as they say," said Miguel.

Zane pulled the throttle back and his boat slumped in the waves. He could see two men in the approaching center console but darkness veiled their features. He had expected the *Coasties* — dock talk for the *US Coast Guard* — but this looked nothing like their large orange cutters that usually patrolled the seaboard. This boat appeared smaller than Zane's, but it did have four outboard engines on the stern compared to his two, which explained how it caught up so quickly.

Who were they, then? FBI? DEA? As the boat edged closer, Zane squinted to read the black lettering on the hull.

"I, R, S," he read aloud. "*IRS?*"

"Death and taxes," said Miguel, now lying on the deck, out of sight. "How many of the bastards are there?"

"Two, I think." What, Zane wondered, would the IRS want with a drug runner?

"Are they packing?"

"Packing?"

Miguel scowled. "Do you see any damn guns."

Zane studied the silhouetted figures on the approaching boat. His heart thudded when he saw that the man to the side of the driver was holding a gun. The shape of it looked similar to Miguel's automatic rifle.

"Well, do you or not?" Miguel's voice was tinged with anger.

"I can't tell," said Zane. "It's dark."

"We can't take a chance. I'm gonna count down from three, and on one you grab that pistol and we take them out. Yours is the driver. Got it? Don't answer—they might see you talking."

Panic squeezed in on Zane. He tried to think of a solution. Should he warn them? Miguel would surely kill him if he tried. Could he try to evade them? That seemed impossible. Their boat was simply too fast.

"Three," said Miguel, his finger stroking the trigger.

An idea hit Zane. He drew a deep breath, put his hand on the throttle, and clenched the steering wheel.

"Two."

Zane looked at the IRS boat. Now only ten feet away, it idled alongside. The men onboard wore black uniforms and appeared to be in their thirties or forties. One of them had short black hair and a well-kept beard. The other had a clean-shaven scalp. Their faces were both stiff with anxiety.

"One!"

It all happened instantaneously: Miguel sprang up with the rifle like a madman, his eyes blazing and his hair blown back by the wind, and the officer with the gun whirled around toward Miguel, and Zane slammed the throttle down as far as it would go and spun the steering wheel away from the other boat. His boat lurched upward and sideways with a tremendous jolt, causing Miguel to tumble backward off the stern and into the water, just as Zane had hoped. But Zane did not anticipate the towering breaker that suddenly charged in and put its shoulders beneath his boat. With the aide of the engine thrust, the wave lifted the boat skyward and slammed it down on top of the IRS boat. A deafening *crack* shot out and shards of fiberglass and splintered wood erupted all around Zane and he felt the deck crumple beneath his feet like wet cardboard. Only blackness and confusion and sloshing water remained.

Somewhere, a man moaned.

CHAPTER FIVE

The oaks shivered as a breeze whispered through them. Their spindly fingers permitted only the slightest streaks of dawn sunlight to trickle through and one beam found Dominic's face. Still bound, he slept beside the waning fire. The light danced across his mouth, crawled up his cheek, and wiggled over his eyes. He woke with a gasp.

"Juan," he said. His face filled with alarm, but despair soon took its place.

Francisco still sat on the stump. "The fear of the Lord leads to life," he said, "so that one may sleep satisfied, untouched by evil."

Dominic tried to scratch his nose on an exposed root. "I am growing weary of your preaching, old man."

"Weariness will be of no help on our journey."

"Journey? You are mistaken if you believe that I would under-take a journey of any sort with some wild man from the woods."

"Would you, then, with a dozen of us?"

"Please, retain some dignity, old man. We both know you're the only person crazy enough to be out here, if you can even be called a person anymore."

"Do you not feel their eyes on your skin?" Francisco looked into the distance where the woods melded into darkness. "Have no doubt they are there, observing from the fringes like spirits in wait."

"I am sorry for you. Senility clearly has its grasp."

Francisco stood. "Perhaps." In the soft morning light he looked sickly. His head sat no higher on his body than his hunched shoulders and his lower back leaned askew, yet he moved with surprising agility when he reached down and picked up a sheathed sword. Dominic stirred. "My —"

"I took it off you before you woke on the beach. For your own safety."

Dominic envisioned grabbing the sword from Francisco and dispatching the old man with one swing. If only he were not bound. Francisco studied the brown leather sheath and ran his fingers over it. To Dominic, it was like watching another man caress one of his lovers. Fiery anger scorched his insides. The old man ran his hand over an etched scene of Spanish countryside near the handle and, farther on, across a long row of crosses carved into the leather.

"Are these your victims?" asked Francisco.

"The memorable ones. I see room for one more."

Francisco extracted the sword from its casing and, with all the precision and swiftness of a skilled swordsman, swung it down between Dominic's ankles. The severed twine coiled back like a snake chopped in two. "Let us hope it's not for you," said Francisco. "On your feet."

The old man plucked his robe from the crux of a nearby tree and cocooned himself inside of it. The hood of the robe created a dark void around his face.

"And what am I to wear?" asked Dominic. He stood shakily, his hands still bound.

"It already adorns you, my friend," Francisco said. "I dressed you last night."

Dominic looked down; his face hardened when he saw the dry mud caked on his body. His shirt was gone and his pants had been rolled up to the knee, yet no part of his skin was visible below the muck. He turned and saw the nearby pond in which he had almost drowned the night before, but it was smaller and dirtier than he envisioned during his blindness. More like a pit filled with sludge and algae, it was dark and stagnant and reeking of moist detritus. Insects flitted about the surface and a filthy turtle basked on the edge. A gloppy crater marked the place where Dominic had gone in and out.

"You're making a mockery of me," said Dominic.

"On the contrary, commander. We will be venturing through mosquito-infested wilderness. They cannot smell your blood through such grime."

As they walked, Dominic studied the twine that bound his wrists, trying to follow the course of the knot and decipher its type. But he had never seen a knot so complex before. He tried to twist his hands free but the knot only tightened.

He could have used such a knot for the slaves; a few always managed to escape during the chaotic auctions and disorderly transfers to merchant ships. The girl never struggled, though. Standing alongside dozens of her brethren while merchants and landowners inspected her, she held a look of grace and resignation, as if she welcomed the humiliation. When she noticed ten-year-old Juan in the crowd of onlookers, however, her expression changed. Tears pooled in her eyes and she let out a long exhale, as if releasing her soul.

Juan, she mouthed. *Juan*. She quivered. She beckoned him with her eyes.

Dominic, sitting at a nearby desk with the auction records and treasury box, watched his son react with indifference. He had taught him well. But then Juan bit his lip. His mouth trembled and a tear seeped from his eye.

Oh, you stupid boy, Dominic thought. Do not dare.

Juan bolted toward her through the crowd. "Mama!"

Dominic erupted from his chair and flipped the desk over, sending papers scattering and coins clinking across the rocky ground. "Juan!" he shouted. "Stop!"

Juan collapsed at her feet when he reached her. He wrapped his arms around her shackled ankles. "Mama, why are you up here?"

"Oh, Juan." She ran her hand across his hair. "I must go with our people."

"Do not leave me, Mama. Take me with you."

"Your father needs you, Juanito. You're his last chance."

"But I hate him, Mama."

"Hatred only wounds the one who harbors it. Fight his anger with your love."

"Silence, woman!" Dominic grabbed the chains from behind her and yanked them; her head whipped back and she fell away from Juan, wincing. "Remember who you are, Juanito. The Spaniards say we are not human. They are right. We are gods and they can never destroy what we have inside."

Dominic backhanded her. Blood gushed from her nose. Later that day, she sold for half of her appraised value because of her battered face. But at least she was gone.

Dominic and Francisco had walked several miles and now trudged ankle deep in the black water of a cypress stand. Francisco had taken the lead for the first time. He used the tip of Dominic's sword to test the depth in their path.

"I demand to know where we are going," said Dominic.

Francisco pointed ahead. "North."

"I asked you where, old man, not in what direction."

"I will tell you when they want me to."

"Who? Your imaginary army?"

"Yes. My imaginary army."

"How far do you intend to walk?"

"Ten days, perhaps eleven."

"You know I will kill you before then."

"And never reach your destination? Never fulfill God's plan? He does have a plan for you, commander. I am certain of it."

"If he does, it's a cruel one."

Dominic studied the surrounding swamp and then looked at Francisco's back. There seemed to be enough distance between them that, if he moved fast enough, he might be able to flee before the old man could wield the sword. "Nothing in this hellhole is worth spending another day with you," Dominic said, and he bolted away.

Francisco did not even turn to investigate the splashing. "That, my friend, is not your decision to make."

Dominic tore through the swamp. Jagged cypress stumps protruded like the teeth of some fossilized beast. Bangs of moss hung from the branches above. Flying insects filled the air. It was hell on earth—a world unfit for humans and animals alike.

Where would he go? The coast could not be far. If he reached it, he could trek to San Agustín where his military superior would greet him as a hero and shower him with the hierarchal respect he deserved. As soon as he arrived, Dominic imagined, he would ask his superior to dispatch a unit that could track down and capture the old man. He smiled when he thought about getting his sword back and running it through Francisco's bowels to ensure a slow, painful death, as every traitor deserved.

The water grew deeper as he slogged. It soon lapped against his stomach. He pushed a small log out of his path with his belly but something felt strange about it; he froze when he felt the log writhe. He looked down; his eyes grew large. What he mistook for a log was actually a water moccasin. Dominic shivered. The snake opened its mouth. A milky bead of venom dripped off one of its fangs.

"I will back up," said Dominic, "and you will not bite me."

Dominic twitched. The snake reared up and hissed. "You will *not* bite me."

He jerked away but the snake puffed up and struck. A clawed hand shot out of the water and grabbed the snake's neck, stopping its gaping mouth from within inches of Dominic's skin.

"Good God." Dominic's mind could not grasp what was happening.

The hand, clasping the snake, continued rising from the black water and soon an elbow emerged and a shoulder and then an entire man. The man's muscles stood erect on thin bones beneath dark, tattooed skin. Water and muck streamed off. His wet hair clung to his chest. His eyes shone as green and vivid as foliage after rain. He was clearly a native, but an extraordinarily large and formidable one. The native brought the moccasin to his mouth and bit into its neck; blood spurted out and the snake twisted into a ball and fell limp. The man looked down at Dominic and spit red saliva into the water.

"Stay where you are," said Dominic. The man did not move. Dominic turned to flee but stopped. Ten more men, their features similar to the first, stood waist-deep in the water and glowered at him.

"Who are you?" Dominic said. "What do you want?"

"Can you see them now, too?" Francisco's voice came from behind. "Behold, commander, my invisible army."

Francisco waded up to the man who had captured the snake. Their eyes met. Francisco said something, his words jolting out with firm consonants and monotone vowels, and the man replied. Dominic could not understand either of them, but he knew that countless languages existed among the tribes of the Spanish Main. It had, after all, been his job to ensure they would all be replaced by one.

"Come, commander." Francisco motioned for Dominic to follow him, which he did without hesitation. He looked back and saw the natives watching them leave.

"You must forgive their caution," Francisco said. "They know all too well that an ordinary malady in a white man could be a deadly one for them. They will travel with us, but they will keep their distance."

"What did you say to the tall one?" asked Dominic.

"I asked him if he could see the fire in your eyes. He said yes, more than he'd ever seen in any man, and that I had done very well to find you."

CHAPTER SIX

D ebris swirled all around Zane and the sharp taste of gasoline
burned foul in his mouth. The silence, at first, terrified him,
but in the short time he had been treading water, a comforting
rhythm had developed—the undulating swell would lift him
high enough to glimpse the dark shoreline in the distance and
then gently lower him into the trough where all he could see
were the backs of waves and flotsam.

Each time he rose up he hoped he would see a boat coming to
rescue him, but he soon realized there were no other boats on the
water that night. It was a weekday, after all, and the conditions
for night-fishing were clearly not ideal. Even if any fishermen
had ventured out, it would have been a miracle for them to spot
Zane amid such darkness.

Something bumped the back of his head and he whipped
around—the bale, stained pink by fish blood, had drifted up
behind him. It looked like the perfect flotation device so he
grabbed hold and slid the upper part of his body onto it. The
plastic still felt cold from being inside the icebox. In contrast, the
ocean water was balmy.

All around him artifacts of his boat bobbed in the sea: chunks
of foam, shattered fiberglass, bits of wood, an empty tackle box.
To Zane, it was like seeing a loved one beaten beyond repair. He
had worked hard to buy his boat and establish his charter business but now it all lay in pieces. He saw no signs of life in the

area. Where was Miguel? And the two officers? He was afraid to look too thoroughly for fear of seeing something he could never delete, like a mangled body or, worse still, only part of one.

"Can anyone hear me?" he called out, but his words were met with silence.

He pounded his fist on the bale. What a terrible captain he had turned out to be. His maneuver was reckless and he should have seen the wave coming or at least been ready for it. Now, several men were probably dead and he was adrift somewhere off a desolate coast. The twinge in his gut felt familiar; this was not the first time he had felt responsible for a tragedy. He knew he stood a good chance of dying as well, but he had no one to blame but himself.

"Hello?" he hollered. But, again, no one answered.

A glare caught his eye and he looked to the west where he saw the full moon sinking toward the horizon. It appeared to be quaking, but Zane realized it was his own trembling that made it seem so. He watched the moon change from yellow to red in an instant. What was happening? He rubbed his eyes and, when he pulled his hand away, he saw blood on it. He touched the top of his head and discovered a hot, fleshy wound on his scalp.

Shark attack capital of the world, thought Zane. And I'm bleeding.

The coast north of Canaveral had earned that title not from man-eaters like whites and tigers but from the hordes of small sharks that swarmed there. The seawater in the area stayed persistently murky from the churning silt of the shoals and it teemed with baitfish; on many days one could see immense schools of menhaden stretching to the horizon. Naturally, the baitfish attracted large numbers of sharks, and fishermen often saw them leaping from the water or charging across the surface as they fed. Most beachgoers who entered the water had no idea that sharks lurked all around them. In the brown obscurity of the surf zone, the palm of a swimmer's hand or the sole of a flailing foot mimicked the flash of a baitfish, and a feeding shark had no way of telling them apart from its prey. As a result, more shark attacks happened in the area than anywhere else in the world.

Zane felt certain that his blood would eventually draw something in. He had used chum enough times to know that it usually did not take long. Would it make any difference if it were ten small sharks or one large shark? Both seemed horrible, and he knew he had to decide whether to stay with the wreckage or try to swim to shore. If he started swimming, he might make it to the beach within a few hours, but if the current proved too strong, it could push him out into the deep blue desert where no one would ever find him. Under normal circumstances, staying with the wreckage was the smartest option; large objects, after all, were easier for searchers to find than a single person. But blood in the water was another issue, and waiting around for the sharks to hone in on its source did not seem rational. He stared at the distant shoreline. The shimmering path cast by the moon beckoned him. He held tight to the bale and kicked toward the moonlight.

"More craters than the moon, I swear it," said Samantha, peering into the mirror. "Just look at my awful skin."

Zane, sixteen years old, stood behind her. "I can't see them, mom. I think you're beautiful."

"Aw, Zane." She turned and looked at him. "Do you mean that?"

"I do. You look really good for your age."

Anger painted her face pink. "My *age?* What's that supposed to mean?"

Zane fidgeted. "Nothing. I just meant, I don't know. I just—"

She spun back to the mirror, fresh tears in her eyes. "Go away."

Zane heard the rattle of a pill bottle as he walked out of the room. Samantha's personality had turned volatile in the years after Skip left. Neither parent had claimed custody of Zane so he spent his time alternating between Samantha's house and Skip's houseboat, although he rarely felt welcome at either place. When he stayed with Skip, he often found himself sharing breakfast with strange women. Staying with his mother, on the other hand, exhausted him. She often interrogated him about his father's relationships. *Who's the latest? How old is she? Is she pretty?*

"You should forget about dad and go meet someone," Zane urged her.

"Please. No one wants an old woman like me. I'm used goods."

"A lot of men think you're great."

"Maybe after I get some work done. When I look pretty again."

Samantha had undergone her first of many facelifts at 36 years old. When the bandages came off, Zane assured her that he could see a big difference. In reality, though, her new face troubled him greatly. After Samantha recovered, she put a deposit down on a tummy tuck. In the days leading up to that surgery, she constantly reminded Zane that it was he who had ruined her figure by the mere act of growing inside her. Where was his gratitude for the sacrifice she had made in giving him life? The damage he had done to her body had destroyed her marriage and instigated her depression, she claimed, and it was only the mound of prescription pills she took daily that enabled her to face the world.

Still, Samantha never dated or spent time with friends. She hardly even left the house except to go to her job as a department store saleswoman for age-defying skin creams and wrinkle-removers. She used most of her days off and vacation time to lie in bed and do nothing. "Beauty rest," she called it, but Zane saw nothing beautiful about a pallid, middle-aged woman stewing in her pajamas for days.

After they had become "an item," Lucia insisted on meeting Zane's mother. He avoided it for as long as he could but Lucia was persistent—*how can I know you if I don't know her?*—so, one day, Zane allowed her to come over. Earlier that morning, Samantha had spent too much time in the tanning booth and her skin shone the color of a carrot when Zane brought Lucia through the door. Lucia smiled, shook Samantha's hand, and congratulated her on raising a gentleman.

"Oh, honey, he might seem like one now," said Samantha, "just like they all do when they're young and stupid. But take it from me, men change, and not for the better."

Lucia did not even flinch. "Well, your son's been nothing but good to me. Probably too good." She laughed.

Samantha scowled. "What's that supposed to mean?"

"Just that he's the nicest boy I've ever met."

Zane, nervous, picked up his *Florida Sportsman* fishing magazine and pretended to peruse it. He turned the page to an article about catching sharks at night. One photograph showed a close-up view of a mako's menacing jaws.

"Let's cut the crap," said Samantha. "What are your intentions with my son?"

Zane looked up from the magazine. "Mom."

"No intentions," said Lucia. "We're just dating."

"But in the future?"

"*Mom.*"

"Well, we've talked about college, Mrs. Fisher, but—"

"Mrs. Fisher? *Mrs. Fisher?*"

"I'm sorry. Miss—?"

"Get out."

Lucia looked at Zane with hurt, questioning eyes.

"I said get out of my house! Go find some other boy to corrupt."

Zane stepped toward his mother. "Stop it."

Tears welled in Lucia's eyes. "No, it's ok, Zane. I should have listened. You warned me, right?" She hurried out of the house, leaving Zane and Samantha in an awkward standoff.

"*Warned* her?" said Samantha. "You *warned her* about your crazy mother?"

"Mom—"

"Next time you bring some little hussy into my house, you should warn *me*. I don't like surprises, Zane. And I don't like that girl one bit."

By the time she turned 40, Samantha's face was incapable of expression; she had undergone numerous cosmetic surgeries. Her swollen collagen-infused lips hardly moved when she talked, and her threadlike eyebrows seemed to have been removed and then reattached an inch too high. The tightness of her skin troubled

Zane the most—stretched over rigid cheekbones, it seemed like it might perforate if a smile reached too high.

During one week toward the end of his senior year in high school, Zane came to Samantha's house to check the mailbox every evening. One night, he found what he was waiting for—a manila envelope from Gainesville, addressed to him. His mother must have seen his excitement because, minutes later, she asked him to come inside and sit beside her on the bed. Her mood was as somber as a raincloud.

"You're not still planning to waste your time at college, are you?" she asked.

"That's our plan," he replied, smiling. "Lucia's already accepted. And guess what I just got?"

"Zane, your college money..."

"What about it?"

"It's all gone, honey."

"Gone? How could it be gone? I thought grandpa left me plenty."

She sighed. "Oh, honey, there *was* plenty, but I had to use it. You wanted me to feel good about myself, right? To get over my depression?"

"Of course, but—"

"My medical bills were so high, Zane. Everything is really expensive, you know."

"You, you spent it on—" he stuttered. The room spun around him.

"I spent it on our future." She looked in the mirror and stroked her hair. Zane could hardly even recognize her any more. "Now that I look young again, I'm gonna meet someone."

Zane put his hand over his mouth, then rushed into the street and let out a scream that cascaded down the block. Dogs howled. Porch lights burst on. He dropped to his knees in the cool grass and felt the acceptance letter from the *University of Florida* Marine Biology department crinkle in his pocket. He knelt there sobbing until a neighbor ran up and shined a flashlight in his face.

"Zane?" said the neighbor. "You okay, buddy?"

The beam flooded his head and he opened his eyes to find himself halfway to shore. The sky was filling with yellow light. Had he fallen asleep? Had morning already come? But then he felt a rumble in his chest and saw the water trembling around him and heard a deep, persistent growl. He looked toward the sound and saw an immense dome of white smoke curling around one of the launch pads. He followed the smoke upward and came to an *Atlas* rocket arcing across the sky. The glow from its fiery tail unfurled over the ocean and lit the night like day.

In the brightness Zane could see everything: the sandy beach and thick forest in the distance, the contours of the waves roiling around him, and the rapid flicks of menhaden on the water's surface. A king mackerel—sleek and shining—shot out of the water with a menhaden in its jaws. Even the marine life thought it was daytime.

Zane spun around in the water and looked east. He could see only ocean as far as the light extended, but then he noticed something peculiar in the water, something out of place, about a hundred yards away. It flailed in an unnatural way. He squinted. Had a shark picked up his scent? Panic brimmed inside him.

The thing stopped splashing, as if it knew someone was looking at it. Zane lost it in a trough but as he rose on the next wave he could see the two eyes and dark hair. It was clearly a man. Zane tried to pick out any features on the man's face but the rocket penetrated the atmosphere and its light dimmed. It became nighttime again, even darker than before because the moon had since set. Zane grabbed hold of the bale and kicked vehemently toward land. He was sure he had seen it on the man's face—that unmistakable glower, and that dark, crooked smile.

He would have preferred a shark.

CHAPTER SEVEN

Striding along the edge of a pungent mangrove swamp, Francisco and Dominic stopped and gazed at a mother raccoon scavenging with her two full-grown cubs. She pulled an oyster from the muck and bashed it against a coquina rock. Her offspring scurried over and licked the dripping meat out of the shell, cooing as they slurped. The animals either did not notice the men or simply did not care.

"Are you hungry?" whispered Francisco.

Dominic glared at him. "I have not eaten in days."

"Let us dine, then."

Francisco bolted toward the raccoons. The animals fled in three different directions but he followed the largest of the cubs. He stomped his bare foot onto its back and grabbed the tuft of fur behind its head. The raccoon hissed and thrashed and tried to bite but Francisco quickly snapped its neck. The animal fell limp in his hands and hung there like a rumpled pelt.

"Good God," said Dominic, stunned. "I thought you meant oysters."

"Glory to the most high." Francisco made the sign of the cross over his body. "Why shuck a hundred oysters when we can make a meal with only one of these?"

He used the tip of the sword to skin and gut the raccoon and then he broke off a mangrove branch and impaled the carcass on it. As he did, the mother raccoon and her cub watched from the dark recesses of the swamp. They paced and grunted and upstretched their noses to sniff the air.

Francisco then prepared a fire and stuck two y-shaped sticks into the ground on both sides of the coals, above which he positioned the animal. Dominic watched, eager and ravenous. When the meat began to pop and ooze liquefied fat, he caught himself drooling. He had never eaten raccoon before but he had no concerns about how it might taste. At this point, any food would do. Trembling and lightheaded, he was even tempted to try some of it raw because he did not think his body could wait any longer for nourishment. He distracted himself by watching fiddler crabs scamper among the mangrove roots.

While the raccoon roasted, Francisco walked along the edge of the woods and picked a handful of indigo-colored berries. He put a few in his mouth and then handed the rest to Dominic. As he did, Dominic noticed that the berries had dyed Francisco's palms blue.

"We use these to color our tattoos," said Francisco, "but they are edible as well."

Dominic took a handful of the berries and scarfed them. Foul, bitter juices filled every crevice of his mouth and he spit them all out in a pulpy wad. "They're awful." He wiped his blue tongue with blue fingers.

Francisco grinned. "I said they were edible, not good."

Once the carcass looked wholly charred, Francisco broke off a hind leg and served it to Dominic. Holding the leg by its curled, blackened claw, he bit into the meatiest part of it and, like a hungry dog, jerked his head to snap off a tough, sinewy chunk. Hot juices ran down his chin. The stringy meat tasted like a blend of smoke and saltwater and the smell of the mangroves, but it could have been rotten and he still would have eaten it. He gnawed it enough to swallow it and then took another bite. He stopped chewing, however, when Francisco snickered.

"What?" said Dominic.

"Nothing." Francisco hesitated. "It's just that you look like a giant squirrel eating an acorn right now."

Dominic gazed down at himself. He was kneeling in the dirt and holding the meat up to his mouth with his bound hands. He did indeed look like a squirrel. Rage filled his gut and extinguished his appetite. "Then untie me and let me eat like a man," he grumbled.

"Oh, commander," Francisco sighed. "We both know what you would do if I did."

"I would eat. Nothing else."

"You are a killer, Dominic. It has not left your eyes."

"I am who God made me. If I am bad, it is simply proof of his malice."

"God gave you freedom. He has no interest in puppetry."

Dominic took another bite. As he chewed, he envisioned crushing Francisco's body with his teeth. "And what has God done for you, old man?"

"He gave me life." Francisco looked up at the sky. A dense flock of swallows streamed across it. "He grants eternity to those who desire it."

"How can you be so certain he even exists?"

"*How?* Just look around you, commander. All of this… *perfection*. At every moment we are in him and among him, but most of us are too blind to see." Francisco reached down and touched an oak sapling protruding from the ground. He massaged one of its waxy leaves between his fingers. "I tell you," he continued, "if you lived long enough to sit and watch a tiny seed grow into a towering tree, you would surely see his persistent hand in the world. He teems in every grain of soil and every breath of air — he dwells in us and we in him — but our lives are simply too passing to recognize that."

Dominic's eyes became red and watery. He grabbed the sapling and ripped it out of the ground, infantile roots and all, and threw it into the fire. "And where is he when the young are dying?" The little tree wilted into a ball and burst into flame.

Francisco frowned. "I know where he is not."

"Oh? And where is he not?

"In you."

Both men watched with desolate eyes as the sapling disinte-grated before them. They sat there for an hour saying nothing until darkness enshrouded them, prompting Francisco to pre-pare a bed of moss on which to sleep.

In the night, after their fire died, Dominic saw the buttery glow of the natives' fire through the mangroves and heard the deep, muffled tones of their voices. Francisco had not been lying; the natives really were traveling with them and, each night, they had made their camp in closer proximity. As the days blurred by, it seemed that their cautiousness was waning, like wild animals acclimating to a settler.

The stars overhead pulsed. Dominic lay there and watched them. He had known the stars as navigation points and noth-ing else; this was the first time he had ever looked at them for any length of time without trying to establish his bearings. They appeared different now—more lurid, perhaps, and far more numerous. He focused on the brightest one and soon felt himself falling toward it and all the others moved past him slow and vac-illating like the lamps of travelers on a dark road until it seemed he was surging through a cave toward its blinding opening. He felt a sudden pang of fear and closed his eyes.

"Old man?" he said.

Francisco rolled over on his bed of moss. "I should not answer to that, but, yes, what is it?"

"Were you sleeping?"

"Better than you, it seems."

"Do you believe in forgiveness?"

Francisco pushed himself up on his elbows and looked at Dominic. "Of course I do."

"Even for horrible things?"

"No sin is too great for God's mercy."

"No sin?"

"Not as long as the sinner is truly remorseful."

"Good. Then I forgive you."

Francisco looked dumbstruck. "*You* forgive *me*?"

"Yes. For taking me captive. I forgive you."

Francisco fell back onto his bed. "*You* forgive *me*." He began laughing and seemed unable to stop.

"Nevermind. I withdraw it." Dominic rolled over and turned away from Francisco. The old man laughed himself to sleep.

Morning came like a slap in the face and both men groaned as they stood. After a wordless breakfast of leftover raccoon meat and a few raw oysters — the similarity of the tastes shocked Dominic — they trudged north again. They came to the end of the mangrove swamp and entered a dense flat of scrub forest. Palmettos sliced their legs and the sparse tops of the sand pines provided little protection against the sun.

Dominic noticed a low, dense bush covered in clusters of red berries. Insects buzzed around and within it. He reached down and plucked a handful of the berries as he walked by. Squishing one between his fingers, a creamy sap leached out. It smelled sweet and plantlike. He put one in his mouth and chewed. The sweetness was there but so was a peculiar acridness he had not detected in the scent. Still, it tasted far better than the berries he tried earlier. He swallowed it and had just put another in his mouth when Francisco looked at him with alarm.

"Spit that out!" said Francisco.

Dominic did. "Why?" he asked, wiping saliva off his lips.

"Half of all the berries in these woods are poisonous. That was one of them."

Dominic looked at the other berries in his hand. "How poisonous?"

"Deadly. Did you swallow any?"

Fear pressed down on him like a wet coat. "Only one." He felt lightheaded but could not determine if it stemmed from poison or panic.

"We had better get the doctor." Francisco cupped his hands and put them to his mouth and made a piercing, hornlike sound. A gaggle of pheasants erupted from the palmettos. Moments later, the natives bounded out of the scrub. They stood there panting, morose with concern.

Francisco and the natives exchanged frantic words and flung panicky hand gestures at the forest. The oldest native—the one who had killed the moccasin—gave an order to the youngest native who then bolted into the scrub. Dominic sat on the ground and held his knees, his stomach tossing and his dizziness escalating.

"Am I going to die?" he asked.

"Maybe," said Francisco.

The young native returned with a sprig of leaves and red berries that he held high, as one would carry a holy relic. The berries on this plant were larger and rounder and altogether different than the poisonous ones.

"Cassina," said Francisco. He took the plant and bent his head solemnly toward it. The natives bowed as well. "The black drink. To my friends here, there is no means of purification more sacred."

The older native prepared a fire which sprang up quickly due to its kindling of pine needles and dry palmetto leaves. He filled a clay bowl with water from an animal skin pouch, and then he took the cassina plant from Francisco's hands and laid it inside. The natives lowered their heads and chanted.

Dominic coughed. He could not get any satisfaction from his breaths. In only minutes, they had become short and painful. Francisco and the natives looked down at him with grave, stone-like faces.

"Is there anything you want to say in case we cannot save you?" said Francisco.

"Yes." Dominic hugged his knees. "Is dying like this part of God's plan for me, too?"

Francisco looked disrespected. "Dying is part of his plan for everyone. Do not think you are special."

The water simmering in the bowl had turned black and the fire hissed every time a drop of it spilled over the side. The older native used a green palmetto leaf to lift the steaming bowl. He put it beneath his nose and inhaled the vapor. It seemed to satisfy him because he quickly handed it to Dominic.

"*Ucu*," said the native.

"Drink," said Francisco.

Dominic took a sip and gagged. "It's revolting."

"If you want to live," said Francisco, "you must drink."

The natives sat around Dominic and watched. He sipped again and tried to make the fluid bypass his tongue but the caustic smell filled his sinuses. He gagged and pursed his lips in an attempt to not throw up.

"All of it," said Francisco.

Dominic looked into the inky blackness of the drink. His reflection — gaunt, dirty, corpselike — stared back. It was like looking at some other man. He took a breath, opened his mouth wide, and tilted the bowl. The bitter liquid poured in and he gulped it down until only a few shriveled berries and some sediment remained. He handed the bowl to Francisco.

"Finished," said Dominic.

Perspiration suddenly broke out on Dominic's forehead. His stomach churned and he vomited all over himself. The drink, it seemed, had not worked. He retched several more times until it felt like his insides should have come out as well. Exhausted and sullied, he collapsed on the ground and gazed up at the men standing around him.

"You did well," said Francisco.

"But I could not keep it down," said Dominic.

Francisco's mouth curved up into a toothless grin. "That was the intention."

CHAPTER EIGHT

The wave rose and bent toward Zane. This was surely the one. He turned toward the beach and extended the bale in front of his body. He held tight and kicked. Soon he heard the roar of the wave and felt its warm breath on his back and, glancing to his side, saw its cylindrical barrel curling in upon itself. The water pushed him, slowly at first, but then it released him like a slingshot and he surged forward with exhilarating speed.

He smiled and savored the salty air in his face. But then the bale angled down and caught the front of the wave like a lipped lure and suddenly he was tumbling underwater. His skin grated against the sandy bottom. Water filled his nose. He came up gasping and coughing, but his distress changed to delight when he realized that it was shallow enough to stand. Solid ground under his feet had never felt so pleasing.

The bale had surfed ahead to the beach and he could see it now sinking into the sand as seawater gushed around it. He waded to the beach and fell to his knees in the foam. He wanted to rest, but he knew he was not safe yet. The man he had seen in the rocket light would not be far behind.

He struggled to his feet. His limbs felt weak and gelatinous, but he managed to drag the bale up the beach and into the tall, powdery dunes. He found a small dell on the back side of the dunes where he concealed himself and looked out at the beach through the sea oats. He sat there and watched the waves pile in, scanning for any signs of Miguel. A movement soon caught his eye—little bursts of sand were shooting up from the other side of the dune—and he heard a sound like digging.

He crawled to the edge of the dune and peered over. It took a moment to recognize what he saw. It was a loggerhead sea turtle, massive and encrusted in barnacles, excavating a pit with its hind flippers. The turtle turned its head and regarded Zane with a massive eye. It breathed through its nostrils, emitting a wet hiss.

"Don't mind me," said Zane.

The turtle turned away and continued digging. Zane receded into the dune and put his hand on the bale beside him. He shivered. A yearning burned inside him. He had not felt such a forceful craving in years. The boat collision was a "trigger event" if there ever was one. He thought of the protocol he had been taught for resisting temptation.

I admit that I am an addict.

I admit that I am powerless over my addiction.

I believe in a power greater than myself.

But did he? Where was this so-called greater power when Miguel hired him for a fake fishing charter, and when his boat inadvertently crushed another? If ever there existed a reality worth escaping, this was it. He looked at the bale with hunger in his eyes. What the hell was in it? It didn't matter—it was surely something good. He clawed at the bale like a digging dog, shredding off layers of plastic wrap in long strips. He needed something to fill the void, and he was certain that the bale contained some form of an antidote to his longing.

When he pierced through the last sheet of plastic skin and was breaking apart the inner layer of Styrofoam, a bright light shone down from above. God's searchlight, he thought, but with Jupiter more than a hundred miles away, he knew that was impossible. He followed the beam. It did indeed originate at a lighthouse, but this one looked different from the one he knew from home. It stood on the coast like a lonely watchman, its lamp slowly scanning the sea. He realized that he had seen it from the water but from that vantage it looked like another launch pad.

Only from the beach could he now see its features. Unlike the Jupiter Lighthouse which always gave Zane a feeling of security, this one — painted white with black stripes like a convict — was foreboding.

He continued ripping into the bale. When he had broken through the Styrofoam he came to a black duffel bag stuffed with a mystery. His hands quivered. He found the zipper. As he pulled it open, a strange sheen emanated from inside. What exotic delight awaited him? He would know soon. Movement, however, caught his eye; he glanced toward the beach and saw Miguel standing in the surf, bent over with his hands on his knees. Something in Miguel's hand glinted.

"No," whispered Zane.

He watched Miguel look down the beach in both directions and then at the ground in front of him. Zane's heart sank when he saw what Miguel was looking at — there, preserved in the sand, were Zane's footprints and, between them, the line left behind where he had dragged the bale. Miguel set off following them.

Zane smacked himself in the forehead. How could he have been so stupid? He looked down at the bale and, aware that only seconds remained, ripped open the zipper. Yellow luster bathed his face.

"Holy —" he said. The beam of the lighthouse crept across the dune and in the radiance he saw the full glory of what lay inside the bag: stacks upon stacks of gold rounds. There had to be a thousand coins, all shrink-wrapped together in stacks of ten. Someone had taken great care in their preparation. He sat there mesmerized. It was too dark to see the features of the coins, but he assumed them to be rounds of bullion. Gold bullion, he knew, was the latest trend in trafficking because — unlike currency — it was anonymous and untraceable. Now he understood Miguel's determination, and it made him even more afraid. But despite the riches that lay before him, he felt an ache of disappointment. He would have preferred drugs. He hated himself for thinking that way.

Zane rubbed his eyes and peered through the sea oats. Miguel had almost reached the dunes. The thing in Miguel's hand, he could now see, was a dive knife, typically carried by scuba divers as a safety precaution but certainly sharp enough to be a weapon. If Zane tried to run now, he would undoubtedly be seen. He felt angry at himself for not fleeing when he had the chance, but his curiosity about the contents of the bale — or, more accurately, his hunger for narcotics — had been too great.

"Where are you, boy?" Miguel's voice was eerily singsong.

Something in Zane urged him to jump out and surrender. If he gave up, maybe Miguel would be merciful. But then he remembered the insane look in Miguel's eyes when the IRS boat had approached, and he crouched lower.

"I know you're up there," Miguel said from the other side of the dune. Zane could hear the shuffle of his feet in the sand, but the sound stopped.

"You've got to be kidding me," said Miguel. "A damn turtle?"

Miguel stormed away down the beach. Zane looked at the tracks in the sand again and realized that they were not even his. What he had mistaken for his own footprints were actually made by the turtle's flippers as it scuttled up the beach; the drag mark was from the turtle's shell, not the bale. Still, Miguel would soon find his real tracks, which were only a little farther down the beach.

Zane looked at the coins. What should he do with them? With this kind of fortune he'd be set for life — a new boat, a new truck, and a big mansion on the water. This was, he figured, the only chance at serious wealth he'd ever get. He had to at least try.

He strained to lift the bag but realized that he would not get far with so much weight. He looked around; his eyes came to the turtle. An idea struck him — he was not sure if it was ludicrous or ingenious but he could think of nothing better.

This is it, Zane thought. Make it happen, captain.

He flung himself over the peak of the dune and rolled down its steep face, dragging the duffel with him. He landed right where he wanted — just behind the turtle. She had finished digging her nest and was now dropping eggs from a pink, fleshy orifice protruding from beneath her tail. Zane had hoped that the eggs would not yet be coming; to prevent crushing them, he would have to improvise. He scooped out the half dozen she had already laid, but they kept coming and he could not clear them fast enough. He looked at their source. There was only one way to stop them—one appalling, disgusting way—and so he stuffed his hand into her chute.

It was slimy and hot inside her and he could feel more eggs pressing down on his knuckles but the turtle did not seem to notice the intrusion. With his free hand he tipped the duffel bag and dumped the stacks of coins into the nest. They fit nicely and left plenty of room. He reached in and pulled out two stacks of coins, hesitated, and pulled out one more. He then pushed a pile of sand into the nest and replaced the eggs he had removed. When he pulled his hand out of the turtle, a large globule of mucous and eggs surged out. Moments later, she continued laying them one by one.

"Sorry, girl." Zane shook his head. He could hardly believe he had just violated a turtle.

He jumped to his feet and tossed the three stacks of coins into the duffel bag. Then he flung the bag over his back, scaled the dune and, crouching on its summit, reached over and stuffed pieces of Styrofoam into the bag until it looked full. He scanned the beach for a landmark—to his left, rising out of the dunes, stood a solitary coconut palm, and to his west he saw a massive structure silhouetted against the stars.

He turned and looked in the opposite direction. Miguel had reached the other tracks in the sand; his head slowly turned as he followed them up the beach with his eyes. For Zane, it was like watching a fuse burn rapidly toward him, with no time to get away. As Miguel's gaze reached the dune, the lighthouse beam found Zane and set him aglow. He felt like a stage performer blinded by a spotlight. When the beam left, he saw Miguel sprinting at him.

"Drop that bag!" screamed Miguel.

Zane bounded across the ridge of the first dune and then turned away from the beach and barreled into the sea oats. Sharp reeds sliced his limbs as he ran. The dunes, and the rhythm of loping over them, reminded him of ocean swells. Each time he reached the top of one he would glance back and, each time, Miguel was a few steps closer.

"You're dead!" shouted Miguel.

The dunes ended at a thick wall of forest. As he approached, Zane scanned it for the clearest entry point. There did not, however, seem to be one — the entire thing looked like an impenetrable tangle of oaks and vines and cabbage palms. He buried his fear and raced headlong into the blackness with one hand outstretched as a probe. Once inside, he could not even see his arm in front of him. Disoriented, he staggered through the dark jumble, tripping over logs, squeezing through bushes, and bouncing off tree trunks like a running back.

The duffel bag jerked backward; he held tight and tugged on it but something with great strength pulled back. He reached around with his other hand and discovered that the bag was entangled in a web of vines. He wrenched on it with all of his strength, grunting and twisting, and the vines snapped all at once. Surging forward, his face smashed into a branch and the force of it flipped him onto his back. Every thought and impulse vanished and an insistent sleep took over against his will.

Chapter Nine

"His name is Ixasatoriona." Francisco gestured to the tall native who had now saved Dominic twice. "But you can call him 'Ona.'"

"Ona," the native affirmed with a bemused smile. He nodded at Dominic as if to say *hello* and Dominic reciprocated.

In the days following the berry incident, the natives had stayed close to Dominic, like overprotective parents afraid to let their child out of sight. Dominic's stomach was still swollen but he had managed to ingest a few fruits without regurgitating them, the nicest of which resembled plums and had been gathered by the natives from a tall tree they seemed excited to discover. Meat, however, still shot back out undigested, and merely thinking about the black drink made him queasy.

They had hiked across a broad expanse of waist-high grass for most of the day. Scattered cypress stands rose out of the plain like hackles on a boar, but otherwise the land was drearily flat. As they approached the edge of the next cypress stand, Dominic studied his captors. What was their motivation for keeping him alive? Where were they taking him? None of it made sense.

He watched Ona march through the grass in the lead. With every step, the native's long legs ate twice as much distance as Dominic's. His black hair sat tied in a tight bun atop his head and, like his companions, he carried a large bow under one arm and a bundle of arrows slung over his back. Small fish bladders—inflated, dried, and painted red—dangled from his earlobes alongside numerous bone piercings. Most striking, though, were his long, claw-like fingernails which had been sharpened into points. Such grotesque hands seemed out of place on what was otherwise a beautiful physical specimen. The other natives shared these features but Ona possessed one distinction—the pearly spire of a conch shell which he wore on a twine around his neck.

Dominic looked at Francisco. "Who do these men worship?" he asked.

"They worship one god," said Francisco. "The sun."

"Why the sun?"

"Why *not* the sun? It makes things grow. It illuminates all. And its power is so great that one cannot even look at it without injury."

"So they are pagans."

"They pray and they fast and, up until recently, they sacrificed the firstborn son from each family because they believed it gratified the spirits. Call them what you will, but the Timucua have profound faith."

As they reached the far side of the cypress stand, a crashing sound arose out of the palmetto undergrowth and a white-tail buck sprang forth. It staggered and skidded and tried to rise again but could not. Its hide was stained by a splotch of blood above its hind leg where the shaft of an arrow jutted out. The natives raised their bows and drew their arrows but they did not aim at the deer—they turned instead toward the cypress stand.

Fifteen other natives with bows and arrows rushed out of the palmettos. They stopped all at once. The shock on their faces made it clear to Dominic that they had been in pursuit of the wounded deer and were not expecting to come upon another group of men with weapons already drawn.

"Who are they?" whispered Dominic.

"Ais," said Francisco. "Our adversary."

With their short, squat stature and narrow eyes, the Ais looked distinct from the Timucuans. Each wore the feathers of some large bird on his head which shook with every movement. Instead of tattoos, their skin was marked by deep scars that looked to have been made deliberately. They wore nothing but loin coverings made of woven palmetto. Hiding their genitals, however, did not seem to be a priority; bits of scrotum hung out all over the place.

The natives exchanged no words as they stood aiming their arrows at each other. Ona's shaky hand struggled to hold his arrow back. Sweat gleamed on his forehead and his nervous breathing sounded like spray bursting forth from the bow of a ship.

A wiry young man emerged from the woods and the Timucuans collectively gasped. He walked languidly—effeminately almost—into the group of Ais and scowled at the Timucuans. His eyes met Dominic's and sent an eerie chill into him. "Who is that?" asked Dominic.

"Urribia," whispered Ona.

"Urribia," repeated Francisco. "Warrior chief of the Ais."

Urribia's eyes were as black as the bear pelt around his shoulders and his hair hung down in one bulky clump as if it were a separate animal. Loose skin drooped off his bones and wiggled when he stepped. He said something harshly to the Timucuans but they did not offer a reply. To Dominic, though, it sounded like the type of statement that probably did not require one.

"We are trespassing in their kingdom, their territory," Francisco translated.

Urribia stepped forward to stand in front of the other Ais. The purple veins on his forehead throbbed and he made another harsh pronouncement.

"What did he say?" asked Dominic.

Francisco looked at Ona, and then at Dominic. "They want us to give them something, as payment for traversing their lands."

"What is it they want?" But Dominic knew the answer before he even finished the question. He watched with terror as Urribia pointed a quivering finger in his direction. Once again Dominic felt that chill in his body, like an infection seething into his bloodstream. Where had he seen eyes like that before? Where had he felt such wretchedness?

....

"Stand up!" Dominic's father grabbed him by the hair and wrenched him to his feet. "Stupid boy!"

"Father," pleaded Dominic. "What harm have I done?"

A creased and yellowed nautical chart was sprawled out on the floor below. Throughout his childhood, Dominic had always been intrigued by his father's maps. Now, as a teenager, his wonder about the New World had become an obsession. Bathed in candlelight, he had been lying on the floor for most of the night, moving his wooden galleon replica over the chart while envisioning how it would feel to stand at the helm of a real ship. The ocean air and violent squalls. Sea monsters and bare-chested mermaids. Exotic lands. Godless peoples. He longed for such adventure.

"My charts are not playthings!" His father squeezed Dominic's head from both sides and twisted it toward him. Dominic glanced away—it was impossible for him to look directly into those eyes. His father's gaze, though, had not always been so menacing. At one time, it had conveyed only kindness. Only upon his father's last homecoming did it seem that he had brought some kind of darkness back with him. Something had happened to him out there in the wilds, something that turned him black inside.

"Please, father," cried Dominic. "I did not mean to offend you."

His father struck him across the face. Dominic could tell right away that a bruise would materialize by morning. "If I catch you in my things again," his father snarled, "I will cut off your goddamn hands."

Dominic did not doubt that his father, in his current state, was probably capable of following through on such a threat. "Yes, sir," said Dominic.

Most of Dominic's schoolmates envied the fact that his father was one of the most famous explorers in Spain. With exploits and discoveries renowned throughout Europe, his father enjoyed regular audiences with the king who peppered him with questions about the New World. Did the savages go about naked? Were their streets paved in gold? Did they worship snakes and crawling things? Whenever his father came home from the palace,

Dominic observed, he looked far more exhausted than he did after returning from a transatlantic voyage.

"I am sorry, father," said Dominic. "I was just imagining. Dreaming."

Dominic's father stood sullen in the doorway. His eyes softened and he looked at Dominic with a tenderness that had been absent for years. "Promise me, my son, that you will never go west. God help me, I have seen the most righteous men lose their souls over there. The devil needs no more laborers in his fields."

"Is that what happened to you?"

His father looked at his own hands for a long time. "So much blood," he said, and then he slunk out of the room, his head hung low.

Dominic looked down at the chart. His toy galleon lay on its side near the meandering line that denoted the coast of La Florida. He picked up the little ship and examined it. One of the masts, no larger than a quill pen, had cracked. His neck swelled and his fingernails dug into the galleon and he hurled it across the room; it smashed against the stone wall and broke into pieces.

"Damn you!" he screamed.

....

The Timucuans gathered in a tight circle around Dominic. He felt somewhat protected but could see that, given their numbers, the Ais had a distinct advantage. Urribia stood in front of them, irate.

"He is not pleased," said Francisco.

"Give me my sword," said Dominic.

Francisco shook his head. "There are too many of them. You would not stand a chance."

"You know so little about me."

Urribia yanked a bow and arrow from the hands of one of the Ais and rushed toward the Timucuans, screaming. He stopped in front of Ona and pointed the arrow at his forehead, shouting something so barbarous that spit flew out of his mouth.

"He said he is getting impatient and that he will take..." Francisco's words trailed off.

"He will take what?" said Dominic.

Francisco looked at Dominic with regret. "He will take what he is owed."

Ona looked back at Dominic with sadness. Then he lowered his bow and let his arrow fall to the ground. He lifted his conch shell necklace over his head and put it on one of the other Timucuans.

"No," said Francisco.

Taking a deep breath, Ona fell to his knees, lowered his head, and extended his arms with his wrists crossed. Urribia looked down at Ona with exultant disgust. He shouted something to the other Ais; one of them ran over and bound Ona's wrists. Urribia then stepped back and kicked Ona to the ground.

"You mustn't," said Francisco.

Ona looked up at Francisco with a determined gaze. "*Ho mi tala.*"

Francisco closed his eyes, and then nodded. "It is time for us to leave."

"What did he say?" asked Dominic.

"He said, he is going."

Francisco ushered Dominic into the vast grassland with the other Timucuans. Dominic struggled to look back at Ona.

"Going where?" he demanded.

Francisco pushed him along. "He is taking your place."

"No!" said Dominic. "Give me my sword!"

"It is already too late."

Dominic watched the Ais surround Ona like a pack of wild dogs. Several of them raised clubs and brought them down on Ona. Dominic lost sight of him amid the pouncing throng. Urribia stood on the edge of the mob, smiling and cackling as if witnessing some joyous event.

CHAPTER TEN

"I want us to try it together," said Zane.

Lucia eyed the two little pills in Zane's hand. "I don't know."

"Come on, Lu, don't be a chicken. We only live once, right?"

"We only die once, too. My parents would kill me if they found out."

Zane closed his fingers around the pills. "Ok." His hand quaked so he jammed it in his pocket.

Lucia touched his arm. Even after five years of dating, he still felt tender warmth in his body whenever she was close. "I'm sorry," she said. "I don't mean to be such a dork. No one gets hurt from one little pill, right?"

"I've never heard of it happening." It had been a year since he asked her to marry him. Her answer had been 'no' but with one caveat—that he ask again in four years. The days could not go by fast enough.

Lucia smiled. "Alright. Give me one."

They downed the pills with swigs of warm *Coca-Cola* and sat holding hands in his parked truck waiting for something to happen. A pleasant, familiar numbness soon blossomed in Zane's abdomen and spread up through his neck and into his head. He smiled and looked at Lucia—she was smiling too, her eyes half-shut like a contented housecat.

"This is nice," she whispered.

He stroked the back of her hand with his thumb. He was elated to have her home, if only for a while. When Lucia went away to college, Zane had taken a job dipping shrimp at a live bait shop with the goal of saving enough money to buy a charter boat. When he no longer had anyone in town to spend time with, he soothed his loneliness with fishing, drinking, and drugs—usually all three at once. He had been sampling various narcotics over the past year, starting with the ones in his mother's medicine cabinet and progressing to things he could only buy in dark alleys. He still had yet to find one that could fill the void.

With each semester that passed, he could see Lucia flowering into someone he could never hope to have in his life. She was slipping away. They would talk on the phone almost every night, but sounds of *Gator* parties and happy people laughing in the background usually tarnished their conversations, and Lucia often had to hang up early. Their monthly phone bills became progressively cheaper. It was only during her visits home—summer vacations, Christmas holidays, and spring breaks—that things seemed like they used to.

"How do you feel now?" asked Zane.

Lucia took a moment to answer. "Kinda weird."

Zane looked through the windshield at the Jupiter Inlet jetty where grungy fishermen stood casting lighted bobbers into the night. Tidewater streamed out of the inlet with tremendous force, creating rapids as it clashed with the breeze off the Gulf Stream. In an instant he felt like he was deep inside the mouth of some terrible monster that was puking out the entire world. He looked over at Lucia. She had fallen asleep.

"Lu?" he said, but she did not answer. "Lucia?"

He woke with a start in the dim forest and felt throbbing in his head. Unlike during the night, he could now make out his surroundings; a gray glimmer to the east indicated where the sun would soon rise. The forest—having been taken over by a greedy vine—looked like one inextricable mass of foliage. He lay in a small den made and abandoned by some large animal; he could smell a faint musk and see dark hairs on the flattened grass around him. It was probably

74

from a boar, he guessed; like so many other introduced, non-native animals, wild pigs had all but taken over the Florida woodlands.

Zane realized that he was still holding the duffel bag. He thought about Miguel. Where was he? How had he not caught up with him? But then Zane recalled how dark the forest had been at night. It would have been difficult to find anyone in such obscurity; happening to fall into an animal's bed had probably saved his life. Now, however, with light creeping in, he knew he had better continue on.

He examined the bag as he stood. All three stacks of coins still lay inside, and he felt confident that Miguel had not deduced where he hid the remainder. He used the direction of the sun to determine his bearings and set off toward the west. He came upon an armadillo feasting on worms, its head buried in the dirt. He tried to give the animal plenty of space but the vibrations from his footsteps must have alerted it — it spooked off, clattering through the undergrowth.

"Shhh..." said Zane, his index finger pressed against his puckered lips. Then he chided himself for thinking that a wild animal would have obeyed him.

Something rubbed against his thigh and he remembered that his mobile phone was inside his pocket. Was it possible that the plastic baggy had not leaked during his swim? He pulled the baggy out of his pocket, opened it, and found the phone dry inside, save for a fine mist of condensation. He pressed the *on* button and stared at the LCD screen as the phone powered up.

"Come on," he said. "Work."

The screen lit up with a background picture of Lucia. There she stood, posing playfully in her bikini on the Intracoastal sandbar near Jupiter. God, he thought. She held a *Corona* as if it were a trophy and smiled her beautiful smile. He had looked at that photo so many times that seeing it did not usually make him sad, but his dream from the night before still hung fresh in his mind and he felt a sudden cramp in his chest.

Don't cry, he thought. Not now.

He looked again at the phone. The battery light blinked — indicating it had only seconds of energy left — and in the top-left corner of the interface two disappointing letters appeared: *NS*. No service.

"Piece of junk," said Zane, but he knew it was not his phone's fault. Cape Canaveral, after all, was cut off from the rest of Florida. Aside from people on tours, it was accessible only to military personnel and space program workers with security clearance. The Kennedy Space Center, though, took up little of the land, and the rest of the area—known as the Merritt Island Wildlife Refuge—remained one of the last great wildernesses in Florida. The only chance he had of getting a cellular signal, he guessed, was picking up a stray one from a distant town like Cocoa or Titusville.

He trudged on, holding the phone high in the air and watching for any signs of a connection. He was paying such close attention to the screen that he did not notice the concrete slab in his path—his foot caught the edge of it and he tumbled forward. He clutched the phone as he fell. The slab, however, was covered in leaves and soil and felt as soft as a mattress when he hit it.

He looked up and was shocked to see an immense, rusty launch pad reaching crookedly into the sky. It seemed like it had been abandoned for decades. Peeling paint drooped off the metal like the bark of a gumbo limbo tree. Veiny creepers stretched up its legs and curled around every extension. The horizontal beams were covered in roosting buzzards, each one of which now examined Zane with black, beady eyes. He felt like a piece of meat in a butcher's display.

He stood and checked his phone—still no service. But then he saw a metal ladder extending up one of the legs of the launch pad. If he could climb high enough, he theorized, he might be able to get a connection. He scrutinized the ladder for a long time. It was severely corroded—a tetanus breeding ground if ever there was one—but all the rungs were intact and did not appear rusted through. With his battery so close to depletion, he knew this might be his only chance, so he put his phone in his pocket and started climbing.

The buzzards departed all at once and he could feel the wind off their wings as they lifted themselves into the sky. A terrible odor remained, though—their waste was splattered all over the beams and it smelled like the rotting dead things that buzzards typically consumed. The stench intensified as he climbed higher into their realm.

When he reached what he thought might be the halfway point, he looked out and was overcome with astonishment and terror. The vast expanse of wilderness that lay before him looked impassable. A dirt road ran parallel to the launch pad but, beyond that, the seemingly endless tracts of swampland and forest were only periodically pierced by space center buildings. The largest structure was the mountainous Vehicle Assembly Building, or VAB, tall enough for rockets and shuttles to stand inside vertically before their transfers to the launch pads. The VAB had an enormous American flag painted on its face. A halo of buzzards orbited above it on an invisible updraft.

He looked in the other direction and was transfixed by the enormity of the ocean and the indescribable beauty of the sun rising out of it. He realized why the most coveted units in ocean-front condominiums were on the highest floors; he had never been in one, but he guessed that the view would look similar. If he pulled this off, maybe he would have to buy one.

He suddenly thought about the wreckage of his boat floating somewhere out there, and about the two men in the other boat. Was it possible they might have survived? It pained him to ponder their fate. If only he could explain to them that he had not intended to crash his boat into theirs. He hated the thought of anyone thinking badly of him.

After climbing a little higher, he wrapped his elbow around the ladder and pulled his phone from his pocket. He looked at the screen, averting his eyes ahead of time to the top-left corner in an attempt to avoid seeing Lucia again. He sighed when he saw the letters *NS*. But then the letters flashed and became another image — an illuminated bar beside four vacant ones. *Service!* He smiled, but then his face hardened with pensiveness. Who should he call? He doubted that he had enough juice for more than one try.

He narrowed it down to two: *911*, or his father. Then he remembered how Skip had repeatedly tried to reach him the previous afternoon, and he could see that his voicemail folder had messages in it. He dialed Skip.

It rang once before Skip answered. "Zane!" he shouted.

Zane had never heard such panic in his voice. "Dad!" he shouted back.

"God, Zane, I'm so happy to hear from you. You're ok?"

"For now."

"I'm so sorry, kiddo. I never thought he'd go this far. I had no idea."

Zane's phone beeped. He wanted to know more about his father's involvement but his battery had little vitality left. "Dad, listen to me, my boat is sunk."

"I know. It's all over the news. You're away from that bastard, right? You're not still in the water, are you?"

"I'm on land. Cape Canaveral. My phone's gonna shut off. Call the police and tell them I'm on an old launch pad, somewhere near—"

"The police? Hold on, kiddo, don't you know?"

"Know what?"

"The police are looking for you. They traced what they found of your boat and pulled up your record. They're saying you killed a federal agent."

Zane's body went cold. "Killed?"

"One of the agents is fine. They found him in a lifejacket. But the other one—Zane, he was dead, floating with the wreckage."

Zane choked on his tears. "It was an accident, Dad, I swear it. When my boat came down—"

"He didn't die in the crash." Skip breathed into the phone. "Somebody cut his throat."

Zane felt dizzy. He hugged the rusty ladder to keep from falling off. He looked down and for the first time saw how incredibly high he had climbed. His legs felt weak and he swooned to one side. His phone beeped again. "Dad, I'm scared."

"I know. Me too. But listen, we'll get you out of this. They'll be looking for you all over the coast, so you have to go inland. Keep a low pro."

"And go where?"

"I'll meet you somewhere and we'll get outta dodge. You're pretty far north. How about Gainesville?"

Zane knew Gainesville well; hearing the name brought such sadness that its name may as well have been Sorrow or Regret. When Lucia did not wake up that night in his truck, her parents thought she would have wanted to be brought back there. Zane tried to go a few times a year. He sometimes came across her relatives or former university classmates — they all knew who he was and never spoke to him — but it was even worse when her parents were there. Whenever they saw Zane, Lucia's mother would sob hysterically and her father would clench his fists. They swore they would never forgive Zane for what he had done, but Zane did not think he deserved their forgiveness anyway.

"Ok," said Zane. "Where in G-ville?"

"How about a bar. Know any good ones?"

It did not surprise him that Skip would want to reunite at a bar. In terms of meeting places, to Skip no other option was ever worth considering. Zane remembered how Lucia always talked about going with her friends to a seedy little lounge famous among college kids because it rotated on its foundation. People got so dizzy inside, she said, that they often spilled their drinks. "Look for the *Spinner*," said Zane. "I have no idea how long it'll take me to get there, though."

"That's ok," said Skip. "I have no problem sitting there every day until you do."

No, Zane thought, you wouldn't have a problem with that, would you?

"Dad? I have to ask you one more thing."

"What?"

"Did you know what was in that bale?"

"Of course I did. I told you everything in the voicemail. Didn't you listen to it?"

Zane's phone beeped again and shut off. He pounded the power button with his finger, but as he did the phone slipped out of his clammy hands. *Bing. Bing. Bing.* It bounced off the beams of the launch pad as it plummeted, hitting the ground and exploding into a thousand shards of plastic and glass. Some of the pieces slid across the slab and stopped at the feet of a man. Where had he come from? The man looked up and Zane's heart leaped — it was Miguel. The knife he held in his hand, Zane guessed, was no doubt the same one he had used to slay the agent.

"Well look at you," said Miguel. "Stuck like a treed coon."

CHAPTER ELEVEN

No one talked around the fire that night. The Timucuans gathered mussels and snails from the slow, gloomy river beside which they had made camp and steamed them on a bed of wet moss placed over the coals. They showed Dominic how to extract the meat from one of the shells and left him to prepare the rest of his supper himself. His stomach could finally tolerate solid foods again, but he doubted he could eat enough of the tiny mollusks to feel full.

All night the natives prayed. When the moon rose they kneeled before it and, with tears in their eyes, delivered up pleas and lamentations in lilting tones that were as beautiful as they were haunting. Somewhere in the distance, a pack of red wolves joined the chorus with their sorrowful howling. While the others prayed, the native to whom Ona had given his shell sloped off to sit alone in the darkness. He looked as despondent as a widower and Dominic watched him remove the necklace, look at it for a long time, and then put it back on.

"Who is he?" Dominic whispered to Francisco.

Francisco, morose, looked at the man. "That is Utina, our new chief."

"A reluctant one, I'd say."

Francisco had been holding a piece of half-eaten snail meat in his hand for several minutes. He looked at it, and then tossed it into the fire. "Utina knows he can never be as just and tireless a leader as Ona. No one can. Ona is — Ona was — irreplaceable."

"Will the Ais kill Ona?" asked Dominic.

"For certain," said Francisco. "But first, he will be beaten and tortured. They will parade him in front of their village like a prize and call a council to try him for trespassing. A spectacle, nothing more. His sentence will be death. The gods, they will say, demand it. Then the real suffering will ensue."

"In what way?" Dominic's appetite had disappeared and he pushed the pile of shellfish away.

"It depends on their mood, I guess. They will most likely cut off his limbs and cauterize the wounds to ensure he lingers for a while. After that they will mount what's left of his body on a pole outside their village and leave him there, until he…" Francisco seemed unwilling to let the word pass from his lips.

"Until he dies," said Dominic.

Francisco frowned. "Yes."

"How do you know all of this?"

Francisco gazed at the river. "Because we used to punish our enemies in the same way. Before Ona became chief."

The next morning, the sound of chopping jarred Dominic awake. The river basin filled with warm sunlight and the thin fog that had materialized overnight swirled away. Dominic looked around the camp; he was surprised to find himself alone. He considered fleeing but decided against it; at this point, he felt safer with the natives than he did on his own. Between the vicious animals, toxic plants and savage Ais, he knew he could never survive in such wilderness by himself.

He traced the chopping sound to a thicket of trees in the distance and set off down the bank to investigate. The fragrance of freshly-cut wood filled the damp riverside air and as he approached he could see the natives hacking the insides out of a felled cypress tree. Francisco leaned on a nearby stump, using Dominic's sword to carve the finishing touches of a paddle. Another paddle lay on the ground beside him.

"*Buenas días*, commander," said Francisco, his disposition much sunnier than it had been the night before. "It's about time we got you back on the water, wouldn't you say?"

Dominic did not respond. It still pained him to see Francisco using his sword. He longed to have it back, if only to give it a good cleaning. The rust accumulating on the blade was a cancer that had to be eliminated; otherwise, he feared, the corrosion would consume the metal entirely. The night before, he had asked Francisco to at least wipe some oil on the blade, but the old man refused. It was only a thing, Francisco had said, and no man should be attached to a thing.

The natives ushered Dominic into the canoe while it still lay on the riverbank. Then they lined up along its sides and heaved it into the water, each one jumping into the canoe when they reached the water's edge. Soon they were gliding across the black water at enough speed to ruffle Dominic's hair. He could tell from the miniscule wake left by the canoe that it had a negligible draft, yet somehow it was buoyant enough to accommodate twelve men. He marveled at the stability and swiftness of the vessel, especially considering it had been standing in a forest as a living tree just hours earlier. The shipbuilders who constructed his galleon could have learned plenty from these natives.

Dominic gazed at the bizarre world around him. Massive alligators basked on the muddy shoreline like dragons turned to stone, too large and otherworldly to be real. Further on, three otters swooped through cattails in a playful game of chase and, nearby, an egret speared a perch with its beak. For the first time since the shipwreck, his surroundings did not seem so hellish. He was beginning to glimpse some sort of covert system at work, a flawless order that disguised itself as chaos to hide from man's recognition, as evident in the biota as it was in the way the natives paddled in perfect unison. Dominic watched them for a while and marveled at their precision.

"Untie me," he said to Francisco, who sat in front of him, "so I may have a turn."

Francisco looked back at him with a skeptical grimace. "You want to paddle?"

"I need to move my arms," said Dominic. "There are eleven of you and one of me. What could I really do?"

Francisco consulted with Utina who then sat silent and pensive for a long time. This, it seemed, was the first chiefly decision Utina had to make. Finally, he nodded.

Francisco turned to Dominic. "Hold out your hands."

Francisco put the rusty tip of the sword against the twine and pushed it down. The severed fibers fell away and Dominic pulled his hands as far apart as he could, stretching his arms and exhaling with relief. He massaged the deep red indentations on his wrists where the twine had dug in to his skin. Then he turned and reached out to the youngest native — the one who had gathered the cassina for him — and motioned for him to hand over the paddle; the native hesitated, but then he gave it to Dominic.

Dominic tried to mimic the motions of the other paddling native but the canoe decelerated and tracked to the left. The young native tried to show Dominic the proper technique by raising his arms into the air and bringing them down across the water in a circular motion. He said something that Dominic did not understand.

"What is this savage trying to tell me?" Dominic asked, frustrated.

"He says that you need to finish your stroke with a curve, as if you are tracing the rim of the moon. And commander, it may surprise you, but this *savage* does have a name."

Dominic put a curve in his stroke. "Not that I care, but what is it?"

"Cual es tu nombre?" Francisco said to the native.

The native smiled. "Mi... nombre... es... Itori."

Francisco nodded. "Very good."

Dominic sat there stunned, his paddle frozen in mid-stroke. "He speaks Spanish?"

"He's learning. I have been teaching him and several others from the tribe. To be effective warriors, after all, they must know everything about their enemy."

Dominic's face reddened. "So I am the enemy?"

"That is up to you."

They stopped to fish at a sandy riverbank beneath the shade of an oak tree larger than any Dominic had ever seen. Its thick branches reached out over the river like claws. A cool northerly wind had developed. As it whistled through the tree, acorns fell upon the water like raindrops. One bounced off Dominic's head; he whipped around to look for what had hit him.

"Angry... squirrels," said Itori, pointing skyward. He repeated it in Timucuan and the others laughed.

Francisco grinned. "Wouldn't that be the perfect Indian name for you, commander?"

"What?"

"Angry Squirrel."

Something like a smile flashed across Dominic's face, but it quickly vanished. "I will kill you if that sticks," he said.

"Then I will ensure it does."

Dominic watched Utina uncoil a long twine that had a fish-hook carved out of a bone at its end. A clamshell was threaded through the line above the hook as a weight. Utina cracked open a mussel and impaled its meat on the hook, and then he turned to Dominic.

"He wants to know if you would like to try," said Francisco.

Dominic took the line. Utina mimicked the motion of swinging the hooked end of the line toward the water. Dominic's first throw launched the bait as far as the twine could reach and Utina nodded in approval. It did not take long before the line twitched and went taut—Dominic held tight as something on the other end pulled back with surprising force. He smiled as he played the fish. The natives whooped and hollered. With one final heave, Dominic pulled a plump catfish onto the bank. Utina patted him on the back and then leaned down to subdue the writhing fish.

"Is it edible?" asked Dominic, his voice flush with excitement.

"Not just edible," said Francisco. "Delicious."

Utina unhooked the fish and held it up for Dominic to see. Its wormlike whiskers quivered as the fish gulped air and flexed its slimy fins. Utina tossed the fish back into the river.

Dominic was dumbfounded. "I thought that was our lunch? What's the point?"

"The first fish is always thrown back," said Francisco. "Next one is lunch."

Before long they had caught enough catfish to make a meal. The natives gutted them with a crude knife—nothing more than a shark's tooth mounted on a wooden handle—and then they wrapped them in wetted palm fronds and laid them over hot coals to cook. The meat came out flaky and moist, although it certainly would have benefited from a pinch of saffron to help mask the mud flavor. Nevertheless, it satiated Dominic's hunger, and he felt a warm sense of accomplishment for having contributed to the meal.

Dominic insisted on paddling when they boarded the canoe again. The natives appeared amused by his enthusiasm for such a mundane task and seemed happy to ignore his lack of skill in exchange for entertainment. They soon came upon a basking alligator that crashed into the water and charged the canoe. Dominic held the paddle up in defense but the alligator stopped before it reached them.

Utina pointed at the alligator and said, "Itori."

Dominic looked at Itori. "I thought that was *your* name?"

Itori smiled. He pointed to himself. "Me Itori. Me Alligator."

"Your name is Alligator?"

Itori nodded and smiled. Then he pointed at Dominic and said, "You Angry Squirrel."

Francisco and all the natives laughed. Dominic's face turned red. "No," he said. Soon, however, everyone in the boat was repeating it and he could no longer repress his smile. He bit his lip to quell it.

CHAPTER TWELVE

Zane clung to the skeletal remains of the launch pad and tried to think of a way out of what had become a desperate predicament.

"You can drop the bag to me," said Miguel, "or I can come up there and get you down the hard way. You have five seconds to decide . . . Five."

If he dropped the bag, Miguel would quickly discover that most of the coins were no longer inside it. Miguel moved to the base of the ladder and gazed up. "Four," he said.

The ladder extended only a few more rungs past Zane, ending at a twisted, rusted-out platform that looked like it could collapse at the slightest touch.

"Three," said Miguel.

Zane thought about climbing out on the nearest crossbeam but he feared he would slip off if he did—it was slick with vulture droppings. He closed his eyes and hugged the metal ladder. There was no way out.

"Two."

Zane tried to calm himself by looking at the phantasmal rafters around him and envisioning how the structure looked when it was still in use. Eager workers checking gauges. Steam rising from cooling systems. A freshly-painted spacecraft aiming for the stars. If only he were a rocket, he mused, when Miguel finished his vile countdown, his thrusters would burn the man to bits.

"One," said Miguel. "Bad choice, my friend." Miguel put the knife blade between his teeth and started climbing up. Zane had to do something. He scrambled up the last few rungs of the ladder and touched the crooked platform to test it but, as he expected, the entire thing lurched to one side and made a groaning sound as it did. Fragments of rusty metal fell off—which gave him an idea.

Miguel stopped and wiped the rust off of his head and then he took the knife out of his mouth. "Your father sold you out, you know. He won't be able to blame anyone but himself for your death."

"You're lying," said Zane.

"Deep down, you know I'm not." Miguel bit down on the knife again and continued up.

Zane's eyes fell on one of the platform's girders. It was rusted through on each end. He reached out as far as he could and grabbed hold of it and strained to break it off. When it finally gave, he had to stop himself from falling backward. He took a deep breath. That was too close.

He looked down. Miguel was halfway up and still climbing with vigor. The knife blade glinted in his mouth and his clenched teeth were curved into what looked like a wicked smile. Zane held the heavy girder chunk over Miguel. "Stop, or I'll drop this on you."

Miguel kept coming, so Zane aimed and let go. It fell silently. Just as it was about to hit Miguel, however, it bounced off the ladder and deflected away. He heard it hit the ground with a solid *thunk*.

Now what?

He looked at the platform again but saw nothing else to detach. All he could hope for now was to kick Miguel away, but that would be difficult with a knife flailing at his legs. He put his head against the ladder and tried to think of a solution and that's when he felt the thrumming of a vehicle engine in the metal.

It soon became audible. Both Zane and Miguel turned to look toward its source at the same time. There, passing by on the nearby dirt road and throwing a plume of dust, was a military Jeep. Large letters on the side spelled out *US Air Force Patrol*. The two men inside it wore full camouflage fatigues. Zane could hear faint music and the driver bobbed in his seat.

Zane waved his hand in a broad sweep and yelled. "Hey! Up here!"

Miguel stopped and took the knife out of his mouth. "Shut up!"

Zane yelled louder. "Help! I need help!"

The Jeep stopped and Zane could see the soldiers looking around for the source of the voice. The cloud of dust overtook the vehicle and concealed it. Miguel hurried down the ladder, half climbing and half sliding; when he reached the ground, he looked up at Zane. "I will find you and I will kill you." Then he ran into the woods.

Zane looked toward the road—the dust had settled and the soldiers had spotted him. They jumped out of the Jeep with M-16s drawn; Zane started going down the ladder and lost sight of them among the treetops. For some reason, the large guns did not bother him. In fact, they made him feel somewhat safe; after all, Miguel was not brazen enough to go up against two automatic rifles with one little knife. Or was he? Zane's hands became moist with nervousness and as he approached the last ten feet of the ladder, he slipped off. *Splat.* He landed in something gooey. Drawing a painful breath, he almost vomited when he tasted the air. He had fallen in a puddle of vulture excrement.

He tried to stand and almost slipped in the glop but he grabbed the ladder and caught himself. He picked up the duffel bag. It, too, was covered in the stinking grime. He tried to shake it off but it clung like some horrid glue.

"Sir, this is a restricted area," said an approaching voice.

Zane looked up. The two soldiers stood at the edge of the slab, their guns pointed at him. He stood up straight and tried to brush the slime off his arms.

"Sir, did you hear me?" said the taller of the two soldiers, an African American man in his mid-thirties. "This is a restricted area." The other soldier, squat and pale in contrast to his partner, looked to be even younger than Zane.

"Restricted?" said Zane, trying to act ignorant. "Really?"

He could tell from the looks on their faces that they assumed him to be some kind of vagabond, and he was not surprised. His ripped shirt hung open and the wound on his head was caked in dried blood. The rest of his skin, covered in dirt, now boasted a generous splattering of bird filth.

"How the hell did you get out here?" said the younger soldier.

"With difficulty," said Zane.

"Where are you from?"

"Jupiter."

"Jupiter?" said the tall soldier, a slight smirk on his face. "Last dude said Mars."

"Sorry?"

"You're in one of them UFO cults, ain't you."

"Cult?" Zane let out a nervous laugh. But then he realized that going along with the soldier's presumption might be a better alternative to the truth. "Well, to be honest," said Zane, "we call it a *religion*, not a cult."

The tall soldier looked at his partner. "See, what I tell ya? Seems like every year we catch one of these nut-jobs trying to stow away in a rocket, wanting to go up and rendezvous with their alien leader or some crazy story." The other soldier laughed, and then the tall soldier looked at Zane. "How'd you get past the gates, buddy?"

Zane put his weight on one hip, trying to look casual. "That was the easy part. Came out on a tour bus and snuck off."

"Then why'd you pick this launch pad? Ain't been no rockets out here for decades."

"Well, I was just waiting, I guess."

"For what?"

Zane had to conjure a more convincing act. He looked at the sky and pointed. "For it to land," he whispered, and then he twirled his fingers in front of his face as if doing something magical. "Behold, earthlings. The mothership is coming to get me, for I am the only being in the universe who can prevent the intergalactic war."

He must have convinced them of his madness because they laughed out loud. A barrage of sarcastic questions ensued.

"So," said the younger soldier, snickering. "Who's your leader?"

"Captain Kirk. James T."

The soldiers guffawed. "And what's your name?" asked the tall one.

"Jeff Skywalker."

"*Jeff?*"

"Luke's nephew." More laughter.

"Okay, Jeff. So how is it you're able to talk with the — what is it again?"

"Mothership," said Zane.

"Yeah, how do you talk to the mothership?"

"Phone home," Zane said in his best imitation of *E.T.*, but when the soldiers raised their eyebrows without laughing, he knew he had gone too far. "Really, though," said Zane, "that's just what I call it. Layman's terms, you know. I actually use a complex subatomic communications device, made with alien technologies that are *way* beyond your infantile minds."

"Watch it," said the tall soldier. He no longer looked amused. "What's in the bag?"

"Just some stuff for my journey. Toothbrush, clean undies, astronaut ice cream."

"Let me see." The soldier stepped closer and reached for the bag but he stopped. His nostrils twitched and his face contorted. "What's that smell?" he asked.

"What smell?" said Zane. He had been breathing through his mouth the entire time in order to avoid it.

The younger soldier smelled it, too. "What the hell is all over you, man?"

Zane tried to think of an answer appropriate to his character. Alien slime? Spaceship sewage? Antimatter? Nothing sounded authentic, even for a lunatic, so he went with the truth. "Vulture crap. I fell in it."

The soldiers took a step back. "Nasty," said the younger one.

The tall one lowered his gun. "We'll have to give you a citation and get you back to the mainland. But you sure as hell ain't riding in front."

Keeping their distance, the soldiers ordered Zane into the flatbed of the Jeep and instructed him to sit against the tailgate. They did not appear concerned about him as a threat—maybe they were convinced that he was a harmless weirdo or were simply afraid to deal with his stench—and they did not even look back at him as the Jeep started bouncing down the road. Zane gazed toward the launch pad as they left and there in the dark woods near its base he saw Miguel glaring out. Zane waved, smiled and held up the duffel bag, but he quickly thought better of taunting a murderer and looked away.

The Jeep turned onto a paved motorway. Zane watched the seemingly endless swampland and forest fly by in a greenish-brown blur, every mile as good as a light year away from Miguel. Eventually the Jeep turned onto a wide four-lane highway. The driver turned on the stereo, but the R&B ballad that burst forth did not seem to agree with him. He scanned the stations until he came to Hank Williams, Jr., drawling out *A Country Boy Can Survive*.

"What's with the cowboy music?" said the passenger.

The driver smiled. "What, a black man can't listen to country?"

"I just thought you had better taste. I'm picking the next song."

The Jeep reached a bridge that spanned an immense lagoon. As it climbed the steep road, Zane could see houses and condominiums on the other side—freedom. He looked at the body of water below and guessed it to be the Indian River. With scant wind, the water was glass. Crab trap buoys of various colors speckled the surface like ice cream sprinkles. A manatee sounded and left a circular upwelling with its tail. A bottlenose dolphin blasted a school of mullet, the front of its body coming all the way out to snare the one that tried to leap away.

When the song ended, a DJ came on to deliver breaking news. "Still no word on the whereabouts of the men wanted in connection with a boating accident and the death of a federal officer that occurred off the coast last night."

Zane froze.

"My turn," said the passenger, and he changed the station.

Zane exhaled.

"Hang on," said the driver, and he changed it back. "Listen."

No, no, no, thought Zane.

"Authorities say that one of the men has a history of drug abuse. They've identified him as Jupiter resident Zane Fisher. They describe Fisher as a 25-year-old white male, five-ten, medium build, sandy blonde hair, and blue eyes."

The Jeep slowed and stopped at the top of the bridge. The soldiers both turned and looked at Zane. He feigned disinterest by gazing at the lagoon. "Police say Fisher may still be lost at sea or has swum to shore," continued the DJ. "He's considered *extremely* dangerous and should not be approached. Now, back to your *Wacky Workday Hoedown* on K-95 FM."

The driver shut off the stereo without looking at it. "They aren't talking about you, are they, Jeff?"

"His name ain't really Jeff, dumbass," whispered the passenger.

"*I know that.* What's your real name, buddy?"

The soldiers angled their guns toward Zane, so he grabbed the duffel bag, jumped out of the Jeep, and ran down the bridge. He stopped, however, when he saw a police car coming up the bridge toward him. He was cornered.

The soldiers leapt out of the Jeep, aiming their rifles at Zane. "On the ground!" yelled the younger soldier.

Zane looked at them with pleading eyes. "The guy you want is back at that launch pad."

"I said get on the ground! Now!"

The police car stopped. A portly policeman stepped out. He aimed a pistol at Zane and inched toward him.

"Who's this dirtbag?" the policeman yelled to the soldiers.

"I think he's the one they're looking for," shouted the tall soldier. "We found him near the beach."

Panic filled the policeman's face and he mumbled something into his shoulder-mounted radio. Then he looked at Zane. "Are they right? Was that you in the boat out there?"

Zane hesitated, but he was tired of lying. The time had come to give up, to come clean. "Yes, sir," he said.

"You piece of crap. You like to kill cops?"

Zane was startled. "No sir."

The policeman glared at him with terrible eyes. "Cop-killers don't get arrested. They get shot. I want you to know that before I pull this trigger."

Zane went damp with terror. Without even looking down to check the height or depth or if there appeared to be any dangers in the water — the three unwritten rules he had learned from a childhood of jumping off Jupiter's bridges for fun — he turned and leapt over the guardrail. A gunshot cracked behind him but he was too distracted by the sensation of freefalling to even wonder if he had been hit.

When he glimpsed the brown water coming up from below, he let go of the duffel bag and curled into a ball. The world around him detonated. The water's impact sent stinging pain through his whole body and the force of the fall propelled him deep into a shadowy gloom where his legs were thrust into cold mud up to his thighs. He tried to extract them but it felt as if they were cemented in. He realized that he would soon drown if he did not get himself unstuck. A stunning thought flashed in his mind — this could be it.

CHAPTER THIRTEEN

The serpentine river twisted and contorted northward until it pushed the canoe across a shallow delta and out onto a vast lake, its waters as black as cassina. Angry little wind-driven waves jostled the canoe and spit in Dominic's face. Licking the rim of his mouth, the water's pleasant flavor surprised him. *Agua dulce* — sweet water — was the Spanish term for fresh water, and the contents of this lake fit that description more precisely than anything he'd ever tasted. He dipped his hand and cupped a sip to his mouth.

"Do not do that," said Francisco.

Dominic stopped drinking mid-sip. "Please tell me the water is not poisonous."

"The water is good, but you should not put your hand in it. You will bring things up from below."

Dominic gazed into the dark water. The sunlight struggled to penetrate its surface. "Snakes?"

"Worse."

"Alliga—" he stopped. "Itori?"

"Close."

"Enough riddles, old man."

Francisco leaned toward him. "Alligator *gar*."

"Gar?" Dominic laughed. "A fish?"

"Not just any fish. These grow as long as this canoe and their teeth will peel the skin right off a man's bones. Splashing brings them in. That is why you do not see any of us dangling our hands in the water."

Dominic cupped another handful and gulped it down. "I am not afraid of a fish." He had never tasted water so delicious and he intended to drink as much as his stomach would allow. He splashed some on his face and ran his wet fingers through his hair. The coolness invigorated him.

"I am not telling stories," said Francisco. "You will attract them."

Dominic grinned. "I cannot help it. I am an attractive man."

"This is not a joke. How do you think I lost my finger?"

"I thought the Calusa ate it."

Dominic leaned over for another handful but stopped; an iridescent eye stared up at him. Dominic squinted. The eye, because of its sheen, was the only thing visible in the murk; the rest of the creature must have been a dark color because it was totally concealed. The eye descended mere inches and vanished.

Dominic leaned back. "I may have just seen a—"

The water exploded near the front of the canoe. A jagged snout with rows of scythe-like teeth grabbed hold of Utina's paddle blade. When Utina jerked back, the thing in the water reacted violently, whipping its tail, arching its thick back, and flexing its spade-like scales. Dominic froze in awe—the fish had to be ten feet long. With one tic of its head, a *crack* rang out and the beast disappeared into the blackness, leaving Utina with the splintered end of a now useless paddle.

Everyone was stunned, but no one more than Dominic. He pulled his hands away from the edge and folded them in his lap. "Good God," he whispered.

"Still not afraid of fish, commander?" said Francisco.

Dominic scowled. "Mock me again and you will be swimming with that thing."

Only one paddle remained, and it was in Francisco's hands. He held it up and said something in Timucuan, and then repeated it in Spanish. "I do not want to be responsible for our success or failure."

Dominic could see by the worry on the natives' faces how dire the situation had become. They all stared at the paddle as if it were both cursed and anointed. None of them seemed to want to take it.

"Give it to me," said Dominic. "I will do it."

The natives watched Francisco contemplate the offer. "No matter what," said Francisco, "do not let go of it." Dominic nodded and Francisco handed the paddle to him.

The natives bowed toward the sun in unison and mouthed a silent prayer. Francisco, in turn, closed his eyes and recited the *Our Father* in Latin.

"Pater noster, qui es in caelis, sanctificetur nomen tuum..."

Dominic put the end of the paddle in the water and pulled it back, remembering to make a curve at the end of his stroke. The canoe lurched forward.

"Adveniat regnum tuum. Fiat voluntas tua..."

At first the prayer repulsed Dominic, but its tempo soon had a calming effect. It was like a relic from his past life in Spain and — as he concentrated on the rhythm of his paddling—his mind wandered across the ocean, across a decade, to the last European foundation his boots ever touched before they carried him to his ship.

"And lead us not into temptation, but deliver us from evil," said the bishop, his arms stretched toward each wing of the cathedral. *"Amen."*

When the time came to receive Communion, Dominic knelt with difficulty on the stone floor. He despised having to wear the cold, unbending armor expected of a conqueror, even on this, the morning of his first voyage to the New World. The garish steel helmet weighed as much as a cannonball and the malformed breastplate pushed in on his ribcage, refusing to let him draw a full breath. He longed to reach the open seas where he could take off the ridiculous outfit without offending the hierarchy. He envisioned tossing it into the sea and watching it sink into oblivion.

The bishop placed the *eucaristía* on Dominic's tongue. Dominic closed his mouth and let it dissolve. That familiar stale-bread taste he had come to love as a child mingled with his saliva and diffused across the nodes of his tongue. He made the sign of the cross, closed his eyes, and swallowed. It may have been his anticipation about the voyage, his lack of oxygen from the armor, or perhaps his delight from having received absolution after an embarrassingly long confession, but Dominic felt something.

It began as a subtle speck of joy fluttering behind the little notch between stomach and breast, and then it expanded into something like a flower. He could see it without seeing it, this white, holy blossom in his chest, and he prayed for God to let him carry it all the way to the New World so that he might be a new kind of conqueror, one who puts the cross before the sword, one who is merciful and just—exactly like his father had not been. At the mere thought of his father, however, the flower wilted and was no more.

Dominic opened his eyes and pondered the striking differences between La Florida and his homeland. Here he was, paddling over a body of water teeming with ferocious monsters, surrounded on all sides by wilderness where even worse creatures probably lurked, and yet to the natives it was all normal. It was simply what they knew. Perhaps similar beasts prowled the wilds of Spain when it was still a land of tribes and huts, but that was eons ago and by now all the dragons had been slain.

The canoe approached a thin lip of shoreline. Dominic's muscles burned from paddling. He was about to request that one of the natives relieve him when a gar burst out of the water and bit down on his paddle.

"Curse you!" Dominic screamed. He strained to pull it out. The fish thrashed and sent a gush of frothy water onto Dominic. Determined to win, he dug his fingernails into the wood with such force that the fragrance of cypress filled the air. The gar, however, would not relent. It shook its head with such violence that Dominic feared the fish would rip his arms out of their sockets.

Itori leapt off the side of the canoe with the shark-tooth knife in his hand. He landed on the gar's back and wrapped his legs around its massive girth and brought the knife down under the fish's throat. At once the gar released the paddle and sounded, taking Itori down into the lightless depths with him.

"Itori!" screamed one of the younger natives. He stood poised to dive in, but Utina pulled him down and said something in the tone of a leader and pounded his fist on the conch shell around his neck.

Dominic, dumbfounded, stared at the deep, pitted teeth marks on the paddle blade. If that had been flesh, there would be nothing left. He gazed into the water but saw no sign of Itori. "He's gone."

"Do not forget what his name means," said Francisco.

A flurry of bubbles stirred the surface and Dominic guessed that the gar had shredded Itori to pieces, but he did not want to suggest anything so gruesome to the others. Suddenly the huge gar broke the surface; Dominic jerked the paddle away from it. Infernal demon—was it coming back for more? But then the gar rolled over, revealing a pearly underside that glowed white against the black water. The gar floated there, undulating in the chop. A cloud of redness spread from a jagged gash beneath its gills.

"Itori?" whispered Utina.

Itori's head popped out beside the gar. He took a gasping breath, then held the knife high and made a whooping sound. He climbed onto the gar and straddled it like a horse and pounded his fists against its sides. He and the other natives burst into jubilant war cries. Even Dominic could not help joining in, but his war cry sounded more like a yodel and the natives playfully mocked him.

Itori climbed into the canoe. Dominic slapped him on the back and said, "Crazy Alligator." Itori smiled.

Twenty minutes later they made camp on a high, sandy bluff overlooking the lake. They dragged the dead gar up the bank and hung it by its tail from an oak branch but the twine broke; the fish flumped to the ground like a body cut from a gallows.

On the second attempt, they used two strands of twine and hung it successfully. Itori slid his knife down the middle of its belly and made a long incision. He stuck his arm into the cavity, felt around for a while, and yanked out the fish's heart. He took a bite out of it and his mouth curved into a dreadful blood-smeared grin. Then he held the dripping heart to Dominic.

"Eat," said Itori.

Dominic's stomach squirmed. He would try almost any food, but not raw organs. "No," he said.

Itori pushed the heart closer to Dominic's face. "Eat."

"It is an honor to be offered this," said Francisco. "He is not just asking you to eat the gar's heart with him—you will ingest its soul as well."

Dominic looked at Itori's eager, wild eyes. Damn it. He took the heart and drew a deep, contemplative breath. He had seen and held plenty of hearts before, but they had all belonged to enemies. This heart was about the size of a man's but it felt heavier, denser. Dominic closed his eyes and bit into it. Lukewarm fluids gushed into his mouth, tasting of iron and bile and fish slime. He severed off a large chunk with his teeth and it slid down his throat like a raw oyster. He gagged once but kept it down.

Itori whooped with joy and grabbed hold of Dominic's hand. "Brother," he said.

Dominic wiped fish blood from his mouth. "Not I."

CHAPTER FOURTEEN

Zane's lungs ached. He could bend his knees without any resistance, but when he tried to lift his legs, they would not budge. His skin was suctioned to the muck. He pushed against the bottom with his hands but it was no more fruitful than pushing against pudding — the only firmness he felt was a cluster of burrowed clams, too scattered to provide any support.

He opened his eyes and the brackish water stung them but the pain quickly conceded. As his vision adjusted, he could see a tea-colored haze, differentiated by a shadowy horizon — the mud bottom. He looked up. Rays of light danced over his head. A few bubbles fled from his mouth and wobbled to the surface. He envied them.

His body urged itself to breathe. He refused to let that happen but he knew he had only moments before he would pass out. His situation was as bleak as it could get and he wondered what it would feel like to die. When he heard the click and whistle of a dolphin, however, a moment of hope struck him. He had heard stories of dolphins saving people from sharks and ferrying drowning children to safety. Maybe this one was coming to help him. He stared into the dinge, expecting his streamlined savior to burst forth with its flippers spread wide like angel wings and whisk him to the surface. But nothing came.

Soon everything within Zane's body was commanding him to take a breath. No part of him but *him* recognized that he was underwater; his functions warred with his reason. He tried again to push himself out of the mud, this time spreading his arms wide to get more surface coverage, and his hand brushed against something rough. He grabbed hold of it and could tell by its shape and texture that it was a rope. He pulled on it and felt only slack, but it soon came taut and he could tell that it was attached to something. He tugged. The thing did not budge. Perfect. He wrapped the rope around his hands and strained to pull himself out of the mud. His legs lifted up.

I might make it, he thought.

But the rope slackened and the mud sucked him back in. He pulled the rope toward him — whatever it was attached to seemed to have gotten dislodged — and soon a black shape came his way. When he tried to touch it, his fingers slid between moss-covered wire mesh. Something pinched his thumb and he realized he had found a *ghost trap,* so called because once its buoy was gone — cut off by a careless boater or an unexpected storm — the crabber could no longer find the trap. When crabs came in and could not get out, they eventually died of starvation and their decomposing carcasses would attract more crabs, and so on through the seasons in a perpetual cycle of waste. Zane could hear the crabs rattling against each other in the trap.

At least I won't die alone, he thought, trying to find humor in his hopeless situation. After thinking it, however, he realized how extremely unfunny it was. Still, he was surprised at how calm he felt. The rays of light swooping around him grew brighter. His chest throbbed and in what he assumed to be his life's last thought he looked at the crab trap and the image of a snowshoe popped into his mind.

Could it work?

At this point, anything was worth a try. He pooled his last morsels of strength, grabbed the trap, and attempted to use it as a brace to lift himself out.

Please, he thought.

The trap sank into the bottom faster than he had hoped but when the mud pushed all the crabs to the top of the mesh, it stopped, providing enough resistance for Zane to put all of his weight on the trap. He strained to push himself up. The mud made a slurping sound when it released him.

As he kicked toward the surface, he felt like he was on the cusp of losing consciousness and was not sure if he would make it. But he swam with vigor, and when his head shot out of the water, he sucked in what he guessed to be the deepest breath he had ever taken, besides, probably, his first. With that one inhalation, he filled his throbbing lungs with all the air they needed and his brain felt suddenly lucid. The ensuing breaths were delicious and the sun felt like warm lotion on his skin.

He looked up and could see the underside of the bridge where, assumedly, the soldiers and cop had looked down and waited for him to surface. When they did not see him after a minute or so, he guessed, they would have considered him drowned. If so, and if he could now reach land unseen, it might work in his favor.

He spun around in the water to analyze his surroundings. The town shoreline was half a mile away and, to his side, monolithic pilings stretched up to the belly of the bridge. He spotted the duffel bag near the closest piling, its contents of Styrofoam buoying it high in the water. Swimming to it, he crossed into the shade of the bridge and the water temperature dropped a few degrees.

In the distance, the dolphin cut across the surface, still busy chasing mullet. "Don't worry, Flipper," said Zane. "The crabs saved me."

He stayed close to the pilings and followed them toward the shore, stopping once to rest against the wooden rafters that marked the channel. The wood smelled of tar; black gunk clung to every part of his body that brushed against it. He continued on. When his ears dipped below the waterline he heard the crackle of the barnacles that covered the submerged buttresses. His fisherman's mind imagined the trophy catches prowling below. Redfish. Mangrove snapper. Speckled sea trout. He wondered if he'd ever get to fish Florida's waters again. The possibility of not being able to made him sad.

He heard the whine of a boat motor. Looking back, he saw a police boat circling the area where he had gone into the water, its flashing lights too bright to look at even in the midday glare. Zane pulled himself around to the backside of the nearest piling and sank into the water until only his eyes and the top of his head were above it. He watched the boat stop. A man on the stern donned scuba gear and flipped backward into the water. This was ideal—they were searching for his body, and with the water so murky, they would probably search for hours. When they did not find him, they would blame it on currents and start counting down the time it would take for enough gases to form.

His friend's body had soaked for three days before it floated. Bobby Nelson was by far the most popular kid in Zane's 5th grade class. A beautiful boy with almond eyes and skin that never burned—it only tanned—Bobby basked in the sun every afternoon while practicing to be a professional surfer. Despite their friendship, Zane was jealous of Bobby's looks, athletic skills, and the fact that his parents loved him so much they would sit on the beach all day while he surfed. The girls, naturally, were crazy about Bobby. But so was David Allen West, who first saw him when he peered over a fence during school recess. Posing as a photographer for a surfing magazine, he befriended Bobby and his parents at the beach.

One day, Bobby was not in class. By midmorning, frantic police officers arrived to interview Zane and his classmates. When had they last seen Bobby? Had he been talking to any strangers? By that afternoon, pieces of the puzzle came together and a manhunt for David Allen West commenced. Two days later, while Zane rode the bus to school, the morning's breaking news blurted out before the driver could silence the radio. David Allen West was in custody and had already confessed—boasted, in fact—to kidnapping, raping, and strangling Bobby, and then dumping his broken little body off the Juno Beach pier, into the surf Bobby had loved so much. And that morning, bloated and corrupt, Bobby had ridden his last wave—right to the feet of a horrified tourist. By the time the busload of distraught students arrived at school, an army of state counselors had already amassed.

"But how did the guy rape Bobby?" Zane asked the counselor assigned to him, a solemn, grandfatherly man with a magnificent mustache that curled up at each end.

The counselor looked at Zane for a long time. "How about let's not focus on the rape part. Let's talk about how you felt when you heard that your friend had been found deceased."

"I don't know. It sucks, it really sucks. But I just don't know why..." Zane's words trailed off.

"Tell me."

"Nothing."

"It's ok, Zane. You can tell me anything."

Zane looked down. "It's just that I don't know why that man chose Bobby. Why not me? I mean, was I too ugly or something?"

The counselor twirled the end of his moustache between his thumb and index finger. His face twisted into a pensive frown. "Are you playing a joke on me?"

"No, sir."

"Then I'm confused. Are you saying you're jealous that a sex offender kidnapped your friend and not you?"

Zane stood. "Can I leave whenever I want?"

"Yes. Please do."

Zane ran out of the room and straight into the bathroom where he locked himself in the farthest stall and cried for over an hour without anyone asking if he needed help. He would certainly miss Bobby, but he was mostly sad for Bobby's parents. Their son, after all, had been the nucleus of their lives. What more did they have to live for? He thought of the time he had seen them sitting on the beach, clapping and cheering whenever Bobby shredded a wave or shot out of a barrel. They were the kinds of parents that otherwise only existed in old movies and TV shows.

Now, watching the police boat, Zane thought about his own father and mother and how they would react when someone came to inform them that he had jumped off a bridge and was likely deceased. That's the word they would use—deceased—as if it were any less awful than telling them he was dead. What would his parents do? His mother, he guessed, would swallow her most potent pills before any genuine grief could set in, and his father would slouch into a quiet corner of a bar to share his laments with a bottle of *Beam* or *Captain*.

But not everyone, he realized, would grieve when they heard the news of his demise. Some would likely find gratification in it, namely Lucia's parents. He could envision their reactions. *We knew he was bad. He got what he deserved. Our daughter finally has justice.* If his death brought some closure to what had undoubtedly been the worst tragedy to ever befall them, then Zane was happy to let them believe it was true.

Zane reached the shore and climbed up the concrete embankment below the bridge, pausing to catch his breath. A yearning buzzed in his body, a mixture of hunger and thirst. He hadn't had any food or water since the previous day. He could not, however, go into town during daylight; the cops would be everywhere. So he crawled up into the narrow, graffiti-scribbled cavity where the bridge abutment joined the underside of the road. Someone had obviously been sleeping there; a piece of cardboard was laid out to the length of a person, empty food tins littered the ground, and a few dirty blankets were balled up in a crevice. The air reeked of urine.

He shook one of the blankets and a syringe flew out. Part of him wanted to see what it held, but the thought of injecting himself with a dirty bum needle revolted him enough to stamp out the craving. He lay down on the cardboard and pulled the stinking blanket over himself. He doubted he had ever felt so tired. Looking out, he could see the police boat in the distance still hovering over the same place. Drawing his gaze in closer, he watched shards of glass glisten on the concrete like a scattering of broken dreams.

CHAPTER FIFTEEN

At dawn the natives carved three new paddles and everyone boarded the canoe, hugging the lakeshore as they journeyed north. The flavors of the previous night's meal lingered in Dominic's mouth. He wished otherwise. The gar meat had been foul and gritty, and the accompanying palmetto berries—which the natives gathered from the surrounding scrub—held the pungency of rotten tobacco. He longed to rinse his mouth. He kept his hands in his lap, though. He had learned his lesson about dangling fingers in dark waters.

"How much more of this?" said Dominic.

"We are not far," said Francisco. The old man looked frail in the morning sheen. The journey had taken an obvious toll.

"And what is in store for me when we get to our mysterious destination?"

"I cannot tell you yet, but trust me when I say that you are not in any danger."

"Trust you? Old man, I have yet to decide whether you are a liar or a lunatic."

"Why is it you think I am either?"

"Do you remember the night of the hurricane? You told me your story about how you came to La Florida. On an expedition with Juan Ponce de Leon, you said."

"Yes."

"Well, I might have believed you if Ponce de Leon did not die over a hundred years ago. It is simply not possible for you to have been on that voyage."

Francisco sighed. "Perhaps my story was not entirely true."

By midday they reached the mouth of a creek that flowed west into the lake. The water in the creek was much clearer, and the confluence looked like a swirl of olive oil and balsamic vinegar, with neither fluid willing to mix with the other. Dominic wished he had a fresh *barra gallega* — Galician bread — to dip into it, even though he knew it would just get soggy and fall apart.

The natives steered the canoe into the creek and paddled rigorously to make headway against the current. They stayed close to the wooded shoreline to reduce the water's resistance and Dominic ducked away from a barrage of low-hanging tree limbs. One of the limbs brushed against the side of the canoe and a swarm of spiders clambered aboard. Dominic spent the next few minutes flicking the hideous things into the water where bream and mudfish quickly slurped them away.

The creek constricted as they toiled on. By late afternoon it had become so narrow that the trees on either shore could reach across and stroke each other's limbs. Soon, their branches conjoined to create a leafy canopy that blocked out most of the sunlight. Not even a gasp of wind stirred inside the dark tunnel and the only sound was of the paddles swishing against water. The natives did not speak, and Dominic had the sense that this was a place where words were not welcome.

Minutes later, Francisco leaned toward Dominic and whispered, "Do you hear it?"

"Hear what?"

"The sound of many waters."

"Do you mean the river?"

He smiled. "No, not the river."

Dominic leaned toward the primeval forest and listened. He thought he heard a child's laugh but it could have just been the call of a bird or wild animal. The canoe came around a sharp curve in the river and before them, half submerged, lay a massive tree that had fallen out of the forest. A naked boy, the same color as the tree, jumped up from it. He looked terrified, but then his face exploded into vibrant joy. He ran up the trunk and bounded into the woods, screaming.

"*Ara Ibi*," said Francisco. "Many Waters — our village."

"I see no village."

"That is the intention."

The natives beached the canoe alongside the tree and hurried out. Dominic followed them up a narrow path. The trail meandered through the woods at several sharp angles so that no one passing by on the river could see what it led to. They came to a clearing in the middle of which stood an immense circular wall made of pine logs that had been sharpened into something resembling fence posts. Coils of smoke rose from behind the walls and the beguiling smell of roasted game wafted through the air.

The only entryway was an opening where each end of the wall ran parallel to the other, as if the entire structure were a circle whose lines continued past one another a good distance without connecting. It created an entrance like a narrow hall which could be defended easily. The boy who had been on the log soon emerged from the opening, followed by a line of natives — mostly women and other children.

The children were naked. The women — wearing girdles of oak moss that barely veiled the dark shadows of their laps — were tall and thin and had long, black hair that hung to their navels. Their bare breasts were the only parts of their coppery skin without tattoos; otherwise their bodies were adorned with ornate indigo bands and clusters of dots that all surely meant something but, to Dominic, were as indecipherable as the words that now poured out of their mouths.

A young woman holding a little girl ran to Itori and wrapped her free arm around him. Itori nuzzled his face into her neck and then kissed her eyelids. A gaggle of children swarmed Utina and gawked at the shell around his neck, none of them daring to touch it. A sullen woman walked to Utina, regarded him sheepishly, and hugged him in an embrace so measured that only her forearms touched his skin.

Another woman, slightly older than the rest, emerged from the narrow doorway and gazed out. Her eyes darted back and forth between the men and the trail. When she saw the shell necklace on Utina, she dropped to her knees and sobbed. "Ona," she cried. "*Onaaa.*"

"She is Ona's primary wife," said Francisco.

Dominic turned to him, puzzled. "Primary?"

"Chiefs are expected to have several wives, but she was his favorite."

Itori helped her stand. The other women surrounded her and took her into the village. Dominic followed everyone inside. What he saw astonished him. The huts were aligned as orderly as houses in a European town, and the roofs, woven from palm thatch, looked like the heads of monks. He assumed the large hut in the center of the village to be the chief's residence, as that was the direction in which the women led Ona's wife. To its side stood seven poles arranged in a circle around a fire pit—a meeting point, it seemed—and feathers, bones and antlers adorned each pole. On the opposite side of the village, a bed of coals smoldered in a large pit, producing a column of thick smoke that drifted across fish flanks and animal pieces arranged on a thatch mat. Nearby, stretched deerskins dried on timber frames.

As the women approached Ona's hut, a maiden more beautiful than any Dominic had ever seen in the New World came to the entryway. Her tawny skin, not yet spoiled by tattoos, still enjoyed the sleekness of youth, although she was clearly not a child. Her thick, black hair waved down across her chest all the way to her thighs and only the curves of her hips and the points of her small, acicular breasts peeked out. She did not wear any moss like the others—her hair was like a dress of its own. When she saw the older woman in tears, she, herself, collapsed. In the throes of grief, she looked primal, raw, and enticing, and in that instant Dominic wanted to both console and conquer her.

"Is she another of Ona's wives?" asked Dominic.

"No, that is Mela," said Francisco. "His daughter, whom he loved very much."

"She is certainly a striking creature."

"She is purity embodied. Many men hunger for Mela. Her fruits, however, are forbidden."

"Are they forbidden now that the tree has been cut down?"

Dominic could feel Francisco's eyes on him, so he turned and met the old man's worried gaze with a look of nonchalance. Francisco relaxed, and then said, "I must tend to something. I will return soon."

Francisco hobbled out of the village and Dominic lowered himself onto a stump beside the central fire and looked around. The place exuded tranquility. The men had dispersed throughout the village to play with their children and enjoy the gentle caresses of their wives. Dominic watched Itori place his sleeping daughter in an outdoor bed of moss and then lead his young wife by the hand into their unlit hut. Next door, Utina's children climbed all over him. His wife brought him a bowl of sliced fruit but he pushed it away and it spilled into the dirt. She stooped and collected the fruit and crept back into the hut.

Dominic looked into the fire and lost himself for a long time watching the glowing embers fissure and crumble. He heard a faint giggle, so he whipped around and startled a pack of knee-high children who had gathered to study him. They scampered away. Moments later, however, they tiptoed back, staring at him in wonder.

"Go away," he said. They did not seem to understand, so he tried to wave them off with his hand. The children laughed and mimicked his gesture, and then the oldest of them, a little girl of four or five years old, crept up to him.

"Blanco," she said. Francisco had obviously taught her some Spanish.

"My skin?" said Dominic, but that did not incite a reply so he touched his bare forearm. "White skin."

"No." The little girl touched Dominic's hair just above his ear. "White."

"My hair is black." And then he said, "*Blaaack.*"

"No." The little girl touched the top of his head and said, "Black." Then she touched the hair above his ear again and said, "*Whiiite.*"

Was there some dried mud in his hair, perhaps? He touched his scalp and felt nothing abnormal, so he grabbed a small tuft of hair above his ear and plucked it out. Sure enough, it was white. Damn it. When had he started going gray? Before long, he feared, he would look just like his father looked in his later years. He turned away from the children and slouched on the stump.

Soon he heard someone whistling and looked up to see Francisco approaching. The old man's face glowed with vitality. His hair looked damp.

"Why do you look like you just bathed?" said Dominic.

"Because I did."

"Perhaps you can get some of these filthy natives to do the same."

"They do not bathe. They swim in the river."

"Which is why they smell like catfish."

"Catfish smell good to them."

"Not to me. I would certainly like to enjoy the luxury of a bath, unless of course you are so selfish that you intend to keep it entirely to yourself."

"In time, but not now. There are important matters at hand."

"What could be so pressing?"

"You must learn our ways."

"And then?"

"And then you can have a bath." Francisco turned and headed off in the opposite direction, his robe curling up in the wind of his walk. "Come with me."

Dominic trailed Francisco to a small, dilapidated hut on the far perimeter of the village. A crooked cross hewn from palmetto sticks jutted from the midpoint of the roof.

Not a goddamn church, Dominic thought as he entered. When he saw the primitive altar made of stacked timber and the three pews fashioned out of cypress logs, his mood turned sour.

"What the hell are we going to do here?"

"First," said Francisco, kneeling at the altar, "we will pray."

"No. I do not pray anymore."

"Then how do you intend to live?"

"I live just fine."

"You are alive, yes, but you do not have *life*. Listen to me closely. The next chapter of your existence will require an ongoing conversation with the one who created what is perhaps the most dangerous and miraculous thing in the world."

112

Dominic sneered. "I thought I was the most dangerous and miraculous thing in the world."

"Do not take this so lightly. Dark forces will conspire against you. You must be prepared. You must put on your armor."

"Old man, my armor—along with my faith—is at the bottom of the sea. I can take care of myself without the help of some vengeful deity. I do not know what it is you speak of, but you cannot make me do something against my will. I answer to no one."

"What if I tell you that if you do everything I ask, you will be rewarded with a treasure more valuable than all the gold and silver in the known world?"

"Of course I would agree, but no such treasure exists."

"On the contrary, commander, it does, and I can show you where it is."

Francisco made the sign of the cross over his body and stood. Dominic could see why the old man's back was so hunched—the ceiling in the makeshift church was not high enough for anyone to stand up straight.

"I suppose," said Francisco, "you think it was mere coincidence that I found you on the beach. That just by chance you were the lone survivor."

"What else could it have been? Do not tell me fate or some nonsense."

"I have lived a long life, commander, and one thing I can tell you for certain is that there are no coincidences. The future unfolds according to a plan. Bizarre happenstances and convergences are supposed to happen. Life is a cosmic drama in which every being plays a part. Especially you."

"If you think you are so wise, then tell me, old man, without all the pious drivel, what the hell is the purpose?"

"It is simple. To learn how to love."

Dominic's eyes became fiery. His voice sharpened. "So what are you saying? That God wanted to teach me to *love* when he took my son?"

Francisco looked at him with tender, knowing eyes. "No, commander. He wanted to teach you to love when he gave him to you."

CHAPTER SIXTEEN

"Who the hell you think you is?" said a deep but distinctly feminine voice.

Zane opened his eyes and tried to discern his whereabouts. Concrete. Graffiti. Filth.

"Why you in my bed? I *know* you ain't been usin' my junk!" said the voice, its pitch and volume increasing with every word.

Zane pulled a deep breath through his nose. Urine. Rotten fish. Stale beer. He threw the blanket off and sat up. The shadowy gloom of dusk had painted the bridge embankment in soft grays and its gaps an impenetrable black, likewise masking the finer features of the African American woman towering over him. Her brow furrowed in distrust and she gripped an aluminum base-ball bat with both hands.

"I'm sorry," said Zane. "I was tired. And cold."

"Dint yo momma teach you no manners? You ain't supposed to touch other peoples' stuff, or sleep in other peoples' beds, unless acourse they invite you in," and she let out a booming laugh that did not seem to gel with her defensive stance.

"Sorry. I'll get up."

"Naw, don't do that." She sat down beside him and put the bat on the ground. "You's little nuff I could kick yo ass, anyway." She laughed again.

Even now, Zane had to look up at her. The woman's cocoa skin was mottled with tiny black flecks, most noticeable on her cadaverous cheeks. Black ringlets of hair hung down the sides of her face from beneath a *Miami Dolphins* beanie cap, and the rest of her clothes gave the impression that she had acquired them by scooping up a random pile from the back steps of a thrift shop. She wore men's *Nike Air* sneakers that had opened up at each toe, purple sweatpants a few sizes too large, a neon-pink *Cancun Spring Break 1997* T-shirt, and a stonewashed jean jacket with a *Bon Jovi New Jersey* button on the front pocket. On anyone else the ensemble would have looked ridiculous. Considering her personality, however, it seemed perfect.

"I'm Mama Ethel," she said, and then she looked up at the underside of the causeway. "Welcome to my wata-front home. Solid concrete construction and close to the highway for them long commutes." She smiled.

"You're homeless?" asked Zane, but then he bit his lip. "Sorry, I shouldn't have said that."

"It don't bother me none. A dog don't get mad when you say he's a dog, do he? What's your name?"

"I'm Zane." He immediately regretted not using an alias. But who would this lady talk to, anyway? And who would listen to her?

"Pleasure," said Mama Ethel, taking his hand in hers so fully that Zane could no longer see it. "You know, Mista Zany, when I saw you in my bed, the first thought I had was to growl at you."

Zane smiled. "Growl at me?"

She leaned toward him with wild eyes and stooped on all fours. "*Grrrr*," she growled, and then she sat back down. "Like a big ol bear. Dint yer momma never read you *Goldilocks*?"

"I doubt it," said Zane.

Mama Ethel's voice took on the whine of a child. "Summun's been sleepin in *my* bed! Summun's been eatin *my* porridge! Summun's been shootin up *my* junk! Ring a bell?"

Zane laughed. This woman was wonderful, if not absolutely nuts. She laughed, too, but then she stopped and the contours of her face drooped into a look of intense sadness.

"Mikaela sho did love that story," she said.

Zane had not even known Mama Ethel for a minute, but he wanted to cheer her up. "With someone telling it like you just did, I can see why," he said.

"Ain't you gonna ask me who Mikaela is?"

"I think I can guess. Your daughter?"

Mama Ethel nodded with slow, broad motions of her head and neck. "It was her birt-day last munf. Fifteen years ode. Prolly be learnin to drive a car soon. Where's the time go?"

"Do you ever see her?"

"Naw. I been on the streets since she was eight. I try to call her sometimes but she don't want nuthin to do with a nappy old homeless woman. I keep on saying that one a these days I'm gonna get my life together and get her back, but like my auntie always said, talkin bout fire don't boil the pot. Mikaela lives with her daddy's momma now — her grandmomma."

"Where's her father?"

"Heaven, I hope, but I doubt it. He killed hisself."

"I'm sorry."

"Don't be. Life is short and full a thorns. The mo you cry the less you piss. You hungry?"

"Starving."

"Most people under bridges is. Let's see what Mama Ethel can rustle up."

She reached into one of the crevices of the bridge and pulled out a can. It had no label and was dented in at the middle like an anorexic. She shook the can by her ear. "You like beans?" she asked.

"I could eat a rock right now."

"They's lots of them round here, too, but I recommend the beans." She laughed, and then used a can opener to open the can. "Sweet blessin a God!" she exclaimed. "She ain't just beans, Mista Zany, she's pork'n beans. Hal-le-lu-jah! Auntie always said, count yo blessins, not yo problems. Hope you don't mind em cold."

"Not at all."

She handed him a *Krispy Kreme* coffee mug filled with beans and a plastic spoon. "Thank you, ma'am," said Zane.

"Call me Mama."

Zane smiled. He took a bite of the beans and looked out at the river. The sun had set and the sky and water looked like identical cobalt mirrors reflecting each other. The police boat was gone and the only movement he could see was from a cormorant making a v-shaped wake as it prowled below the surface. He wondered if the cops had given up, or if they would resume their search in the morning. He resolved to find a newspaper as soon as it came out.

"So what you runnin from?" said Mama Ethel.

Zane felt suddenly nervous. "Who said I was running?"

"I dint say you did nothin wrong. Plenty a good cotton plants get chopped down from associatin with weeds. I can see you ain't trouble. You just *in* trouble."

Zane looked out at the river and watched the ghostly streaks of fish cruising through phosphorescence. Mama Ethel hummed a tune he guessed to be from a gospel hymn. When she finished, she picked up a hypodermic needle, but after looking at it for some time, she wrapped it in a napkin and set it aside.

Zane blurted, "Last time I talked to my mother, I told her I hated her."

Mama Ethel leaned back and looked at Zane down the bridge of her nose. Then she nodded her head. "I sho know how it feels to be on the other end a that. But you don't really hate her, do you?"

"No. I could never hate her. I just wish she was different. I wish she was... more like you."

Mama Ethel's booming laugh echoed off the bridge rafters, driving out a few pigeons. "Why in the world would you wish that on yo momma?"

"Because you don't blame your daughter for your situation."

Mama Ethel looked at Zane for a moment, and then she stood and said, "I know zactly what you need." Zane watched her go up the embankment. He hoped that she would not offer him drugs because he doubted he had enough strength to resist, dirty needle or not. But she simply grabbed two blankets and a sweater from one of the crevices. She laid the blankets out on a piece of cardboard and gently smoothed them down with her large hands, and then she rolled up the sweater and placed it as a pillow. "Come on, child, let me tuck you in."

Zane felt uncomfortable about her offer but the unwavering smile on her face made it impossible to decline. He carried the duffel bag up the embankment and set it down beside the bed, and then he lay down. Mama Ethel pulled the top blanket up to his chin and folded it in under his sides until he looked like a pastry. Then she lay next to him and ran her fingers through his hair.

"Now I lay me down to sleep," she whispered, "I pray the Lord my soul to keep."

Zane closed his eyes and savored the feeling of Mama Ethel's warm, calloused hand caressing his scalp. To the world she may have been a homeless drug addict who lived under a bridge, but at that moment to Zane she was nothing less than an angel.

"If I die before I wake," she continued, her whisper waning, "I pray the Lord my soul to take."

Her hand stopped moving. It sat motionless on Zane's head for a long time before the tips of her fingers started trembling. She sniveled, and then in a low murmur she said, "Goodnight, Mikaela."

"Goodnight, Mama," whispered Zane.

Zane slept a hard, dreamless sleep and woke to the sound of singing. "*I once was lost but now am found...*"

It was Mama Ethel, belting out *Amazing Grace* as she prepared their breakfast: two coffee cups full of stale *Cheerios* with water instead of milk.

"*When we've been here ten thousand years, bright shining as the sun, we've no less days to sing God's praise than when we've first begun.*"

119

The morning sun, floating low in the east, had not yet been obstructed by the bridge and in the gleam Mama Ethel seemed almost ethereal. When she noticed him awake, she brought him his cereal.

"You know what, Mista Zany?" she said. "Last night I dint need no dope to sleep. First time in years. I think you brought me some hope, or sumpin like it."

Zane smiled. "You're a good mama, Mama."

She sat beside him and put her cereal down. "You know, *Goldilocks* wasn't Mikaela's favorite book."

"No? What was?"

"*Billy Goats Gruff.*"

"Tell me about it."

"Well, these three goats start to cross a bridge one by one, but a big ugly troll lives under it. 'Who's that trampin over my bridge?' the troll says. 'Now I'm comin to gobble you up!' But when that troll finally goes up, the biggest a them billy goats knocks him right smack in the water." Mama Ethel's chestnut eyes flushed with tears and she gazed down. "Sometimes I wonder if Mikaela thinks a me as some nasty ol troll, hidin in the darkness while life just passes over me like a long line a billy goats."

Zane put his hand on her back. He suddenly realized that he had the ability to help her. He unzipped the duffel bag and pulled out one of the stacks of coins.

"I want you to get back on your feet and go spend some time with Mikaela," he said. He handed her the stack. She looked at it cautiously.

"What's this?"

"A gift. They should be worth enough to get yourself a place to live, maybe even buy your daughter a car for her next birthday."

Sunlight glinted off the coins and Mama Ethel gasped as if she had just seen God. Her hands shook and her breaths quickened into something like hyperventilating. "Mista Zany, is these real gold?"

Zane smiled. "Have a look."

She dug into the shrink-wrap with her long, dirty fingernails and wrestled out a coin. This was the first time Zane had seen one of them in daylight and, without the obscurity of the plastic wrap, it did not resemble a round of modern bullion as he thought it would. Instead, its edges and width were uneven, and the crude design on the front looked familiar.

"Oh my God," said Zane, taking the coin from her.

He pulled his doubloon necklace out of his shirt and his face contorted in confusion and shock as he compared the two coins. They were identical, even down to the text around the edge: *Nuestra Señora de los Dolores*. How was it even possible? He ripped open the stack and held the coins in a pile in his hands. *Nuestra Señora de los Dolores. Nuestra Señora de los Dolores.* All of them *Nuestra Señora de los Dolores.*

He stood abruptly. "I have to find a telephone."

CHAPTER SEVENTEEN

D ominic was overcome with grief as he watched Mela cutting off her hair with a conch-lip knife. He wanted to grab the knife away from her. Given the somberness of the other natives, however, he thought it unwise to interrupt the ritual. Slowly, methodically, she held her hair in thick handfuls and sliced it as close to her scalp as possible, dropping each bulky strand into a woven basket, until the basket overflowed and her face looked boyish. Without her locks to cloak her, she stood there completely and unashamedly naked, until one of the women brought a girdle of moss. She seemed loathe to wear it and only upon her mother's urging did she finally wrap it around her waist.

Mela's mother, too, had sliced off her own hair, as did three other women whom Dominic guessed were Ona's lesser wives. They gathered each of their baskets of hair and walked in a straight line out of the village wall with the entire tribe trailing them. A somber chant rose from the row of people. Francisco and Dominic followed.

"Why did they do that?" asked Dominic.

"Widows cut their hair," said Francisco, "and do not remarry until it has regrown."

Dominic stepped to the side of the line and stared at Mela walking in front. Without her gown of hair to cover her, he could run his eyes down the arc of her back and around the curvature of her hip and all the way to the nape of her knee which flexed as she walked. "And what about daughters of widows?" he said.

Francisco did not answer.

The procession ambled through the village entryway and came to a three-way fork in the trail. The path on the right, Dominic knew, led to the river, but he had not yet explored the other two. A disconcerting feeling overcame him when he saw that the trail to the left was demarcated by two poles sticking out of the ground, each with a human skull on top. He was relieved to see the natives take the middle path.

The surrounding oak trees, with moss sagging from their twisted limbs, looked as dreary as the natives. The middle trail tapered and soon became so narrow that the ferns on either side brushed against Dominic's legs. The air grew dim and cool. He shivered.

The procession passed a knoll of higher ground, comprised not of earth but of empty shells—clams, oysters, mussels, snails. The shells toward the bottom of the hill were bleached white by the sun, while the newer, darker ones near the top were still cloaked with beards of algae. It was the village trash heap.

As they came around a bend in the trail, Dominic heard a shrill, fanatical chanting, and as they entered a clearing, he saw that its source was an old man jumping and twirling around a small mound of dirt. Other mounds were spread throughout the clearing, but only this one bore the dark moistness of being freshly dug. The old man wore the preserved face of an actual panther over his head like a skullcap, making it look like he had four eyes and four ears, half of them feline. His long white hair stuck to his face like a spider's nest. Most of his body was stained red with some earthen pigment, and he held an ironwood staff adorned with shells, bones and other forest trinkets that rattled when he waved it over Mela and the women.

"He is Yaba," said Francisco, his voice gruff with disdain. "The village shaman."

"And what is in the mound?" asked Dominic.

"For a normal funeral it would be Ona's body, but it is too dangerous to retrieve it from the Ais, so they buried some of his possessions instead. His spear. His ceremonial headdress. And the bones of his firstborn—and only—son, who was sacrificed fifteen years ago."

Yaba motioned toward the mound and the women came forth and spread their chopped hair over it in clumps. Before long it was impossible to determine whose hair belonged to whom, except for Mela's. Hers stood out because of its thickness and sheen. Dominic watched tears stream from Mela's eyes. Despite her newly unfeminine look, he ached to hold her.

Mourn for your father, he thought, while I mourn for your beauty.

With her basket now empty, Mela bowed her head and handed what looked like a cup fashioned from a conch shell to Yaba. He danced around the mound and set the shell on its highest point. "*Ah ah ah aye,*" he chanted. "*Ah ah ah eh.*" He suddenly threw down his staff and leaned back in an unnatural, contorted posture, with the back of his head touching the top of his shoulders and his arms twisted straight out behind. It looked as if his back had become his front.

His eyes, rolled back in his head, were as opaque as fish eggs, and his eyelids fluttered over them. He yammered out a rash of words that, to Dominic, sounded like gibberish. The natives gasped. A few women cried out.

"What did he say?" asked Dominic.

Francisco stared at Yaba with contempt. "Nothing. He is trying to frighten them."

"*Tell me.*"

Francisco sighed. "He says the spirits warn that Ona will return from the dead, but at a terrible price."

"What price?"

"A rain of fire. A great dragon rising out of the sea. Pestilence and mass death." He sent a dismissive backhanded wave toward Yaba. "Pay no attention, though. Yaba is a charlatan, a soothsayer."

Later in the afternoon, Dominic found himself sitting around the central fire with the men of the village, including Itori and Francisco who sat on either side of him, and Utina, who sat in the center with an air of detached pride on his face. The men seemed to be telling stories about Ona — Dominic heard the name repeatedly. Everything else they said was indecipherable and Francisco was too involved in the passionate conversation to translate.

Mela entered the circle carrying a large wooden bowl and a conch shell cup almost identical to the one atop Ona's memorial. Dominic admired the gentle grace of her walk, but when a dribble of black liquid spilled out of her bowl, a wave of nausea surged through him. "Cassina," he groaned, as if the drink itself were one of his worst enemies.

Itori looked at him and smiled. "Cassina."

"Not for me," said Dominic. "Never again."

"This cassina will not make you ill," said Francisco. "It has been prepared by the women, as it is supposed to be."

"I do not care who prepared it. I will not drink."

"Commander, it is an important part of learning how we live. They expect you to partake. Otherwise you will not be invited on tomorrow's hunt."

"So they will shun me if I do not drink their awful swill?"

"They simply want you to be of clear mind. Self-awareness and purification are the keys to being a good hunter. When you look into the black drink, they say you see yourself as God sees you, and when you drink, you are cleansed."

"It involves God? Even more reason to decline."

Mela kneeled in front of Utina. She dipped the cup into the bowl and held it out to him. He bowed toward her, took it, and drank. When he gave the cup back to her, he stroked her hand. Prickles of jealousy erupted inside Dominic, but when he saw the look of anger that Mela shot at Utina, he relaxed.

Next, she came to Itori, and as he drank, Dominic's body hummed with anxiety. This was the closest he had yet come to Mela. When Itori returned the shell to her, she stood, hesitated, and then kneeled in front of Dominic and presented it to him. With her ample pink lips, obsidian eyes, and lean, willowy body, she was far more breathtaking up close, even without her long hair. She could have asked him to drink poison and he would have agreed to it. She put the shell in his hands and cast her eyes to the ground. His heartbeat hastened and he breathed her in. Her scent was strong — water lilies, pine sap, tilled earth, sweat — and her chest heaved with an anxious catlike pant. She seemed as nervous as he was.

"Look into the bowl," said Francisco.

Dominic did not want to look away from Mela, but at Francisco's second urging, he did. It took a moment for the ripples in the black liquid to disappear, but when they did, he simply saw himself. He appeared as dirty and disheveled as he had ever been, and the white streaks above his ears made him seem older, but it was exactly the reflection he had expected to see. He laughed inside. If this was how God saw him, then God's eyes were no more exalted than any of the people around him.

"Drink, and look again," said Francisco.

Dominic took a deep breath. He feared that Mela would be disappointed if he did not drink. He would have to try, and he hoped he could at least hold it down until she was out of range. Closing his eyes, he gulped the cassina. It went down with the bitterness of vinegar and left an aftertaste like rotten fruit. He felt the fluid hit his gut and his insides burned, but, to his surprise, the nausea did not come. Perhaps he was getting accustomed to it.

"Now look," said Francisco.

Dominic sighed. When would the old man admit there were no visions to be seen in a bowl of cassina? He decided to humor him one last time. When he looked into the shell this time, however, he saw nothing — no reflection, only a black sheen. He squinted and looked closer. Still nothing. He looked up to see if the light had changed but the sun still blazed overhead, unobstructed.

"I see only blackness," said Dominic.

"Decipher the meaning," said Francisco.

Dominic felt dizzy. Perhaps the cassina was having some strange effect on him. Who knew what kind of herbal hallucinogens the natives might have infused into it? He gazed deeper into the black drink and it seemed as if the gloom suddenly sprouted tentacles that wrapped around the back of his head and pulled him down into a darkness unparalleled. He had the sensation of falling through something even thinner than air and the only light he could see was from the erratic flicker of the memories of his great many misdeeds and all around him in the inky void he could hear the whispers and moans of charred creatures who claimed to have once been men.

"Help me," he whispered.

At once the head of a panther appeared out of the dimness and he found himself again sitting among Mela and the others. He shivered. She put her hand on his shoulder. It felt like ice. The panther, still in the black drink, stared up at him with vacant soulless eyes. Dominic jumped up and threw the shell. Cassina splashed all over Mela.

"Be calm," said Francisco.

"*Yaraha*," said a voice from behind. Dominic whipped around and came face to face with Yaba, still wearing his panther head-dress. Dominic stopped shaking. Perhaps he had simply seen Yaba mirrored in the cassina. But even if that were the case, why had his own reflection been so black?

CHAPTER EIGHTEEN

Zane had not used a payphone since his childhood, but he was happy to discover that at least one still existed in the world. He found it on the outside wall of a rundown gas station. As ancient to him as a medieval artifact, the payphone's heavy, bricklike receiver glistened with human grease. When he brought it to his face, the smell of alcohol and stale breath overcame him. He inserted the money and dialed his father's number.

Moments earlier, Mama Ethel had given him the two "quottas" he would need for the 50-cent phone call. It did not feel right to accept money from a homeless person, but she insisted, and "beside," she said, "it ain't nothing compared to what you given me, and I ain't talkin bout gold." She promised she'd have lunch ready for him when he returned. He intended to leave that night under the cover of darkness, although part of him wished he could stay with her forever.

"Just rememba two things, Mista Zany," she said as he left. "First of all, the worm betta not find nothin pretty in the robin's song. And don't you dare forget that the cat's gotta eat if he smells any meat. Go on now. Do whatcha gotta do."

He tried to decipher her idioms as he walked but he finally decided that he should not get lost in what were probably just the ramblings of a lonely woman who had spent too much time in squalid seclusion.

The riverfront town he found above the bridge — Titusville — had certainly seen better days. Like other communities populated by Space Center employees, this one had sprouted up out of nowhere in the fifties, but now, after the end of the *Shuttle* program, Titusville was a tired old man wearing the same clothes he did as a teenager.

Zane tried to act and appear as normal as possible while he searched for a phone, and when a police cruiser zoomed by on the road, he stood up straight and pretended to look into a furniture shop window. The Spanish coins in his pockets — two shrink-wrapped stacks — were so heavy that he had to hold up his shorts by sticking one of his fingers into a belt loop. Having been worried that the cops might be looking for a man with a duffel bag, he had emptied the bag and left it under the bridge with Mama Ethel.

He came to a man nailing a plywood plank to the window of a barber shop. At first, Zane guessed that the business was another victim of the ailing economy, but when the man came down from his stepstool, Zane saw the words spray-painted on the wood: *Juan, Juan, go away! Don't come again no other day!*

"Who's Juan?" asked Zane.

The man looked surprised. "You been living under a bridge or something? It's a cat two already, sprang up yesterday from that depression out there."

"Really? Is it coming this way?"

"Why else would I be boarding up? Supposed to hit just north of here, couple days from now."

....

Now at the gas station payphone, Zane was met with a long silence after dialing his father's number, followed by the recording of a nasally operator: "We're sorry. Your call cannot be completed as dialed."

"What am I doing wrong?" said Zane, as if the recording might answer him. A pit bull popped its head out of a sidecar attached to a *Harley Davidson* motorcycle parked nearby. The dog watched him with skeptical eyes.

"I wasn't talking to you," said Zane. A long drip of drool oozed out of the dog's mouth and splattered on the motorcycle's license plate. When Zane noticed that the license plate read Brevard County, he understood the problem with the phone — he was in a different area code. Calling anyone in South Florida was long-distance. When he hung up, the phone did not even return the quarters. What an archaic piece of junk; he might as well have been trying to use a telegraph.

Frustrated, he followed an old, bespectacled woman through the door of the gas station. The tantalizing smell of coffee and donuts enveloped him and he wished he would have spent the 50 cents on a snack instead of feeding it to a stupid payphone. The woman glanced back at him. He knew he probably smelled as bad as he looked. He walked up to the clerk behind the counter, a spiky-haired brute of a man adorned with piercings and elaborate tattoos. Zane flashed the best smile he could muster.

"May I use your phone?" he asked, his tone higher and more feminine than he had intended.

"Payphone's outside," said the clerk, his voice as deep as a trench. Zane noticed the *Harley Davidson* eagle tattoo on the man's arm and remembered the motorcycle parked outside the gas station.

"I see you're a Harley guy," said Zane.

"Sure, I'm into Hogs. You ride?"

"Do I *ride*?" Zane had never even sat on a moped, let alone a motorcycle. "Every day, bro. Bike's in the shop, though." Zane cringed when he realized he had accidentally rhymed.

"What kinda bike?" said the clerk.

"What kind?"

"Hold up, let me guess. Fat Boy?"

"Hey, who you callin' fat boy?" Zane laughed and the clerk did, too. "Yes, my man, that's my ride. I love Fat Boys."

The woman, now perusing the magazines, looked up at him.

"I'm Shady," said the clerk.

Was the man describing himself or making an introduction? But then Zane saw his nametag: Lucas Shademan. Now, it was Zane's turn. He tried to think of a good biker nickname for himself, one that would not divulge his real name, but something that was at least vaguely personal. Fisher. Fisherman. Fishizzle.

"I'm Fishy," he blurted. He immediately regretted it. Shady, however, smiled.

"Well alright, Fishy," said Shady. "Hey, you and I should hoon it up some time. Go find us some hardbellies out at *Lone Cabbage*. Pound a few *Natties*, ya know?"

Oh, Zane knew—not one of Shady's slang words. He did his best to look like he understood, but in reality Shady spoke a language altogether foreign.

"Listen, my friend," said Zane. "I really need to use your phone. Payphone's not working for me."

Shady shook his head. "No can do, brother. Wish I could, but I'd get fired." He pointed up at a closed-circuit security camera. Funhouse renditions of the two of them stretched across its bulging eye. "Bossman might be watchin."

Zane looked around, then reached into his pocket, pinched a gold doubloon off the top of the stack, and slapped it on the counter. The woman peeked over the magazine rack so he cupped his hand over the coin. "Would this make it worth it?" he said in a hushed voice.

Shady leaned forward and gawked at the coin. "Is that—?"

"Solid. I don't know how much it's worth, but it's probably more than you make here in a year. So, can I use the phone?"

Shady slid the coin into his pocket. He leaned over the counter to look out the window, and then he grabbed the phone handset from behind the register and handed it to Zane. "Be quick," he said.

Zane began to dial his father again but stopped. What if the police were tracing his father's calls? Was it worth the risk? He suddenly remembered his last conversation with Skip. Starting over, he dialed his own cellular number and entered his passcode—4321—to reach his voicemail.

134

His father's voice burst out with frantic urgency. "Zane! Why won't you pick up? I know you're on the ocean right now. Listen, it's about your client. He's not really out there to go fishing."

"No kidding," Zane muttered.

Shady tapped on his skull-shaped watch.

"I'm so sorry, buddy," said Skip's message. "I gotta come clean. Remember that coin you found when we went diving? I never told you, but I saved those GPS numbers that day, and I went back there without you after that. Took me an underwater metal detector. Turns out there were more of 'em down there. Brought up a dozen or so over the years and sold 'em all, for damn good money, too. But eventually I wasn't finding no more. Figured I'd got 'em all. Word got out on the dock—you know how it is—and not too long ago I was having a drink at the *Lager-Head* when this guy comes up, says his name is Miguel and he's been looking for the wreck of the *Señora Dolores* for years."

Shady tapped on his watch again. Zane gave him a pleading look. "Please, just one sec."

Shady crossed his arms.

"So this dude tells me," continued Skip, "that he heard I found some of the coins he's been looking for, and that he's got a salvage boat, dredge equipment, the whole deal. Said we'd split whatever he found if I just showed him the spot. So, I took him there. He anchored up, dug for a few days, and I'll be damned if he didn't find the mother lode. Zane, I'm talkin' hundreds of millions of dollars worth."

"Time's up," said Shady.

Zane slapped another coin on the counter. Shady stuffed it into his pocket. "Thirty seconds. I mean it."

"Two problems," said Skip. "Number one, Uncle Sam wants a piece of the pie. It's illegal to salvage treasure without a permit, and one day these two IRS agents started asking around the dock about what he was up to. Second problem is that Miguel was such a greedy pig he wanted to cut me out of the deal. I told him I'd spill the beans to the IRS guys if he did. Well, he knew I'd be waitin at the dock when his boat finally came in with the loot. So, what did that bastard do? He hired himself a floatplane to transport the treasure at sea so his boat would come in empty. He chartered you—knowing you're my son—just so I wouldn't talk. But Zane, I found something out about him tha—"

The line went dead. Zane looked up. Shady had his finger on the base of the phone. "Sorry, Fishy, but the law's comin for his mornin coffee. He's friends with the boss, so..."

Zane spun around and looked out the window. The same roundish police officer who tried to shoot him on the bridge humped out of his police cruiser and waddled toward the door. His face had the ruddiness of an Irish alcoholic. Reflective aviator sunglasses veiled his eyes. Zane buried his face in the candy aisle as the officer entered. *Starburst. Milky Way. Payday.*

"Mornin, Shady," said The Law. "Stayin outa trouble?"

"You'd know if I wasn't," said Shady.

"You guys gonna board up for the storm?"

"Ain't everyone? Bossman says I gotta close early today and go buy some plywood. Hey, we got some fresh glazed with sprinkles up there for ya. Any speed traps I should know about before I leave?"

The Law poured coffee into two paper cups. "You know I don't eat donuts, Shady. I refuse to be a cliché. You probably don't know what that means. Anyway, speed traps? Not today. Nope, got me some company from the federal government riding along."

Zane glanced out the window. A uniformed man with a bald head sat in the passenger seat of the police car. He looked vaguely familiar. Where had he seen that face before? It hit him just as The Law said, "The tax man. IRS agent. Scary, right? And boy is he hot for revenge. He was out on that boat. His partner's the one who got killed."

"I heard about that," said Shady.

The Law tossed two one-dollar bills on the counter. Holding a coffee in each hand, he backed up to the door and pushed it open with his rear end. He paused, however, to finish talking. "Turns out this punk kid didn't drown under the bridge like we thought. Nope, last night, Air Force lost two soldiers out there by one of the old pads. Little sicko cut their throats, stole their Jeep and a handgun. We just found the vehicle parked down by the river.

I tell ya, if I catch that guy..." The Law shook his head and pushed himself through the door. "Gotta run."

Zane's body felt weak. Not only were the cops looking for him again, but Miguel lurked nearby as well. He had to get out of town, but he couldn't flee without warning Mama Ethel about the hurricane. She had no way of knowing otherwise.

"You okay, Fishy?" said Shady.

Sweat effused on Zane's forehead. "Yeah."

Somewhere, glass broke. A clear, greenish liquid spread across the floor, splashing onto Zane's bare feet. Pickles? He looked up to find the old woman standing over a pile of dropped groceries. Her lower jaw trembled as she stared at a *Florida Today* newspaper on a rack. There, glaring back at her from the front page—his eyes ice blue against the inflammation that encompassed them—was the mug shot of Zane from his final night with Lucia. The woman looked at Zane, then at the police cruiser now pulling out of the parking lot.

"Please don't," said Zane.

"Criminal," hissed the woman, and she bolted out the door, hobbling after the car. Zane looked at Shady. "Please help me."

Shady glanced at the newspaper with disbelief. "It's *you*? Did you really do what they're sayin?"

"Do I look like I could kill someone with a knife?"

Shady paused. "I guess not. But I can't help you."

"You can take me on your bike. Take me to Gainesville."

"Gainesville? You're nuts, man. Get outta my store."

Zane took out the stack of Spanish coins. "I'll give you all of these. You'll be set for life."

Shady stared at the coins with a look of temptation and unease. "Dang. I don't know, man..."

Zane slammed his fist on the counter with such force that it startled Shady and knocked a chewing gum display to the ground. "Listen to me," Zane said with commanding passion. "Do you want to be a gas station clerk for the rest of your life, or do you want to be the badass you were born to be? You call yourself a biker, right?"

Shady nodded.

"Then come on. Let's ride."

25

CHAPTER NINETEEN

The stench inside the dead deer's face was appalling, but when Dominic watched a massive buck prance out of the forest on the other side of the brook and regard him like an old friend, his mind became fixated on the hunt. Holding its antlered head high as if it thought of itself as royalty, the buck strutted toward him through tall grass. Dominic's body tensed and his breathing accelerated, but with the nostrils of his deer costume sewn shut to keep its face from tearing apart, each breath ricocheted back at him as hot, gamey vapor.

He gazed to his side through the eyehole. Even though he knew it was Itori hiding within the other hollowed-out deer carcass beside him, it appeared so lifelike and natural that he had to look for the human eye peeking through to be sure. Itori held steady as the buck extended its neck over the brook to sniff him. Dominic had never been so close to a wild deer before — so close that he could hear its breathing and smell its pungent odor and see the black-legged ticks that groped through its fur.

The buck swiveled its neck upward and sniffed the air, then lowered its head to the brook and drank. Its cheeks bulged with each sip and Dominic could hear the water gushing down its throat like a torrent, but then, mid-gulp, the buck froze. Dominic became worried when he saw what the deer saw on the water's surface — it was his reflection as seen from beneath his deer disguise.

"Now," whispered Itori, and at once the native lifted his bow from the grass and drew its leather string and — *thwack!* — sent an arrow into the buck's fleecy neck. At the same time, Dominic lifted a spear and, lunging forward, rammed it into the buck's left haunch and pulled it out. The buck rose on its hind legs and whipped its head, trying to shake Itori's arrow.

"Again!" said Itori. Dominic reared back with the spear and slung off the deer costume as he did. Time seemed to decelerate. He looked into the frantic eyes of the buck and could envision its thought: *My brother has become man. Nature has come undone. All is lost. All is lost.*

The confusion in the deer's eyes brought forth a gust of memories; in a blur, Dominic saw the faces of all the people he had ever slain, their eyes rife with fear. *Let them tremble before you.* How many had he killed? For the first time in his life, he wished he knew the number. *Seek gold, glory, and God — and only in that order.* His superior's foul ranting echoed in his head. It was a voice he had not heard since his first day in the New World, when his ship sojourned in San Agustín to take on supplies and orders. *You are to be a subjugator of barbarous peoples, Dominic, and never their equal.*

"Now!" yelled Itori. The buck came down on its front hooves and Dominic rammed the spear into its chest, using all of his weight to thrust it in. Dark blood pooled around the spear shaft and the buck collapsed around it like a piece of skewered meat and Dominic pushed and pushed and let out a terrible, animalistic scream that only relented when the spear burst out of the deer's back. He found himself leaning against warm fur. A legion of ticks — as if somehow sensing the death of their host — clambered onto Dominic like rats abandoning a sinking ship. He shoved the buck off and brushed the ticks away before they could burrow into his skin.

Dominic felt a hand on his back. He spun around and almost struck Itori, who stood looking at him with fear and concern, obviously troubled by Dominic's excessive aggression. "Brother?" said Itori, as if to ask if he were alright.

"I told you," snarled Dominic. "I am not your brother."

Dominic looked down at the crumpled buck, its face half-way submerged in the brook. A steady stream of redness flowed downstream out of its nose and waved in the current like a water snake. The rest of the deer's body was sopping with blood and three of its legs were bent beneath it in a disturbing and unnatural position; the other leg jutted into the air. What had he done? He felt sick and bolted into the woods.

When has it ever occurred, mused his superior, *that exploits more remarkable have been achieved over such vast distances and cultures?*

Dominic kneeled beside a poplar tree, in a leafy alcove on the bank of the same small brook, completely shrouded from the world. In the water crayfish and minnows faced the current, snaring miniscule bits of flesh that flowed toward them from the kill. They were plucking life out of death, he perceived, entombing the deer within their pea-sized gullets one particle at a time, never questioning the innate desire to prolong their brief but crucial stints in the world, eyes as cold as undertakers' while they gorged.

Whose deeds compare to Spain's? Not even the ancient Romans or Greeks.

He shuddered when he saw his own reflection in the water. Was it even him anymore? His face and hair glistened with deer blood. His shirtless body looked no more civilized than a native's. He splashed his head and scrubbed feverishly. The minnows went silly with the deluge of tasty sustenance that rained down from him. They swarmed in a tight ball around the largest chunk, tails lashing.

I have seen the wilderness. I know what to say. Conquest is simple, if you use my advice.

Dominic heard the *chk chk chk* of Itori butchering the buck with a whalebone adze and soon the brook ran red. All he could see of the minnows now were raindrop-like dimples on the surface. *First, kill their chief to prove your power*, said his superior, *and if that does not pacify them, kill some women and children, too.* Dominic dipped his hands in the rosy water and brought them so close to his face that he had to cross his eyes to focus. Red droplets plummeted back to the brook. *And their blood – let it run through your fingers.*

Somewhere, something moved. He jerked up to look, still not sure if it was something he heard, glimpsed, or sensed in another way. He scanned his surroundings but saw only palm fronds and oak foliage. Still, it was clear to him that some living, intelligent being drew near. Dominic could feel eyes on him. His body went cold.

"Itori?" he said.

He heard a stick break deep in the dimness. Had the scent of deer flesh lured in some predator? Was the panther of his vision stalking him? A dry leaf crunched. He squinted into the forest and poised to flee. "Hello?"

A human figure, clothed only in shadow, melted out of the foliage and limped into view. A shroud of knotted hair obscured the man's face and a scabby gash ran from his neck to his navel. His right arm was missing from the elbow down. The man parted his hair with his only hand, looked at Dominic, and opened his mouth to speak—but Dominic heard the sound of the flowing brook and nothing else. Who was this broken person standing before him? Dominic studied the man's features for anything familiar and his eyes came to the man's chest where a patch of lighter-colored skin bore the shape of a conch spire.

"Good God," whispered Dominic. "Ona?"

The man turned away and stepped into the forest and vanished in its obscurity. Dominic jumped across the brook and started to pursue the man, but he suddenly stopped. If it were Ona, wouldn't he have approached? Wouldn't he have made contact? A chill leached up the middle of his back. Something was not right.

At dusk, Dominic and Itori returned to the village with arms full of deer meat. They gave it to the women at the cooking fire, and then Itori ushered Dominic to the chapel where they found Francisco praying inside.

"Tell," Itori said to Dominic, and Dominic did. Francisco listened with his hands folded across his lap and his head facing downward as if still in deep prayer.

142

"I do not believe in ghosts," Dominic concluded, "but I do not understand what else it could have been."

Francisco looked up at him. "Itori says you were like an animal when you killed the deer."

"Angry," said Itori, nodding.

"So perhaps your mind simply tricked itself," said Francisco. "Let us not tell anyone."

Dominic glared at him. "Are you saying I did not see him?"

"I am simply saying that the woods can play games with a tired mind. Our journey was long. Perhaps you simply need more rest. The women have prepared a place for you, a place of your own. Come."

They walked along the inner wall of the village. Dominic noticed a circle of women around the central fire. Dripping with firelight, they threw their arms in the air to the booms of a drum. Yaba flailed about in the shadows beyond them, thrusting his staff in the air and shrieking. "*Ayyyyeeee!*"

"The crops need rain," said Francisco. "When it comes, they will think Yaba's invocation worked. They do not know that I have been praying for rain all day."

Francisco led him to a small hut. When they entered, dry, comfortable warmth embraced Dominic. He saw a hardwood cot covered in animal furs. Below it, a shallow pit filled with coals emitted a specter of smoke and a pleasant light. On the opposite side of the hut, a clay bowl filled with water and a basket of roasted hickory nuts sat atop a table carved from a single piece of wood.

Dominic lay on the cot and ran his fingers through the soft fur. His body hummed with a feeling like warmth and coolness combined, something he never felt in any of the Spanish villas and colonial mansions he had ever lived in. Despite its simplicity—or perhaps because of it—he liked his new home.

"This will do," he said.

"For now," said Francisco, "it will have to."

Dominic crossed his arms. "When will you give back my sword?"

"When God tells me to. Goodnight." Francisco swirled out of the hut.

Dominic stared up at the finely-woven thatch roof. "My hovel," he said.

He closed his eyes but behind his eyelids he saw the mysterious figure in the woods. In an ongoing loop, the man staggered into view, looked at Dominic, said something inaudible, and then stepped into oblivion. Dominic knew he would not be able to sleep—whenever his mind entangled itself around something, it did not relent, no matter how exhausted he was.

He slunk through the low doorway of his hut and crept out of the village, not breathing until he made it through the village entrance. The direction to the hunting grounds took him down the middle trail, first past the shell mound, and then along the perimeter of the burial ground. The partial moon overhead strew droplets of silver on the tall grass, giving him enough light to follow the trail. Mosquitos whined in his ears. He batted them away. As he came to the far end of the burial ground, he froze. There, beside Ona's grave, stood a figure.

"Hello?" he said. The figure turned to him and in the gleaming moonlight he saw that it was Mela. He stepped toward her, but she backed away.

"Do not be afraid," said Dominic. "I may have seen your father."

She did not respond.

"I am sorry," he said. "I know you do not understand me."

"I understand you," she replied in flawless Spanish. "But one can lie in any language."

Dominic suddenly felt angry at Francisco. Why hadn't the old man told him that Mela spoke his language? What other secrets was he keeping?

"I am not lying," said Dominic. "I saw your father, I think, during the hunt."

Mela looked at the grave. "My father is dead."

"I thought so, too, but remember—his body is not in there."

"You're a Spaniard. Why would I believe you?"

"I hardly believe myself. I have seen many strange things lately. But this was different. It seemed... real."

Mela stared at him for a long time, and then at the grave. "Take me there."

Distant lightning sent white flickers through the woods as they trekked. Growls of thunder shook the ground beneath their bare feet. Thick clouds rolled in and extinguished the moonlight. Mela whistled a mournful tune.

"Please whistle, too," she said.

"Why?"

"It calms storms."

Dominic puckered his lips for a moment but then he stopped and shook his head. He wanted to please her, but he would only go so far. "You can whistle for both of us."

When they reached the brook, Dominic shivered against a cold breeze that carried the sweet, earthy scent of looming rain. They came upon a family of foxes huddled around the blood-stained patch of grass where Itori had quartered the buck. The animals scampered into the forest, leaving behind gnawed bits of bone and sinew.

"How did he look?" said Mela.

Dominic paused to choose his words. "Not well." He gazed at her. "I am surprised you came with me."

"I love my father." She leapt across the brook and turned to face Dominic. "I am one of the few who want him to be alive."

Dominic jumped across, stumbled in the soft ground, and fell toward Mela. She caught him by his shoulders. He looked into her eyes. "Who would not want him to be alive?"

"Can you not see? Chiefdom has blackened Utina's heart. He has fallen in love with power. He wants to bring back the old ways. He wants to take me as a lesser wife. My father would never allow these things."

"Wife?" Dominic felt a knot form and tighten in his chest. He took Mela by the hand and led her toward the place where he had seen the man. Could they run off together? Find the coast and walk to San Agustín? She pulled her hand away, but he took it again and this time she did not retract it.

"Francisco asked me not to tell anyone what I saw," said Dominic. "Why?"

"Because of Yaba's vision," said Mela. "He and Francisco are jealous of each other, I think. They are both shamans — but with different sorcery."

All at once the rain came heavy and cold. Dominic felt Mela's hand trembling, so he put his arm around her and pulled her close.

"We should go back," she said.

"Alright," said Dominic. In truth, he wanted to stand there and hold her all night.

As they turned back toward the brook, a vein of lightning flashed across the sky and brightened the forest. They both gasped when they saw him — the man standing behind a curtain of rain on the other side of the brook — but just as quickly the lightning faded and darkness pervaded the forest.

"Father?" said Mela. She clenched Dominic's arm so tightly that he could feel her sharp fingernails digging into his skin. The rain was deafening.

Another streak of lightning lit the night, and in that instant they could see the man clearly. It was Utina, holding a spear and staring at them with a livid pout. A crack of thunder reverberated in Dominic's chest and Mela pulled out of his grip.

CHAPTER TWENTY

On the day Zane planned to kill himself, a tropical depression had formed off the coast and the seas were far too rough for his boat to make it through the inlet. Besides, no one would have believed that he intended to fish on such a blustery day. According to the marine forecast, though, the following day would be calmer, so, to pass time, he plopped himself on a stool at the *Lager-Head* and ordered a draught beer and a basket of stone crab claws — the perfect last meal.

Zane cracked open a claw, pulled out the meat and dipped it in a blob of creamy mustard. He rolled it on his tongue and savored the sweetness. He figured he could eat a hundred *stonies* in one sitting, but at $25 a pound, he could only afford a few.

He looked around the bar. Like most unfishable days, it was packed with drunken captains and mates. They reserved their best fishing tales for such times. Zane noticed Leather Heather sitting alone in a corner booth, leaning on a table and holding her head in her hands, the smoke from her cigarette swirling around her face like a bridal veil. He almost wanted to check on her.

This, he mused, was the last day of his life, and he could not think of a better way to spend it than with the people he had grown up around. Would they miss him? Maybe.

It had been five years since his arrest. The seven months of prison he served, however, did not feel like nearly enough time to atone for what he had done. His life itself seemed a more fitting compensation, and that was a sentence only he could impose.

His plan, though, was not entirely selfish; in fact, he had designed it to inflict the least amount of suffering on the few people who still cared about him. He would make it look like an accident. First, as if preparing for any other day at sea, he would load his boat with fishing gear, bait, ice and even a turkey sandwich never to be eaten. After clearing the inlet, he would drive due east, past the tepid waters of the Gulf Stream, until his depth finder — with its range of 1,500 feet — went batty because it could no longer detect the seabed. He had a hundred feet of anchor line tied to four cinderblocks stowed in a bow hatch and after placing the blocks on the edge of the gunwale, he would fasten the other end of the line around his ankles. Then, with his boat still motoring forward, he would jump into the water and watch the line come taut and his weight would yank the blocks off the side and their weight, in turn, would drag him down, down past the place where blue fades to purple, down past the realm of swordfish and giant squid, and down to the moonrock floor of the abyss where angry pressures would shrivel his body into a crumpled likeness of itself and blind crabs would prune the meat from his bones and every molecule of his body and soul would be diffused into the ocean like so many lost mariners before him. When someone found his empty boat still putting around at sea, everyone would assume he fell off and drowned while fishing alone. It was something that happened sometimes.

"Are you Captain Zane Fisher?" said a voice from behind. Zane spun around on the barstool and found a dark, well-dressed man standing there. In his three-piece suit and shiny dress shoes, the man looked out of place at a waterfront bar.

"Yes, sir," said Zane.

"And that's your boat out there at the dock, is it? The Lucy?"

"Lucia."

The man sipped a banana daiquiri garnished with a cocktail umbrella. "I'd like to charter it tomorrow."

Zane hesitated. "I may have other plans. What are you looking to catch?"

"Something exceptional."

Zane was eager to follow through with his original plan, but would one extra day really matter? If he took the job, then at least he could leave the world with no unpaid debts; the economy was so bad that people had all but stopped paying to go fishing and his bar tab was closing in on absurdity.

"Be at the dock at 7 a.m.," said Zane, and then he smiled, "but don't bring any bananas, okay?"

The man shot him a confused look. "Why not?"

"Because they're bad luck." Zane was equally confused. Keeping bananas off a boat was an age-old fishing superstition he thought every angler knew.

Now, as he hid inside the cramped leg compartment of Shady's sidecar, his face pressed against the reeking belly of the pit bull that sat in the seat above him, Zane could hardly believe that his first conversation with Miguel had taken place only two days before. Now in danger of losing his life, he felt grateful he had not ended it himself. Leather Heather, in fact, had saved him.

"Are you sure, bro?" Shady yelled over the roar of the Harley.

Zane poked his face out between dog fat and the sidecar seat. "I have to say goodbye to her. It'll only take a second."

"You're the boss." Shady reached into the sidesaddle of his bike and pulled out a wad of black leather and a red bandana. "Put this on so no one recognizes you. It's my chick's, so it should fit."

Back at the gas station, Shady had agreed to take him to Gainesville only after Zane assured him that—if the cops caught them—he would say that Shady had no knowledge of him being a so-called *person of interest*. The Law had pulled out of the parking lot without even seeing the frantic old woman chasing after him, giving Shady enough time to lock up the shop and usher Zane into the sidecar.

Zane pulled the pants over his legs and the jacket over his arms, trying not to disturb the dog. The clothes were almost too big for him; Shady's girlfriend, he surmised, was a fairly hefty woman. He wrapped the bandana around the top of his head. If he were not hiding in the cramped leg area of a sidecar beneath gigantic dog balls that bounced like a jogger's breasts every time the bike hit a pothole, he might have felt pretty cool at that moment.

The bike jerked to a stop. "Hurry up," said Shady.

Zane squeezed past the dog and jumped out. Shady had stopped at the edge of the bridge, enabling Zane to descend the narrow trail of concrete to the underside of the embankment without anyone seeing him from the roadway. When Zane reached the bottom, he turned the corner and stopped.

"You okay, Fishy?" yelled Shady.

"Yeah," said Zane, but he wasn't. Nothing looked the same under the bridge. Blankets and trash were strewn all over the place.

"Mama?" he called out, but the only sound he heard was a boat wake clapping against the seawall. He stepped into the dimness of the bridge's shade. Most of the debris scattered about were pieces of the Styrofoam that had been inside the duffel bag. Had Mama Ethel rifled through it to look for more coins? He barely knew her, but it did not seem like something she would do.

"Mama? It's me, Mister Zany." Still no response.

He found the empty duffel bag hanging from a finger of rebar protruding from the concrete. He picked it up, thankful he had removed the coins before he went topside. His shorts sagged beneath his new leather pants, so he pulled his last stack of coins out of his pocket and put it in the bag.

"I almost didn't recognize you," said a voice that he instantly recognized. He turned and found Miguel standing in the deep shade beneath the embankment. "Going to a costume party?"

"Where's Mama Ethel?" said Zane.

"You mean the negro? She wouldn't tell me where my coins are, so I insisted she go for a dip. Who knew she couldn't swim very well—not with a bullet in her back and all."

Zane looked toward the river. There, pressed up against the seawall, a multicolored mass swayed in the waves. When he saw the purple pants and *Nike* shoes, his stomach knotted up. "Mama," he whimpered. She was face down in the water, her arms spread wide like a child pretending to fly.

He had brought this evil to her. He was, once again, at total fault.

"Now," said Miguel, pointing a handgun at Zane, "unless you're keen to join her, you need to tell me where my coins are."

"I hid them."

"I see. Well, maybe you *are* smarter than your father. Perhaps we can make a deal. How about you tell me where they are and then we split them. Fifty fifty."

Zane heard Mama Ethel's sweet voice in his head. *The worm betta not find nothin pretty in the robin's song.* He took a step backward and said, "I'm the worm."

"Pardon me?"

"I know all about your deals, Miguel. Go to hell."

Zane bolted up the embankment. He heard Miguel clambering after him. How had Miguel found his hiding place? What were the odds?

"Go!" said Zane as he jumped into the sidecar, squeezing himself and the duffel bag in beside the dog. Shady gave it full throttle and they skidded onto the highway, narrowly missing a *U-Haul* moving truck, and two shots rang out behind them. One bullet struck the motorcycle's taillight while the other whizzed past and hit the moving truck's rear view mirror; glass shattered and the truck skidded to a stop.

Zane looked back. Miguel, standing beside the bridge, slid his gun into the waistband of his pants. Zane had to look again to be sure he saw it correctly—and there it was, a crooked smile on Miguel's face. Why in the world was he smiling?

"Who *was* that guy?" said Shady.

Zane thought for a moment. "I'm still trying to figure that out."

"You know, I could have left you. It wasn't smart to give me that gold in advance."

Zane was not sure how to answer. "Thanks, I guess."

They took a right onto *US1* and The Law zoomed by in his cruiser, lights flashing and sirens howling, without even noticing them. Zane hunched deeper into the leg compartment of the sidecar and wiped dog drool off his face. He heard the sound of rain and thunder. Peeking out, he discovered that it was playing on the motorcycle stereo. The squally sound eased into jazz instrumentals and Shady nodded his head while *The Doors* grooved out *Riders on the Storm*.

Shady turned onto a side street and then rocketed onto the I-95 ramp. They zoomed north on the highway at a constant 79 miles per hour, passing gargantuan SUVs and family sedans and smears of dead animals, the Brazilian pepper trees on the roadside a lime-colored blur in their periphery.

"Are you ok?" Zane asked Leather Heather. He had gone to check on the moping woman after he finished eating his crab claws. He still had not decided whether he would take the well-dressed man fishing the next morning as he had agreed or leave an hour earlier to follow through with his suicide plan. He was leaning toward the latter.

"It's caincer," wheezed Leather Heather.

He lowered himself onto the opposite bench of the booth and looked at her for a moment. What do you say to a person who tells you they have cancer? "I'm sorry," he said. "What kind?"

Heather looked at him with eyes darkened by yesterday's mascara. "It's metastasized."

Zane did not know that word. "Is that a lady part?"

Heather let out a raspy laugh, but then she sulked again. "It means it started somewhere's else — for me, my left tit — and then it spread. My throat. My lungs." She pointed to the areas on her body as she spoke of them. "My stomach. My liver. Doctor said it's all a big mess in there. They're sending me to *Shands*."

"For treatment?"

"For hospice."

Sadness swept over Zane. Few people would miss him, but what would the *Lager-Head* be without Leather Heather? "What will you do?" he asked.

Heather thought for a moment, and then took a drag of her cigarette. "Die, I guess," she said, blowing smoke in his face.

CHAPTER TWENTY ONE

The sunrise that morning bore the color of an old wound, casting a deep red flush over a growing throng of natives. The crowd parted as four of the stoutest warriors in the village approached carrying Mela on a litter. A thin, androgynous person walking in front of them fanned her with palm fronds. In the wake of the litter, a dozen teenaged girls—all virgins, Dominic assumed—dropped flower petals on the trail.

Francisco shook his head. "Utina has found a way around the custom."

"Pardon?" said Dominic. He had just joined Francisco in the assembly of onlookers.

"Instead of waiting for Mela's hair to grow back before marrying her, he had a wig made from an otter pelt. See for yourself."

As Mela passed by on the litter, her gaze met Dominic's. The wig was unsightly, but otherwise—in her garland of white flowers, her gown of moss, and her bracelets and anklets made of cowrie shells and oyster pearls—Mela looked heavenly. She was crying, though, and her eyes pleaded with Dominic. *Do something.* But what could he do besides further anger Utina and get himself killed?

Utina had screamed fiercely at Dominic and Mela when he found them together in the woods the previous night. Then, red-faced and furious, he marshaled Mela back to the village, woke all the women, and ordered them to prepare a wedding.

Dominic saw Utina's primary wife standing along the path of the litter. The morose look on her face matched the feeling in Dominic's heart. He watched the bearers lower the litter; Mela stepped out onto a platform and stood beside Utina. Boasting a feather headdress and a bear pelt cloak, Utina found Dominic in the crowd and shot him an arrogant glare, as if to say *I win*.

I have to find my sword, thought Dominic.

Mela wiped tears off her face. Dominic craved to comfort her. He had never suffered such feelings for a woman before, and he was irritated with himself for caring about a full-blooded native so strongly. What had started as a whim of lust had developed into something much more cumbersome.

"*Aayyyeee!*" Yaba's shriek was unmistakable. A drumbeat exploded out of the crowd and Yaba broke into a turbulent dance in front of Mela and Utina, pointing his staff at them and then whirling it around toward the rest of the village. He lit a clump of some herb and threw it burning into the sky. Ash rained down on him.

"He is calling on the spirits of the dead to bless their union," said Francisco. "To the Timucua, the supernatural is the natural. There is no separation."

Next, Yaba pointed at Utina's primary wife and she approached the platform. She bowed toward Utina, and then toward Mela. Dominic watched the eyes of the two women meet. He could see the words behind their faces.

I am sorry, said Mela.

I know, said Utina's wife.

Could he truly perceive peoples' thoughts? He had not always had such stirrings going through his mind. He feared he might be going mad.

The maidens that had followed the litter now joined hands in a circle around the platform and shook their hips in smooth, sensual gyrations. The dried fish bladders hanging from their belts rattled. Dominic could not look away. As the tempo of the drumbeat hastened, so did their motions, and their bodies, sparkling with perspiration, went into a judder, and their hips quaked in rapid convulsions that screamed of carnality and raw passion. Dominic turned to see Francisco's reaction, but the old man stared at the ground.

"The spirit is willing," said Francisco, "but the body is weak."

The dance subsided into a gentle swerving and a soft chorus levitated out of the maidens' mouths. Yaba climbed onto the platform and pulled a shark-tooth knife from his belt. Utina presented his hand, palm up, and Yaba pricked it with the tip of the knife, enough to draw a few drops of blood. When Yaba turned to Mela, however, she did not offer her hand, so he grabbed it and pressed the knife deep into her palm. Blood flowed out and dribbled off her fingertips. Rage filled Dominic; he envisioned jumping onto the platform and turning the knife against Yaba's smug face.

"This is the moment they will be forever joined," said Francisco.

Dominic trembled. "Tell me where you put my sword."

Francisco eyed him with concern. "You must not repay evil with evil."

"It has never failed me in the past."

Yaba took Utina's wrist in his left hand and Mela's blood-soaked one in his right and brought their hands toward each other. Gasps, however, hissed out from the rear of the crowd and in a great and sudden movement every head turned away from the platform. Utina jerked his arm away from Yaba and looked out over everyone with alarm.

"Glory to God," said Francisco. Dominic followed Francisco's gaze to the village entrance in time to see a figure stumble sideways and collapse.

"Father!" screamed Mela. She ripped off the wig, leapt off the platform, and ran toward the entrance. Dominic and Francisco followed.

When they reached Ona, Mela cradled him in her arms and her mother—Ona's primary wife—held his hand, sobbing. Francisco fell to his knees beside them. "Ona," he sighed. "What have they done to you?"

Mela kissed Ona's swollen face. He opened his eyes and whispered something to her. She pulled him closer and stroked his hair with her fingertips. "*Shhhh.*"

Dominic had never seen a man so destroyed and yet still alive. The nub of Ona's elbow, where his right arm had been, oozed green fluid; a piece of shattered bone protruded from it. Dirt and puss filled the enormous scar on his torso, and copious other cuts and boils were spread about his body. His hair, previously black, was now gray. His eyes were swollen and bloodshot.

Yaba and Utina approached and looked down at Ona with disgust. Yaba gave some kind of order to a few boys standing nearby.

Francisco stomped his foot. "No," he said with clenched teeth. "*Yati.*"

Yaba and Utina glared at him. Francisco turned to Dominic and said, "We cannot let them take Ona. Help me bring him to the chapel."

They stooped and lifted Ona by his underarms and helped him step forward. Dominic, however, stopped. "Does this mean that Ona is chief again?"

"Yes," said Francisco. "As long as he is alive, he is chief."

"Then hold him a moment." Dominic walked back to Utina, stared into his eyes, and tried to let him see all the fire within. Then he ripped the conch spire necklace from Utina's neck and said, "This belongs to the chief."

Utina stepped toward Dominic with his fists balled but Yaba put a hand on Utina's shoulder and whispered something in his ear. Utina stepped back.

Dominic could see the words burning in Utina's dark eyes. *I will kill you, Spaniard.* Dominic, in turn, sent him back a thought of his own. *Not before I hang you from a tree with a noose made from your own intestines.*

They laid Ona on a pew inside the chapel and Francisco went around the room lighting beeswax candles. He made the sign of the cross over his body and knelt beside Ona. Ona's wives remained outside, tendering prayers and burnt offerings to the sun god, but Mela came into the chapel and stood over her father, holding his only hand so tight it looked as if she were trying to prevent him from falling into a chasm.

"*Father*," she whispered.

Francisco and Mela hovered around Ona for the entire day, praying and singing and pacing in the small and increasingly suffocating chapel. Dominic watched from the back corner. As nightfall charred the outside air, Ona woke and tried to speak. Instead, he coughed up a wad of bloody phlegm. Again, he tried to talk, and this time he was able to whisper something into Francisco's ear. When he had finished, he lay back on the pew. His wheezing was like wind through a barren tree.

"He says that the Ais were following him," said Francisco, "and he hid in the woods so as not to lead them to the village, until he saw Utina's rage last night, and then he knew he had to save the tribe."

Ona pulled Francisco close and whispered again. Francisco looked at Mela and Dominic. "No, I said it wrong. He came to save the two of you."

Ona coughed violently. His body shuddered and his mouth foamed and he let out a long, dreadful wail. In all of his suffering, however, he never took his eyes off Mela.

"He is dying," Francisco said with urgency. "Mela, go get my holy water from the rectory."

Mela looked at Francisco for a moment, and then she looked down at her trembling father. Tears welled in her eyes.

"Now!" yelled Francisco, and Mela ran out of the chapel.

"Do not be so harsh," said Dominic. "Her father is going to die."

"He is not going to die," said Francisco.

"You just said he was."

"No, I said he was dying, but we can—God can—still save him."

"*Save* him?" Dominic looked at Ona. The native's breaths had become long and drawn out, with at least ten seconds now lapsing between each one. Dominic had seen plenty of people die throughout his career. These, he knew, were clearly Ona's final moments. "God cannot save this one. He may as well be in the ground already."

Francisco looked at Dominic with certitude. "Such little faith, but are you really as rigid as you portray? Tell me, commander, if God saves this man, will you make a confession?"

"God cannot save him!" said Dominic.

"But if he does, will you confess your sins?"

Ona's eyes had rolled back into his head and his complexion was fading to blue. "Sure, old man," said Dominic. "If he lives, I will tell you every filthy thing I have ever done. But that will never be. He is practically a corpse."

By the time Mela returned, Ona was unconscious and looked as gaunt as a beggar. "Father?" she whimpered.

"In this moment," said Francisco, "it is important that both of you refrain from doubting God's unfathomable mercy." Francisco's lips quivered out a silent prayer. He took the clay bowl from Mela, dipped his hand into it, and made the sign of the cross over Ona's body. Droplets rained down as he did, but Ona did not react. Francisco then poured some of the water into his hand and dribbled it over Ona's most prominent wounds. Ona looked as lifeless as ever.

Mela knelt beside her father and looked at Francisco. "Do you think he would want this?" she asked.

"I do not know," said Francisco.

Mela dipped her hand in the bowl and spread the water over Ona, massaging it into his lesions. Even in her anguish, Mela looked enticing to Dominic. He hoped that when she finally realized her father was dead, he might get the opportunity to hold her and let her cry against him. He hungered to touch her again. He also pitied her—Francisco was leading her to believe that a miracle was possible, but the moment of hope had clearly passed.

"He is *dead*," said Dominic.

Francisco frowned at him. "Do you even know the definition of faith?"

"False hope?"

"Faith, commander, is the assurance of things hoped for, and the conviction of things not seen."

"No. It is a cruel lie."

"Get out." Francisco pointed at the doorway. "Go!"

160

As Dominic exited, he looked back to see if Mela was watching him, but she gazed only at her father. He felt a ping of jealousy as he plopped down on a bench outside the chapel, but it was nothing compared to the fury he felt toward Francisco. "Superstitious fool," he muttered, and he remembered Yaba's prediction from the funeral. *Ona will return from the dead, but at a terrible price.* Dominic dismissed it, though, certain that the old shaman was no more intuitive than a catfish, and no more Godly than Francisco.

Having not slept for several days, Dominic was too exhausted to even carry himself to his hut, only a spear's throw away. He gazed at the stars for a while. In his fatigue, however, he saw nothing beautiful about them. His eyes began to shut but something caught his last sliver of vision and he jumped up, gazing at the heavens. He had seen plenty of shooting stars in the clear tropical nights of the Spanish Main—some of them miniscule flecks that fizzled almost instantly, and others large radiant flares that scorched the ether and disappeared behind the horizon, leaving swaths of incinerated stardust that resembled the wake of ships in phosphorescence—but those had all been whitish in color. The one now coursing over the village shone bright orange.

"Old man?" Dominic called out. "Have a look at this."

The illuminated object angled down in a broad noiseless arc and plunged to the roof of a hut at the far end of the village. A great blossom of flame leapt up, coating everything in a sinister glow. Shouts and screams preceded natives who ran naked from their huts just in time to see a deluge of flaming objects descend from above. It looked as if the stars themselves had decoupled from the sky.

What price?

A rain of fire…

CHAPTER TWENTY TWO

"Fake titties," as Shady called them, swung to and fro. Zane covered his eyes by pulling the bandana down over the mirrored wraparound sunglasses that Shady had given him to wear. Looking at a naked woman he had never met before—or in this case two of them—felt like a crime.

Shady punched him in the arm. "You some kinda queer?"

Zane pulled the bandana up and pretended to be interested. "They're just not my type," he said. In truth, he only felt pity for the two girls. Their song cut off early and, confused, they danced to silence before scuttling off the stage.

"Please welcome Destiny, our next lovely lady about to take the stage," crooned the DJ in an impossibly deep voice. "Destiny loves foreign films, poetry, and red wine. She gets weak in the knees when she reads about the mysteries of the universe and she's studying to be a cosmetologist. No, sorry, a *cosmologist*. Ain't that the same thing? Well, whatever. Destiny got her name from a quote by—do I really have to read this?—a quote by some French dude whose name I won't even try to pronounce which says, '*A person often meets his destiny on the road he took to avoid it.*' Okaaay, whatever that means. Note to management… it's time to stop letting the dancers write their own bios. Anyway, come on out, Destiny, but leave your brain in the back… We just wanna see your body!"

Tom Petty's *American Girl* bellowed out of the tired, muffled speakers and Destiny flounced onto stage wearing a short negligee dress and stiletto heels. Shady leaned forward in his chair, his eyes wide and eager as if looking at a shiny new motorcycle or a chargrilled steak. "Check this one out," he said.

With curly, rust-colored tresses and creamy skin, Destiny would have looked far more attractive had she been in regular clothes and not dressed like the hookers Zane sometimes saw lurking on *A1A*. When he was a child, his mother told him they were real-life witches in search of young boys to mutilate and eat. Even though he had long ago realized that was not true, prostitutes — or anything resembling them — still made him uneasy.

Destiny leaned off the chrome pole with one hand and rolled her hips in a circular motion. Zane tried to keep his eyes on her face — above her neck at least — and as she swung closer to him he noticed a tear on her cheek. Their eyes met.

"Take it off!" yelled Shady, holding up a $1 bill.

Destiny wrapped her legs around the pole, arched her back, and lowered herself to the ground. Lifting herself up, she let go of the pole and tore off her dress, revealing a black lace bra and G-string panties. She took the pin out of her hair and shook her head from side to side as if auditioning for a shampoo commercial.

"Yeah, baby!" shouted a gray-haired trucker in the back row. He looked old enough to be her grandfather.

Destiny unfastened her bra and held it over her chest for a moment, and then she let it fall away. She grabbed an *Everlasting Springs* water bottle off the edge of the stage and poured it over herself. Her body glistened in the red floodlights.

When she crouched down on all fours, Zane smiled — it reminded him of Mama Ethel doing her bear impression — and Destiny must have seen his smile because she zeroed in on him. But then Zane remembered Mama Ethel's big body floating in the river and sadness swept over him. "Mama," he said.

"That's the spirit, Fishy!" hollered Shady. "Hot mama!"

Men held dollar bills out to Destiny like kids trying to feed a zoo animal, but she paid them no attention. Instead, she gazed at Zane and crawled toward him. He wanted to look away but was afraid that anything resembling disinterest might embarrass her. Her face within inches of his, she stopped, stared into his eyes, and mouthed the last verse of the song. Suddenly Zane could not take it anymore — he broke eye contact and looked at the ground. Destiny danced to the back of the stage and disappeared through the red velvet curtains.

"Oh, she's got it bad for you," said Shady. "I'm gonna buy you a lap dance!"

Zane shook his head. "Please don't."

"Don't tell me *she's* not your type. I saw the way you was lookin at her."

Without waiting for a response, Shady jumped up and hurried to the bar. Zane cringed when he saw him hand over a hundred dollar bill. Moments later, Destiny walked into the crowd and took Zane by the hand.

"Come with me," she said.

"Where?" asked Zane.

She smiled. "In the back, silly. Don't be scared. I don't bite." She bent down and whispered in his ear. "Unless you want me to."

....

Zane and Shady had spent that entire day on the road, stopping only at a Daytona pawn shop, *Hock Your Socks Off*, to sell one of the doubloons. Shady said he wanted to be sure that the coins were worth something before he continued transporting a fugitive in his sidecar. Zane did not object; he was eager to know their value, too.

"Three hundred," said the bearded man behind the pawn shop counter.

"Three thousand," said Zane.

The man rolled the coin in his hand. "Fine, three thousand." He counted out the money in hundreds, fifties and twenties.

Shady gazed at the cash as they left the shop. "He didn't even counter offer."

"Which means he would have paid a lot more," said Zane.

Cruising west on *Highway 40*, they came to a pack of other bikers. Shady gave them a hand signal that, in road code, must have indicated he was on the run because the bikers encircled him and Zane. They escorted them through the Ocala National Forest up until Shady left the pack to head north on *I-75*. For the next thirty miles, Shady kept the bike just above the speed limit and stayed between two semi-trucks. They passed a rancid landfill obscured by seagulls and smoke, but otherwise all Zane saw were billboards and woods.

Twenty minutes outside of Gainesville, Shady spotted a billboard for *Café Risque* with its tagline *We Bare All* and insisted that it was "bad mojo" for bikers to pass by such a legendary establishment without stopping. Zane protested, but he changed his mind when Shady told him that the *Café* had free trucker showers they could use. Despite his initial trepidation about bathing in something prefaced with the word *trucker*, Zane could not remember ever enjoying — or needing — a shower so much.

....

"Relax," whispered Destiny. She led him into the dim, cavernous *Paradise Room* and pushed him down on the couch. Putting her hands on his shoulders, she straddled him and pressed her chest against his face. It felt nice, and, for a moment, he closed his eyes, but then he thought about Lucia.

"Destiny," he said.

"Yes?"

"Can I pay you *not* to do this?"

Destiny leaned back and looked at him. "What's wrong, baby?"

"I have a girlfriend."

Destiny's eyes swelled with tears. She lifted herself off and sat beside him on the couch.

"I'm sorry," said Zane. "It's not that I don't like you. I think you're real pretty —"

"That's not why I'm crying, baby." She took his hand in hers. "It's just that after working here for a few years, I was starting to think there were no good men left in the world. I'm happy there's still one."

Zane shook his head and looked down. "I'm not a good man."

"Yes you are. And your girlfriend, whoever she is, is a lucky girl. I bet the two of you were high school sweethearts."

"We were."

"I knew it. That's so cute. Will you get married?"

"No." His voice became raspy. "She's…"

Destiny looked at him with angelic compassion. "She's what, baby?"

"She's…"

Loud yelling erupted from the main room of the strip club. Destiny jumped up and peered through the curtain. "It's the cops," she whispered, wrapping a silk robe around her body.

Zane went cold with fear. He peeked through the curtain and saw Shady struggling beneath several police officers. The Law and The Taxman walked through the front door, scanning the crowd as they approached Shady.

"I thought you'd outgrown your penchant for crime, Shady," said The Law. "Where's Fisher?"

Shady strained to break free of the cuffs. "Where's who?"

The Taxman stomped his boot on Shady's neck and said, "He killed my partner. Tell me where he is, or I will break your spine, right here, right now."

Zane picked up the duffel bag and retreated to the far corner of the Paradise Room. He looked at Destiny. "How can I get out of here?"

"Why, are they looking for *you*?"

"Yes."

Destiny backed away from him. "Tell me you're not the guy they were talking about on the news."

"Yes, I mean no, but—"

Destiny pulled the robe tight around her body. "You stay back!"

"*Shhhh!* I mean yes I'm the guy they're after, but it wasn't me. I didn't hurt anyone. I swear it. They think I did, though, and if they catch me, they'll kill me."

Destiny scrutinized his face. "You promise?"

"I won't tell you I'm a good person. I'm not. But I'm no murderer."

She grabbed his hand and led him through a hidden door on the far side of the room which looked like part of the wall. "Our escape hatch from perverts."

They entered a long hallway lit by buzzing fluorescent bulbs and then burst into a dressing room packed with lingerie, wigs and skimpy costumes.

Destiny cracked open a door in the back of the room. Afternoon light shone in as blindingly as a searchlight. She peeked out but shut the door quickly.

"Cops're outside, too," she said, and then she looked around the room. "I have an idea. Blonde or brunette?"

"What?" asked Zane.

"I think blonde." She grabbed a wig off the rack and put it on his head.

"What are you doing?"

"Take off your clothes."

"No!"

"I'm trying to help you! Take them off."

Zane pulled off his jacket and pants and stood there holding himself. She looked at him and smiled. "See how *we* feel?"

Next, Destiny dug through a bin and pulled out a padded bra. "Hold still," she said, and she moved behind him and put it over his chest and fastened the clip. Then she hunted through the rack of dresses until she found a long sequin gown. "Marilyn Monroe was blonde," she said, and she yanked out the dress and pulled it over him.

She pushed him to a lighted makeup mirror and opened a box filled with brushes, pencils, creams, and all sorts of womanly things he had seen many times but could not name. "Be still," she said, and she swept his face with a soft brush.

"This is the police," said a voice from the other side of the door.

"Hold on!" yelled Destiny. "I don't have any clothes on!"

"Please get dressed, ma'am. We have to come in."

Destiny applied mascara to Zane's eyelashes. With his face only inches from hers, he looked at her autumn eyes and watched her pupils track the mascara wand. He felt an intimate, electrifying sensation — one he hadn't felt since Lucia. Sure, Destiny was a stripper and there were cops lurking outside the door and he was wearing women's clothes, but, in that moment, none of that mattered. He leaned toward her. Lost in her work, however, she turned and plucked a lipstick tube from the makeup box without noticing.

"Wait a minute," said the voice on the other side of the door. "She's a stripper. Who cares if she's dressed?"

And then another voice, "Ma'am, we're coming in now."

The door cracked open just as Destiny finished applying Zane's lipstick. "You look beautiful," she whispered. Then, turning to face the door, she ripped open her robe. The Law stepped into the doorway with two police officers behind him. Their eyes locked onto Destiny's breasts which shone pink under the fluorescent lights.

"Pardon me, ladies," said The Law. "But we're looking for someone. Have you seen a young man round here?"

Destiny crossed her arms over her chest. "Men aren't allowed back here. Just me and Marilyn in here."

Zane trembled with fear. Destiny took his hand and, whether she knew it or not, stroked the back of it with her thumb. A soothing warmness came over him. The Law glanced at Zane but his eyes went back to Destiny. She pulled her robe around herself and said, "Seriously, do you guys mind? Like I said, men aren't allowed back here."

"We're sorry, ladies. Pardon our intrusion." They backed into the hallway and shut the door.

Destiny's face filled with excitement. "It worked!" she exclaimed in a loud whisper, jumping up and down and wrapping her arms around Zane in a hug he hoped would never end. She released him and grabbed a set of car keys out of a drawer. "We've gotta go before the other dancers see you. Come on." She led him through the back door and out into the sticky Florida heat.

CHAPTER TWENTY THREE

Vast plumes of smoke impeded the morning sunlight and cast undulating shadows across the charred and smoldering blight. More than half the huts in Many Waters had burnt to the ground. Others were only partially scorched, while, somehow, a few looked untouched by flame.

Dominic, catatonic, sat on the ground with an arrow sticking out of his arm and a severed head on his lap. Dozens of bodies lay around him. Some of them had succumbed to the smoke and flames, but most of the victims were bludgeoned, speared or hit with arrows when the Ais warriors overran the village walls and went to work slaughtering every person they found. In their cruelty, they had targeted the women and children first.

....

"Give me my sword!" Dominic had yelled as soon as he realized they were under attack.

Francisco and Mela emerged from the chapel, the deluge of flaming arrows reflected in their eyes.

"God be with us," whispered Francisco.

Mela gasped. "The Ais — they must have followed my father."

Francisco backed into the chapel doorway. "We know what they have really come for, and we cannot let them have it."

Dominic marched toward Francisco and screamed in his face. "My sword!"

Francisco looked again at the fires erupting in the village, drew a pensive breath, and hurried into the chapel. Dominic followed and watched him remove a carved wooden crucifix from the wall. Behind it, hanging over a cross-shaped patch where the wall was unstained by candle smoke, was his sword. Francisco reached for it but Dominic pushed him aside and ripped it off the wall. When he wrapped his fingers around the grip, his body shuddered. He lifted the sword over Francisco.

"If you ever touch it again," he said, "I will butcher you."

Dominic heard a cough and spun around, ready to swing the blade. His face, however, contorted in shock and he lowered his arm. There, sitting on the pew in a stupor, was Ona.

"How?" said Dominic.

"God's grace," said Francisco.

Dominic shook his head. "Impossible."

Ona rubbed his eyes, stood shakily, and stumbled to the doorway. His wounds no longer looked infected. His face burst into concern when he saw the flames. He turned to Francisco and uttered a flurry of brusque words, and then he hurried out of the chapel.

"What did he say?" asked Dominic.

Francisco looked stunned. "He asked why I brought him back...from all the beauty."

Dominic rushed out of the chapel and into the burning village. A shout caught his attention—his eyes darted toward the village entrance where Ais warriors were spilling in over the bodies of slain Timucuan guards. A chill of terror washed over him. Where was Mela? He scanned the village. Terrified women and children stood huddled against the opposite wall. Ona ran to them, scooping up crying toddlers with his one arm and rolling them through a narrow passageway in the wall.

"Angry Squirrel!" Dominic spun toward Itori's familiar voice and saw him huddled with a group of Timucuan warriors in the center of the village, near the meeting circle, holding their weapons high. The Ais, having stopped to assess the Timucuan warriors, paced back and forth just inside the village entrance, their dark faces dripping with vitriol. Dominic ran up and took a stand beside Itori.

"Brother," said Itori.

Dominic did not respond. He lifted his sword but its rustiness troubled him—the metal gave off no sheen whatsoever. How could he go into battle with something so unsightly? He bent down and grabbed a handful of ashes from the edge of the central fire and rubbed them over the blade, and then he spit on his hand and wiped the blade again. The metal sparkled, and everything felt right.

A savage yell rang out from the Ais. They broke into a charge. Dominic turned to face them. There looked to be about twenty attackers compared to the ten Timucuans beside him. The three Timucuan archers drew their bowstrings; the others reared back with their spears and clubs.

"Wait," said Dominic, and Itori repeated it in Timucuan.

The approaching Ais, lit by the hellish glow of the burning village, resembled demons pouring out of the netherworld in some apocalyptic church painting. Dominic caught a whiff of their sweat and knew it was time. "Now!" he said, and Itori translated it with equal ferocity.

The Timucuan archers released their arrows, hitting two Ais and hurling them onto their backs. "Again!" yelled Dominic, but at that moment, a voice rang out and the oncoming attackers split into three groups. One cluster of Ais warriors maintained their course toward Dominic, while two groups on each side broke away and took an outside track.

Dominic saw that the source of the order was a little native strutting in the distance. It was Urribia, warrior chief of the Ais.

When the middle group of warriors was nearly upon them, Dominic reared back. "Send them to hell!" he screamed.

He swung his sword and cut a long gash across the chest of the closest Ais. The warrior collapsed to the ground. Blood bubbled out of his wound and quickly formed a puddle around him. Itori swung a club against the face of another warrior and pieces of the man's head splattered out. To Dominic's side, an Ais drove a spear into a Timucuan; Dominic swung his sword across the Ais warrior's calves, severing bones and tendons, and the man collapsed to the ground and writhed. Dominic stood over him and drove the sword into his chest. He turned to look for Urribia, but the wicked little man was gone.

A woman screamed behind them. Dominic and the Timucuans spun around. The other two groups of Ais had surrounded the remaining villagers. Itori gasped—an Ais warrior held his wife by the hair. Urribia, standing in front of her, plucked the little girl from her arms and held her up by her legs and pressed a conch shell knife to her neck.

"No!" screamed Itori. He bolted toward them. Dominic followed.

The little girl screamed and Urribia smiled sickly as he pressed the knife into her neck but his eyes suddenly widened and blood gushed out of his mouth. He looked down at the spearhead protruding from the middle of his chest. The spear retracted back into his body and he tumbled to the ground. The girl fell with him, her landing cushioned by his torso. Mela dropped the spear and embraced the girl, who was now slick and shimmering with Urribia's fluids, and carried her past several stunned Ais warriors before disappearing through the passageway in the wall.

Blind chaos ensued when Itori, Dominic and the other Timucuan warriors reached the remaining Ais. An arrow hit Dominic's arm but in his fury it felt like nothing worse than a wasp sting. Amid the fray, Itori clubbed the warrior who held his wife and continued clubbing the man until his head was like a trodden gourd.

Two Ais warriors approached Dominic. He wielded his sword. Reflecting the surrounding fires, the blade was like a shaft of flame.

"You like to kill women and children?" said Dominic, but the Ais did not respond and continued approaching with their spears held high. The native on the left lunged forward and in one motion Dominic swung and sliced off the spearhead and whirled around and cut a deep gash across the native's thighs. The native collapsed, screaming. The other warrior looked at his fallen friend and then dropped his spear and retreated toward the village entrance.

"To...hell," said Itori, and he sent an arrow into the fleeing native's back. The man folded to the ground and a cloud of ash rose up like his spirit leaving.

Dominic looked around. All the Ais lay in the dirt, scattered among the bodies of Timucuan children, women, and warriors. A voice caught his attention and his eyes found Ona cradling his primary wife. Someone had clubbed the back of her neck and her head dangled to one side. She breathed laboriously. Ona stroked her hair and spoke into her ear.

"She...go...beauty," translated Itori. "She...no...afraid."

Ona suddenly looked up at something behind Dominic. Dominic heard the sound of an impact and Itori crumpled to the ground beside him. He started to spin around but something struck the back of his head and he glimpsed blood-soaked dirt rushing toward him and then his world went dark. In that darkness he heard hushed voices, and then silence.

"Dominic! What have you done!?"

Dominic's mind clawed out of the gloom. The first thing he saw was Francisco screaming in his face. Dominic's head pounded and he struggled to think. Why was Francisco so frantic?

"You killed him!" bellowed Francisco, sobbing.

Dominic felt something heavy and spherical in his hands. He rolled it around and felt hair and teeth and a fleshy nub with a sharp bone sticking out of it. He looked down. His eyes saw the disconnected head in his lap but his foggy mind strained to identify it.

"He loved you, Dominic," cried Francisco. "Ona loved you and you...you...."

Dominic's brain snapped into coherence. He threw Ona's head off his lap and jumped to his feet. "It was not my doing!" he screamed.

Francisco bent down and held the head by both cheeks. The rest of Ona's body lay on the ground nearby, his wife's limp body beside it. Dominic's sword lay between them. "Then who?" pleaded Francisco.

Dominic put his hands over his face. "I do not know," he muttered. "I do not know." His murmurs became sobs and he leaned forward until his forehead touched dirt.

By the time the fires had consumed the afflicted huts to ash, the sun sagged low on the horizon. Thick, acrid smoke sullied the air and mingled with the mounting smell of decay. Francisco darted from body to body like a bee among wildflowers, giving Last Rites and anointing the cold foreheads of the dead with oil in the shape of crosses. Yaba sat in front of the central fire, chanting. Somewhere off in the distance, mourning women yowled like coyotes. There was a dreadful peace about the whole scene. Watching from the bench in front of the chapel, Dominic was trying to replay the events in his mind when Mela slumped down beside him.

"I know you did not kill him," she said, her face raw from a day of crying.

"How can you be sure?" said Dominic. "I am not. You cannot trust me. I am a wicked man."

"Urribia was the wicked one. Do you know why he attacked at night?"

"Surprise, I presume."

"He attacked at night so that God would not see his evil." She pointed at the sun.

"I would have done the same."

Mela moved closer to Dominic and placed a bundle of moist herbs and bark against his arrow wound. It felt cool on his skin. His pain morphed into numbness.

"I must ask something of you," Mela said.

Dominic looked at her. "Anything."

"Marry me."

CHAPTER TWENTY FOUR

"Did you know," said Destiny as she drove her car down a dusty road, "that all the matter making up the human race could fit in one little sugar cube?"

Zane smiled. "Sorry?"

"Make a fist."

"Why?"

"Just do it!"

Zane did.

"Now," said Destiny, "imagine that your fist is the nucleus of an atom, enlarged of course. Get this. The nearest electron would be miles away. *Miles*. Everything between is just empty space—a void."

"That's crazy."

"With all that space, it seems like my hand should just slide right through anything, right?" She karate-chopped her steering wheel. "I mean, come on, everything we touch is almost a hundred percent empty space. But it doesn't go through, because of all the energy. In my body alone there's enough energy to keep the whole country going for fifteen years!"

Zane laughed. "I think your customers would agree."

"Oh, shut up!" She laughed. "And listen to this. There are more atoms in one glass of water, than there are glasses of water in all the oceans! Seriously, doesn't that freak you out a little?"

Zane nodded. "A lot, actually."

"If people only knew how crazy it is to even be…"

"Be what?"

"Just *be*."

They were taking a wooded back road in Destiny's clunky old *Buick* to avoid the highway. Doing so would add an extra hour to reach Gainesville, she had informed him, but they both knew that cops would be swarming the main roads. The plume of dust trailing them shone orange in the waning light. The car's interior smelled of hot leather and gasoline. Soda cans, fast food wrappers, quantum physics books and dirty clothes littered the floorboards. He wondered if she lived in it.

The ailing radio garbled out *Tuesday's Gone* by Lynyrd Skynyrd, and then the DJ announced that he had breaking news. Zane's body tensed, but it was only a weather update. "Time to batten down the hatches, folks," said the DJ. "Hurricane Juan is now a *nasty* category three storm. He's expected to make landfall within the next 48 hours, somewhere near Saint Augustine. Its projected path will bring it right across the interior of the state. Mandatory evacuations for low-lying areas are to be announced soon."

"That'll bring it right through here," said Destiny.

"What will you do?"

She grinned. "Hurricane party, of course."

The road took them through Micanopy, a quaint centenarian of a town preserved in the formaldehyde shade of drooping oaks, then along the shore of a spring-fed lake, and eventually past an open wetland signposted as *Payne's Prairie*. By nightfall they were zooming down a gravel road through a corridor of forest. *Gainesville-10 miles,* read a road sign peppered with buckshot.

"I want you to know," said Zane, "I appreciate what you're doing."

She looked at him and laughed. "Sorry. For a second I forgot you were in drag."

Zane had, too. He ripped off the wig, wiped off the make-up, and rummaged through a pile of clothes on the back seat to find a plain black t-shirt and some khaki shorts which—although tighter and shorter than he would have preferred—did not seem *too* girly.

After he dressed, he pulled his last stack of doubloons out of the duffel bag, took one coin off the top for himself, and put the rest inside Destiny's glove box. "You won't have to dance anymore," he said.

She looked at him sideways. "Who says I don't want to?"

"I saw you crying on stage."

"Oh, that? No, I just get overwhelmed with my thoughts sometimes. Right before I went on, I'd been thinking about the fact that every person I know, eventually, is gonna croak. You. Me. Everyone. It makes me want to go around campus screaming at people, *you're all gonna die!*"

Zane laughed. "Probably not the best idea."

"I just wish people would make the most of their time in this world, you know? Too many of us just kind of…exist."

White smoke came pouring out of the car hood and Destiny pulled over. "Just a sec," she said, and she popped the hood, grabbed a jug of water from the backseat, and dashed to the front of the car. "Radiator leak," she said, and soon they were rattling down the road again. Judging by her nonchalance, refilling the radiator was part of her normal routine. They continued on for another few miles in silence, and then Destiny blurted a question that seemed to have been brewing within her for some time.

"So how'd you get mixed up in all this?"

"Wrong place, wrong time, I guess," he said.

She looked at him for a moment, and then smiled. "Everything will work out like it's supposed to."

Was he putting her in danger by getting help from her? Was he being selfish? He wasn't worried about Destiny being charged if the cops caught them. After all, he could deny that she had any knowledge of his alleged crimes. He was more afraid of her ending up like Mama Ethel and the IRS agent. Miguel wasn't just some average criminal — he actually seemed to enjoy killing. Thankfully, though, Miguel had no way of knowing their whereabouts. It was not like the man had some supernatural gift or something.

Smoke poured out again. "That's not good," said Destiny. She pulled the car over, shut it off and looked at Zane. "We're out of water. I didn't think I'd be driving so much today."

With his window down and the engine off, Zane could hear the night sounds of the surrounding forest. Crickets. Tree frogs. Buzzing things. "What do we do?" he asked.

"Someone'll eventually come down the road. When they do, I'll flag them down and ask for some water, and you can hide in the woods until they leave."

Without opening her door, Destiny lifted herself through the open window. "Come on," she said. Zane stepped out and found her lying on the roof, gazing at the stars, just like Lucia had always done. She pointed up with excitement. "Look, a satellite!"

Zane climbed up and lay next to her, the metal roof cool against his back. He followed her finger to a point of light, no larger than a star, sliding across the firmament. "They're probably spying on us," he said.

She flashed her breasts. "Spy this!" They both laughed. For the next twenty minutes, they lay there and stared at the cosmos, called to silence by its terror and glory.

"Did you know," said Destiny, her soft voice breaking the stillness like a scream, "that if every star in the Milky Way was a grain of salt, packed together they could fill an Olympic-sized swimming pool? There's a hundred billion stars just in our galaxy alone, and more than a hundred billion *galaxies* in the universe. Makes you feel small, doesn't it?"

"How do you know all this stuff?"

"I like to learn. I have this nagging curiosity about the world and how it all works. What do you like to do?"

Zane thought for a moment. "I like to fish."

She smiled, and then took his hand in hers. "The Big Bang is even crazier. Did you know that fourteen billion years ago—give or take a few hundred million—everything started from one teeny-tiny singularity?" She held up her fingers as if pinching an ant. "Something so small, and then—*pow!*—it exploded into something so vast, and it's still expanding! But the thing with the Big Bang—for it to have even happened—it means there had to have been something that caused it, right? Something beyond time and space and everything we know as reality."

"And what do you think that is?"

"I don't know. Maybe one day we get to find out. I hope so. All I do know is that the smartest physicists in the world say there should just be nothing. But there's *something*. Something beautiful, and we're all so lucky to be part of it."

"No offense, but how can you do the job you do if you believe that?"

"Easy. When I'm up there, I just remind myself that none of it is real, in the sense of it being part of some ultimate truth. I'm just up there shaking my atoms, which happen to be aligned in a shape that men like, but in reality I'm just a vast empty space held together by bits of energy." She smiled. "Plus, the money's good."

Zane raised himself on his elbows and looked down at her. "Did you know," he said in the same tone she had used for her scientific diatribes, "that your eyes look amazing right now?"

"Oh, shut up."

"Seriously. It's like they're glowing in the moonlight."

Concern filled her face. "The moon shouldn't be up yet." She looked down the road. "Headlights!"

They both scrambled off the car and Zane ran into the woods. He hid behind a tree and watched Destiny wave her hand as the headlights approached.

Please don't be a cop car, Zane thought. But as the vehicle approached, he relaxed — the headlights were high off the road and the engine had the deep hum of a diesel. The vehicle stopped beside Destiny. Moths and eddies of dust swirled about the beams.

"Hi!" yelled Destiny as she walked to the driver's side of the truck. "You got any water?"

Zane's eyes adjusted enough to see *U-Haul* written on the side. There's no way, he thought. But when he saw the broken rear-view mirror, he knew. He bolted out of the woods. "Destiny! Get away from him!"

She turned and smiled at Zane, holding up a jug. "Relax, he's got wa—"

The truck's door swung open and knocked Destiny to the ground. The jug of water fell out of her hand and emptied into the road. Miguel jumped out of the truck and aimed a pistol at her. "Please don't," she said.

Miguel smirked. "Sorry, señorita."

Zane barreled out of the darkness and lunged at Miguel, slamming him against the truck. The pistol flew out of Miguel's hand and landed in the road. Zane reared back to punch him, but Miguel grabbed Zane's arm and twisted it back. Zane whimpered.

"Where are the coins?" said Miguel.

"I told you. I hid them. Kill me and you'll never find them."

Miguel grabbed Zane in a chokehold. "I won't kill you yet—but you'll wish I had."

A shot rang out. Miguel collapsed backward against the truck and slid down the fender and hit the gravel. Blood streamed from a hole in his side. Destiny stood there holding the pistol. A whisper of smoke emanated from its barrel. "Take it," she said. And then, in a horrified scream, *"Take it!"*

Zane grabbed the gun and put his other arm around Destiny's back. She cried and quivered. "It's okay," he said. "It's all okay now. Just atoms, remember?"

He helped her to the car. When he turned around, Miguel was gone. Only a puddle of blood remained. "Where'd he—"

"Zane!" screamed Destiny.

Miguel wrapped his arm around Zane's neck, compressing it like a snake, and ripped the gun out of Zane's hand.

"Run," wheezed Zane, and Destiny bolted toward the woods.

Miguel fired three wild shots into the darkness. "I'll find you!" he shouted, and then he forced Zane toward the truck. "Get in," he said, and Zane did.

Miguel struggled to climb in and keep the pistol aimed in Zane's direction at the same time. Miguel's shirt, sopping with blood, clung to his body like a wetsuit. He leaned against the passenger door and aimed the gun at Zane. With his other hand, he dug around in the glove box and pulled out a plastic bottle. He unscrewed the cap and held the opening over his mouth, but nothing came out.

"Dammit," he growled, and he threw the bottle down. He plucked a greasy rag from the dashboard. When he put the rag on his wound, it instantly turned red.

"Drive," said Miguel.

Zane put the truck in gear. "Where?"

"You're going to help me retrieve what is mine." Miguel winced. "But first I need to get fixed up. That bitch who shot me—what was her name?"

Zane did not reply. Miguel jabbed him with the pistol. "Her name."

"I don't know."

"Doesn't matter. I'll find her, same way I found you."

Zane followed Miguel's glance to a GPS unit sitting on the middle console of the truck. It looked identical to the one Miguel had used to track the IRS boat. Two green dots on the screen moved away from each other.

"How'd you get a transponder in her car?" Zane asked.

"I didn't," said Miguel. "You did, when you put my duffel bag in it. How do you think I found you under the bridge?"

Zane sighed. Why had he not even checked the bag?

Miguel grinned, his teeth red. "Maybe you're not so smart after all."

CHAPTER TWENTY FIVE

T he skull atop the wooden post at the trailhead rattled in the breeze. Dominic stopped. The two cavities that once held someone's eyeballs stared back at him, and the lower jawbone dangled open like it had a secret to tell.

Who were you? Dominic wondered.

I am you, said the skull.

Dominic took a breath and continued on. In the early morning darkness, the overgrown trail closed in around him. A thin mist blanketed the ground and obscured his feet. Other skulls and bones hung off tree limbs. Some looked human but most had belonged to deer, bears and creatures altogether alien to him.

He came to a bend in the trail where the branch of an old oak stretched over. He ducked under it. When he emerged on the other side, his face filled with fear. All around him, hundreds of small, human-shaped effigies woven from palm thatch swung from branches. Each one had a sun-bleached bird skull for a head. Their slanted eye sockets and sharp beaks gazed down at him with ire.

What is this God-forsaken place? he wondered.

Where you belong, said the things.

The previous night, as part of their secret plan, Francisco had instructed Dominic to take the left trail—the forbidden path, he had called it—before first light and follow it to the end. "Do not be afraid," Francisco had said, but the old man did not warn him about the macabre things he would encounter along the way.

He continued past the dangling figurines. Around the next corner he came to a rotted pine stump atop which a Spanish *conquistadore* helmet sat impaled with a sword. An armor breastplate leaned against the stump. The helmet looked similar to the one he once wore, except for a few markings on the side which included an etching of *Nuestra Señora del Pilar*. Dominic ran his fingers over the Virgin. When he was a boy, his father had taken him to the shrine of Our Lady of the Pillar in Zaragoza, along the river Ebro, where the *Madre de Dios* supposedly appeared. They went as pilgrims for her feast day. After saying their prayers and attending Mass in the basilica, he and his father gorged on *paella* and danced with strangers in the streets until dawn.

He picked up the helmet and turned it over—the top half of a man's skull was still inside, skewered to the helmet with the sword. A black widow spider had made a nest inside the brain cavity, and her offspring scurried out in a cloud. Dominic dropped the helmet; it clinked to the ground and the skull rolled out, coming to rest on its front teeth. It lay there gawking at him, seething with miniature spiders.

I, too, am you, said the skull. *As are we*, said the spiderlings. Dominic shivered and hurried down the trail.

After he had walked half a mile or so, the trail became so narrow that the foliage on each side and above him brushed against his arms, sometimes as a gentle caress, other times as a harsh scratch. One sharp twig scraped against his arrow wound and he cringed. He startled some foraging animal and sent it crashing through the undergrowth, but he was certain that the unseen creature scared him more than he scared it.

Just as Dominic began to fear he was lost, he noticed a subtle glow in the distance and his ears caught an enchanting song warbling through the woods. The trail broadened and then opened into a clearing in the middle of which a fire roared. Candles placed on tree limbs formed a perimeter of softer light around the clearing.

"Mela," whispered Dominic. She knelt before a wooden table, singing. Her sweet voice fit perfectly with her appearance.

She wore a gown of oak moss dyed white and a garland of beige flowers around her head. Her eyes danced in the firelight. She looked exquisite. She looked pure.

Francisco walked up behind the table and placed a freestanding cross upon it. "Kneel with your bride," he said.

Dominic knelt beside Mela. She glanced at him sideways but otherwise kept her eyes locked on the altar. Francisco held out his arms as if to embrace the entire night and said, "This is why a man leaves his father and mother, and the two become one flesh."

Francisco came out from behind the altar and extended his hand to Dominic. "Take this," he said, "and plant it together as a symbol of your union." He dropped an acorn into Dominic's hand and continued, "Blessed are those who wash their robes, so that they may have the right to the tree of life."

Mela dug a small hole and Dominic dropped the seed into it. Together they covered it with soil.

"Dominic, do you take Mela as your wife, from this day forward, in sickness and in health, until death do you part?"

Dominic nodded.

"Say, I do," said Francisco.

"I do."

Francisco looked at Mela. "And Mela, do you take Dominic—"

"I do," she interrupted. "Until death."

Francisco traced an invisible cross over them with a broad sweep of his arm. "So then, what God has united, let no man divide. You are man and wife."

Mela kissed Dominic's cheek. He turned to her.

"It may be futile for me to ask now," he said. "But did you want this because you love me, or so that Utina cannot have you?"

She touched the side of his face but did not answer.

"I am usually not the one being used," said Dominic. "But as I walked here, I realized that it does not matter why you want to marry me. Damn me for my weakness, but I think I would do anything for you."

"There is another reason," said Mela.

"Tell me."

"When my father came back to us last night, he asked me to help you on your next journey."

"Where am I to go?"

"It is not that kind of journey." She gazed into the darkness. "It is only steps away."

"No, Mela," said Francisco. "He is not ready."

"Ready for what?" said Dominic.

A shrill birdlike sound blared out of the forest. They all turned toward it. The sound grew louder and soon another cry accompanied it. "What is that?" asked Dominic.

Francisco's eyes widened. "Screaming!"

"The village!" Mela jumped to her feet. Flowers and moss streamed from her body as she sprinted down the trail. Dominic followed and caught up to her. At the intersection of the trails, they almost collided with Itori and two warriors. Hurrying toward the river, the frantic natives carried a post they had dislodged from the village wall, its end sharpened to a point.

"Come!" shouted Itori.

Mela and Dominic followed Itori to the riverbank where several other Timucuan men had surrounded a massive alligator; longer than two canoes put end to end, it was the largest alligator Dominic had seen in La Florida. Each time the natives prodded the beast with their spears, it opened its mouth and hissed, but their spears could not penetrate the thick hide.

"Alligator...eat...boy," said Itori.

Mela put her hand over her mouth, and then she hurried to the crowd of onlookers where one woman among them wailed with particular intensity. Mela put her arm around the woman and wiped tears off her face.

Itori looked at Dominic. "We hold!" he said.

Dominic grabbed the dull end of the post behind the other natives. Did they plan to spear the alligator? The thought seemed absurd; the end of the post did not look sharp enough to impale such a well-armored creature.

Itori shouted something and the natives surrounding the alligator jabbed it again with their spears. The animal opened its mouth wide in fury.

"Now!" shouted Itori, and the natives rushed toward the alligator and pushed the end of the post into its mouth. Dominic suddenly understood. "Push!" screamed Itori, and Dominic and the natives thrust the post down the alligator's milky-white throat. The alligator twisted around it and the natives rotated the pole until the beast flopped onto its back, exposing its soft, white underbelly. Almost instantly the natives with spears jabbed the alligator's abdomen; their spearheads pierced the supple skin and soon the creature stopped struggling altogether. It released a long exhale that sounded like a growl.

"Dead," said Itori. He straddled the alligator and carved open its belly with an adze. Mela shielded the crying woman's eyes, but the woman pushed her hands away. Itori stuck both arms deep into the alligator's chest cavity and grabbed hold of something. His muscles strained as he tried to pull it out. Dominic stepped closer. His stomach roiled when Itori pulled out the boy. Covered in fluids and viscera, limp and broken but still intact, the boy looked like he was being born anew as he slid out of the greasy cleft. His face, although partially digested, was familiar even in its grayness.

Dominic recalled that this was the same boy who was sitting on the log in the river when he first arrived at Many Waters. He had also seen him the previous night, in the chapel.

………………………………

"Do you not want God's forgiveness?" asked Francisco.

"I want nothing from God," said Dominic.

"Not even to be pure for your wedding day? You made a promise. If Ona lived, you agreed, you would confess your sins and be made anew."

"And tell me, old man, is Ona alive now?"

Francisco sighed. "Let us start another way. Just tell me, commander, the worst thing you have ever done, and allow me to give you absolution for it."

"Does it count if I have not yet done it?"

"I do not understand."

"Well, if I hereby confess that I want to kill you, and then I do kill you, will I be forgiven in advance?"

Francisco sighed again. "I cannot let you marry her."

A snivel drew their eyes to the chapel doorway. The boy was standing there. "Yes?" said Francisco.

Fear coursed through the boy's eyes. He looked at Francisco, and then at Dominic.

"What is it?" demanded Francisco.

The boy crept to Francisco and whispered something into his ear. Then he turned quickly and scurried out. Francisco sat staring at the dirt floor for a long time.

"What did he say?" asked Dominic.

"He said he saw who killed Ona."

Rage filled Dominic's face. "Who? Tell me!"

Francisco hesitated. "No. Not yet. I must confirm it first." Francisco stood. "Tell Mela that I agree to officiate the wedding. We must do it with haste."

At that moment Dominic knew. Utina had killed Ona, or at least that was what the boy must have told Francisco. There could be no other explanation as to why Francisco changed his mind so quickly about the wedding. Avenging Ona's death, Dominic mused, would feel as nourishing as a royal feast, and he fantasized about how he would do it. He was always at his most creative when plotting *venganza*.

……………………………

"*Nihi*," Itori said sadly. "Dead." The boy's mother slipped like liquid through Mela's arms. Other village women surrounded the grieving mother. Their hair, like hers and Mela's, was cut short. Nearly one-third of the village—about seventy souls—had been slaughtered by the Ais during the attack. Every survivor had someone to grieve for.

Dominic gazed at the dead boy. "How did this happen?"

"Yaba…see," said Itori.

Dominic searched the crowd of onlookers for Yaba but did not find him, so he walked down to the riverbank. The belly imprint and claw marks in the mud indicated where the alligator had lunged out of the black water to snare the boy.

What price?

...a great dragon rising out of the sea...

A foul, familiar whiff caught Dominic's nose. It was the unmistakable odor of rotting flesh. He traced it to an oily sheen on the water's surface, shimmering around a twine tied to a cypress stump. A few bullfrogs hopped away as he bent down and grabbed the twine. When he pulled it, the severed leg of an adult man rose to the surface.

CHAPTER TWENTY SIX

They had taken dirt road after dirt road through the night, each narrower and more potholed than the previous. The one they now traversed had been used so little that grass grew in the center, and its two tracks were scarred with such deep washboard ruts that Zane thought the truck might lose a wheel or rattle apart at the joints. It would not be such a bad thing, he figured.

Holding a blood-soaked t-shirt over his wound, Miguel flinched at each bump. "Slow down," he said. His other hand held the gun pointed at Zane. Three rags lay on the floorboard near his feet, all of them red.

Zane brought the truck down to twenty miles per hour, but the roughness of the road seemed worse at the lower speed; instead of zooming over the bumps, the tires now caught each one and caused the entire frame to quake. Zane's teeth rattled.

"Slower," said Miguel. His lips were blue, his skin pale. He had nodded off several times in the past hour and, each time, Zane watched in hopes that sleep or unconsciousness would grab hold. Every time, however, Miguel jerked awake in seconds.

They had been driving for over an hour through parts of Florida that few Floridians had likely ever seen. Dense woods bordered both sides of the road. Red eyes would appear out of the darkness and, as the headlights approached, materialize into deer, wild pigs or bobcats. The animals did not flee from the oncoming truck as Zane expected; instead, they stood there transfixed, staring into the headlights like zombies.

Miguel glanced at a crinkled yellow map on the dashboard. He had been looking at it throughout their drive. "It should be near," he said.

Where was Miguel taking him? Zane was certain there were no clinics or doctors out in such wilderness. He wished he had surrendered to the cops at the strip club. But then, he realized, he never would have gotten to know Destiny.

They came to a side road marked by an old wooden signpost with two arrow-shaped signs. Zane squinted to read them. The first arrow, pointing in the direction they were going, read *Church – 2 miles*. The other arrow aimed down the side road. *Cowhead Ranch – 4 miles*, it read.

"Turn here," said Miguel. "If you see anyone, stop the truck and let me deal with it."

The woods encroached on the new road and branches screeched against the sides of the truck. This road felt smoother than the previous, save for the occasional judder from an exposed root or coquina rock. They passed an old, weathered sign nailed to a pine tree that read *No Trespassing*, and then, moments later, another. *Turn Back Now*, it said.

"Are you sure this is the right way?" asked Zane.

When he did not get a response, he looked over. Miguel had fallen asleep.

This is it, thought Zane. Do or die.

Zane's heart raced. He eyed the pistol in Miguel's hand. With one hand on the steering wheel, he leaned over and pinched the barrel of the gun between his thumb and forefinger. He tugged gently, hoping to pull it away undetected, but Miguel's grip tightened and his snoring stopped. Zane released the gun and the snoring resumed.

Plan B, thought Zane.

His fingernails dug into the rubber steering wheel as he tried to envision his escape. Could he pull it off? What if Miguel woke up too soon? It did not matter. This might be his only chance to flee. He spotted a clearing in the trees ahead. He pulled the doubloon out of his shirt and rubbed it between his fingers, and then, easing his foot off the accelerator, threw open the truck door and vaulted into the blackness.

As his feet left the floorboard, he caught a glance of Miguel waking with a start and lunging toward him, but Zane was away and soaring through the air. He slammed into the grassy ground and flipped several times before landing on his back. The surrounding woods glowed red from the truck's brake lights, and he heard the truck shift into park and its door squeak open. He froze in the darkness, hopeful that Miguel would not see him if he kept still and silent.

"You think you can outrun me?" Miguel shouted, and then he let loose a harsh, hacking cough. "I *will* find you! You cannot hide—you don't know the wilderness like I do!" Miguel coughed again, and then the door slammed shut and the truck pulled away.

Zane exhaled with relief, but in the ensuing quietude of the woods, his fear mounted. Judging by how far they had driven—and by the total lack of civilization along the way—it was not like he could just walk to a town to get help. They had not even passed another vehicle at any point during the last thirty miles of dirt roads.

What now? Zane remembered the other arrow-shaped sign at the intersection, the one that indicated a church. What better place to find help? And so, he started down the road, back the way they had come. The stars emitted enough light to help him spot the low branches before any could whack him in the face. He felt thankful for that.

He came to the intersection. As he turned to head toward the church, a dark figure stepped onto the roadway in the distance. Zane froze. He could see only a silhouette, but it had the shape and stature of a human, wearing some sort of cape or robe that came up over its head and hung to its feet.

"I need help!" shouted Zane.

The figure stopped in the middle of the track, crouched for a moment, and then bounded into the woods on the other side. "Hello?" said Zane, but he heard no response. As he came to the place in the road where the figure had stopped, he found a large arrow drawn in the gravel, pointing toward the woods. He gazed into the darkness, and then shook his head and hurried down the road. What had just happened?

He shivered as he walked, both from fear and due to the occasional pockets of cold air that hovered over the road in random places. His eyes caught a white glow in the trees and he hoped it came from a house where he could find help, but soon the light breached the treetops. It was the moon rising. He was grateful, however, for the light it provided, and he quickened his pace.

He came to a gravel driveway and noticed a sign engulfed in foliage. He pushed away the branches and wiped the dirt and dust off the lettering. *Church of the Living Waters*, it read. The poor state of the sign and the overgrowth that choked the driveway made him doubtful that the church was still in use, but it was likely his only chance to find help within many miles. He crept down the driveway. The hollow of surrounding vegetation blocked out most of the moonlight. He held his hands in front of him to feel for any stray branches in the darkness.

Soon, however, another light appeared in the distance. This one looked warm—the distinct yellow glow of an electric bulb. Walking farther, he came to the source of the light: a tiny church. Zane doubted the narrow building was capable of holding a congregation any bigger than a few families—but out here, he guessed, overcrowding was not a problem. As he drew closer, he realized that the structure was an old mobile home trailer, converted into a church with the addition of a plywood spire. Bordered on all sides by thick woods and covered in mold and vines, the church looked like some dreary woodland animal just roused from its slumber; the two rectangular windows in the front were its gleaming eyes and the vertical spire a great horn, like that of a rhinoceros or unicorn.

Zane heard a deep, muffled voice from inside the church—so loud that it shook the walls. If he were high on weed or tripping on acid, he thought, he would have feared that the church itself was speaking to him. For once, he was happy to be sober. The voice increased in volume as Zane walked up the creaky steps. He opened the plastic door.

"I am the Alpha and Omega!" boomed a man behind the pulpit. "The beginning and the end! It is written—to him that thirsteth, I will give of the fountain of the water of life!"

The preacher glanced at Zane but did not seem surprised or distracted by the presence of a stranger, nor did he appear to care that all the pews were empty. Dressed in a skintight collared shirt and a black tie that seemed to be strangling him, the man's plump, sweaty face shone hellfire red. His body bulged several feet past both sides of the pulpit, and his hair flowed up in a vintage pompadour shimmering with pomade.

"And he showed me the water of life, says the Book of Revelation," continued the preacher, "clear as crystal, proceeding from the throne of God!" His arms flapped as he spoke, spraying beads of perspiration into the church like a lawn sprinkler.

"Sir?" said Zane.

"And the Lord said, whosoever drinketh of the water that I will give him, he shall never thirst again!"

Zane stepped forward and raised his voice. "Sir, I need help."

The volume of the man's preaching increased to a shout. "The water that I will give him shall become in him a fountain, springing up into life everlasting!"

Zane cupped his hands over his mouth. "Sir!" he yelled. The preacher stopped and glared down at him.

"Where are your manners, son?" the man said in an effeminate Southern accent that sounded nothing like the commanding voice he had been using.

"I'm sorry, sir, I really am, but I'm in trouble and I need some help."

The man scanned Zane from bottom to top. "No trouble is too much for the Lord. Have you been baptized, son?"

Zane thought about the preacher's question for a moment. He did not know the answer. "I can find out for you, but first I really need help. Do you have a phone?"

The preacher stepped out from behind the pulpit and put his hands on his hips. His rotund body eclipsed the lamplight

behind him. "Of course I have a phone, but it's only for members of this church—"

"But, sir—"

"Do not interrupt me, son. As I said, it's only for members of this church, *my* church, and therein lies your solution. Tell me, son, do you wish to join the congregation?"

Zane felt uneasy. Something was askew. Florida had plenty of so-called *rednecks* and *crackers*—the most extreme of them might be called *hill people* in states with more hills—but the preacher seemed different from the many countrified Floridians Zane had known through the years, the ones who almost unanimously hunted feral hogs, stuffed *Copenhagen* into their lower lips, and raced airboats on the weekends. This man seemed more genteel but far less trustworthy. Even his accent sounded unusual— it had a pluckier drawl and somewhat of a melodic tone—and Zane guessed that the man was not even a Floridian at all. A transplanted Georgian, maybe, or a South Carolinian. But what was he doing in a trailer church out in the boonies?

"What do I have to do to join?" asked Zane.

The preacher smiled, revealing a mouthful of teeth that were all too perfect and white.

Chapter Twenty Seven

"Twins!" shouted Francisco. He slapped Dominic on the back.

Dominic's eyes narrowed. "Pardon?"

"A boy *and* a girl! Perfect in every way. God has blessed you twofold, commander. Now I can call *you* father."

Earlier that day, when Mela's screams from the maternity hut became too upsetting for Dominic to bear, he retreated to the far side of the village to busy himself with his normal share of daily work: stretching deer hides, flipping the smoked meats, husking corn, and binding arrows. Lost in the monotony of his chores, he did not even notice that Mela had stopped screaming until Francisco shuffled over.

"*Twins?*" Dominic whispered. He dropped a half-husked ear of corn and ran to the hut.

Inside, curled up on a bed of moss and surrounded by three smiling midwives, Mela held two infants against her chest, their mouths glistening with colostrum. She beamed at Dominic. The midwives hurried out of the hut. He inched forward, put his hand on the baby boy's back, and lost his breath when he felt the faint heartbeat. It was like the flutter of small wings.

"As their father," said Mela, "you must name them. It is our custom."

Dominic looked away until he felt certain he could restrain his tears, and then he kneeled beside Mela and the infants.

He put his hand on the baby girl's tiny body and gazed at her rosy checks and her glossy eyes and her black, downy hair that wimpled when he breathed on it.

"How do you say the word beauty in your language?" asked Dominic.

Mela smiled. "*Isa.*"

"Then we will call her Isa."

Mela kissed Isa's forehead. "Isa," she whispered.

Dominic touched the other infant's head. The little boy twitched and made a sucking sound with his mouth. "As I understand it, the lineage of chief is passed down through the mother," said Dominic.

"Yes," said Mela.

"Then he should have a name befitting of a leader. What is the strongest and smartest animal in these woods?"

"The panther. *Yaraha.*"

"Yaraha. Perfect."

Francisco entered carrying a bowl of water. "Pardon my interruption, but I am here to administer the baptism."

In a spasm of anger, Dominic knocked the bowl out of his hands. Holy water sprayed the walls. "I did not request any baptism!"

Mela put her hand on Dominic's arm. "Be calm, husband. I did."

"You? Why?"

"Because I fear what Utina will do when he finds out we have a boy child. He likely already knows — one of the midwives is his niece."

"How will dribbling some water on our baby's head help that?"

"They may not worship our God," said Francisco, "but they do fear him, and they respect what is his."

Yaba burst into the hut, knocking Francisco down as he approached Mela. His eyes darted about. The severed raccoon tails on his headdress swung as he walked. Mela pulled the infants close.

"Stay back," she said.

Dominic glared at Yaba. "What do you want?"

Yaba dipped his finger into a small clay bowl filled with some red substance, and then he lunged past Dominic and poked Yaraha in the chest. The infant wailed.

"No!" shouted Francisco.

"Be gone!" Dominic pushed Yaba out of the hut and onto the ground outside. "Go away, you snake!"

Yaba scurried off, cackling.

....

A year had drifted by since Dominic and Mela were wed. Life at Many Waters had been both blissful and difficult. In the months following the Ais attack, the memories of the dead had faded and the hair of the women gradually grew back. At the same time, however, the reign of Utina—and that of his most trusted adviser, Yaba—had become dark and oppressive. Most of the natives accepted the changes. Many even embraced them. They saw obvious benefits to the old way of living.

Slavery, for example, was brought back. It started one bleak winter day when Utina sent a group of warriors to the northwest to raid an Appalachee encampment. One week later, they returned with seven captives: two men, two boys, and three women, the latter of which, it was made known, were available for the pleasure of any Timucuan man who desired them. Many did. Utina severed one of the Achilles tendons of each slave to prevent them from escaping. Dominic could not even look at the poor things as they toiled and limped among the crops. Sometimes, he stopped to help them.

"Devilry," as Francisco called it, flourished. The age-old custom of bartering with the dead was renewed. Late at night, natives would kneel beside the graves of loved ones and ask favors of them, including, at times, to put vexes on their rivals within the village. If a native wanted an enemy to die, for example, all he or she had to do was present an offering of raw meat at the grave of a warrior and murmur a series of incantations. In time, the graveyard became a stinking mess of rotten food and, on most nights, it was filled with hunched-over natives, the sound of their collective prayers burbling out of the darkness like an ill wind. Mela no longer went there to mourn her parents.

Violence burgeoned. Small war parties were dispatched into the wilderness as part of a campaign to broaden Utina's kingdom. They would return with scalps and limbs severed from members of neighboring villages; these trophies were then displayed on the posts in the center of the village. From then on the odor of death pervaded every tribal meeting. The most vicious warriors were treated as heroes. If, however, members of a war party showed cowardice or mercy during their raids, they were brought before Utina upon their return. First, he made them kneel and beg, and then he split their heads open with a canoe paddle.

One day a hunting party returned with a wounded panther that had fallen into a pit trap. Utina requested that a cage be built for it beside his hut—panthers, after all, were godlike in their cunning and beauty. Utina would spend hours taunting the animal with chunks of raw venison and prodding it with a stick, laughing every time it lashed out. On many nights, Dominic considered releasing the miserable beast, but the consequences of getting caught were too grave.

As things regressed throughout the year, Francisco became increasingly despondent. He spent most of his time at prayer in his chapel, or in his rectory which was supposedly at the end of the gruesome trail where Dominic and Mela were wed. Dominic had still not seen the rectory, though. He guessed that the treasure Francisco had spoken of was out there and that the old man slept near to guard it.

Lost in his new life with Mela, however, Dominic had no urge to go looking. For the first time he could remember, the ambition that had always thundered inside him was now as calm as a windless sea. His thoughts were no longer clouded by avarice. He reveled in the peace, a peace that had begun to flower as soon as he and Mela moved into their hut together. Dominic constructed the hut by hand, with Itori's instruction. In exchange, Dominic allowed Itori to tattoo him, the most painful thing he had ever endured.

Apparently, the tattoo—which consisted of concentric bands and animal shapes wrapping around Dominic's arm—meant something about hunting deer and battling alligator gar, but one of the animals looked suspiciously like a squirrel.

Regardless, every bit of discomfort from the tattoo was worth Itori's guidance with the hut. The roof leaked and the walls were crooked, but to Dominic—having built it for the woman he cherished—it was nothing less than a palace. Mela decorated the interior with things she salvaged from her father's hut before Utina had taken it over, including an owl totem, a clay panther effigy, and her great-grandfather's femur, which still bore the tooth marks of the bear attack that killed him. Day after day, Dominic sensed, Mela worked her way into him, softening his heart and coaxing out little morsels of kindness. Her most effective tool was food; Mela, he discovered, was a skilled cook.

Breakfast in their little home usually consisted of corncakes drizzled with honey or maple sap and topped with whatever wild fruits were in season. Mela would wake before Dominic and, in the pre-dawn darkness, scour the woods for blackberries, persimmons and hog plums while they were still crisp and glistening with dew. Whenever she found a goldenrod flower, she added that to the dish as an edible garnish.

After breakfast, Dominic would go to work with the other men of the village. His day often consisted of hunting deer, trapping otters, setting snares and carving new canoes, but he always came home for lunch. Mela would usually catch a perch or bream from the river and serve it to him roasted on a clay platter with mushrooms and beans. Other dishes included boiled snails with squash; fritters made of corn flour and crayfish tails; dandelion greens with hickory nuts and fish oil; and, what was perhaps Dominic's favorite, swamp duckling roasted over an open flame. How he loved her duckling.

Supper was generally a communal feast shared in the center of the village, and—despite the copious amounts of smoked game, steamed shellfish, corn on the cob, whole roasted turkeys, and desserts of honeycomb and muscadine grapes—this was the least pleasant of Dominic's meals. He always felt like he was being watched. Members of Utina's entourage would scowl at him and lean toward each other throughout the evening, their whispers slithering from mouth to ear like invisible snakes.

When Utina had learned about their clandestine wedding the day after it took place, he had stormed off to his hut and pushed his wife inside; no one saw her for the next three days, and when she emerged, she was bruised and scarred and looked like a corpse. Dominic was certain that he would, one day, avenge Ona's death by killing Utina, but as he became more accustomed to his life in the village and to the sweetness that his new bride showered on him, that resolution moved to the very aft of his thoughts. Still, he always slept with his sword at his side.

He never forgot finding the leg in the river on the day the alligator ate the boy. Judging by the decorative scarring and the lack of tattoos on the severed limb, it belonged to one of the Ais warriors who had been killed during the battle. But how did it end up in the river, tied to a rope? So many things about that day made no sense. He tried not to think about it too often.

One night, not long after Mela's belly began to swell with pregnancy, Dominic woke with a start and reached over to make sure she was still there. He relaxed when he felt her warmth. Pulling the deer hide curtain away from the window to let the moonlight stream in, he lay there staring at the soft silvery features of her face. She quivered, and he hoped she was having a good dream full of beautiful things and that he was as present in her nighttime thoughts as she was in his. Why was she so good to him? What was her motivation? He decided that night to never ponder such questions again. Mela and her love for him were mysteries he did not want to solve.

"Let us run away from here," Dominic said to Mela one cold evening as they sat together wrapped in a deerskin blanket beside the hearth.

Mela put her head against his shoulder. "But we are meant to be here."

"We are meant to be wherever we are. We can go to San Agustín and I will take you to Spain on a sailing ship. I have a house in the Pyrenees with seven rooms and two servants. You will see things there that you can never imagine."

"If you go, you will have to go without me. I was born at Many Waters, and I will die at Many Waters. That is how it must be."

....

As soon as Yaba was out of sight, Dominic hurried back into the hut. He found Mela bawling, cradling the babies. Francisco knelt beside her, his face filled with gloom.

"What's wrong?" said Dominic.

Francisco looked up. "Yaba marked him."

"What do you mean?"

"Before I could baptize him, Yaba put the mark on him."

Dominic tried to rub the red spot off of Yaraha's chest but it would not even smudge. He lifted the baby out of Mela's arms and took him to the other side of the hut and used water from a clay pot to try to wash off the spot—but it seemed to be ingrained in his skin. "What does this mean? This mark?" asked Dominic.

Francisco hesitated. "It means he is reserved for *tacato*."

"What is *tacato*?"

"Sacrifice."

"*Sacrifice?*" Dominic's face filled with shock.

"Many years ago, the tribe would sacrifice every firstborn son on the first full moon of the year. The next such moon—is four nights from now."

Dominic rubbed his forehead. "Four nights?"

Mela quelled her sobs. "I had a baby brother, but he..." Her words turned into weeping and she buried her face against Isa.

"An offering, they believe, will bring good fortune to the tribe." Francisco shook his head. "Everything Ona tried to change. All for naught."

Dominic's eyes filled with fury. "They will not sacrifice my son."

Chapter Twenty Eight

"The book of Revelation describes the Son of Man as thus," boomed the preacher. "His hair was white as wool…his eyes were a flame of fire…and his voice was like the sound of many waters!"

Zane kneeled beside the improvised baptism font—a five-gallon pickle bucket filled with water—and the preacher stood over him, reading from a ratty old Bible.

Get it over with, thought Zane. He just wanted to use the phone.

Moments earlier, the preacher had explained the simple process of joining his congregation. Judging from the dusty pews that had not seen a rear end in years, the so-called congregation consisted of only one person—the preacher himself.

"All you need to do," the preacher had said, smiling like a traveling salesman, "is be baptized." He waved a cordless phone at Zane.

"Can't I just use the phone and think about getting baptized?"

The preacher dropped the phone on a pew and put his hands on his hips. "Son, don't you want eternal life?"

"Doesn't everyone?"

The preacher's face reddened and his voice changed into the deeper, fiery one he had used on the pulpit. "Unless a man be born again of water," he roared, "he cannot enter into the kingdom of

God! No way, no how!" And then he relaxed and softened his tone. "Just let me baptize you, son. It'll only take a minute."

"And that's it?"

"That's it. That and you need to make an offering to the church, of course. Give me cash, get a splash, and the phone's all yours. Easy peasy, right?"

"I don't have any money."

The preacher's face soured. "Well, that is a problem. Eternity has never been free, you know."

Zane felt around in his pocket and realized he had one doubloon left. He pulled it out and flashed it at the preacher. "I do have this," said Zane.

The preacher's eyes lit up and he reached for the coin. "Let me see that."

Zane stuffed the coin back into his pocket. "Not until I use the phone."

The preacher exhaled. "Fair enough. Let's get to it, then, shall we?"

Now, kneeling beside the bucket, Zane hoped it would be over soon.

"A spring rose out of the earth, watering the surface!" yelled the preacher, his mouth frothing. "And the Lord God formed man of the slime of the earth, and breathed into his face the breath of life, and man became a living soul!"

The preacher grabbed Zane by the hair and yanked his head back. "Let me go!" screamed Zane, but the preacher ignored him. Sweat dripped off the preacher's chin and onto Zane's face. With his other hand, the preacher reached into the bucket with the chalice—a *Miller Light* can cut in half.

"Zane Fisher! I now baptize you and wash you of all sin!"

Warm water splashed onto Zane's face. He felt nothing but regret for stepping into the church in the first place.

"And last but not least," yelled the preacher. "The Lord said that whosoever shall drink of his water will have life everlasting! Can I get an amen, brother Zane?"

Zane trembled. "I want to stop."

The preacher tightened his grip on Zane's hair and yanked his head. "I said, *can I get an amen!?*"

"Amen," whimpered Zane.

"Hallelujah! Now drink, son—drink the water of life!" He thrust the beer can chalice toward Zane's mouth, but Zane shook his head.

"No."

"Drink!" yelled the preacher. "Drink for eternity!"

The preacher pulled Zane's head backward and down, forcing Zane's mouth open. The doubloon rolled out of Zane's pocket and wobbled on the floor. The preacher squinted and leaned closer to it. When the coin stopped moving, the preacher's mouth fell open. He dropped the beer can.

"*Señora Dolores?*" he whispered. His grip on Zane's hair loosened and Zane pulled away.

The preacher picked up the coin. "Where did you get this?"

"I found it."

"Nay," said the preacher, shaking his head. "He sent you, didn't he?"

Zane inched away. "Don't come any closer."

"Do you know the secret? Is there more gold out there?"

"I don't know what you're talking about." Zane spotted the cordless phone on the pew beside him. This had gone too far. Even though the cops seemed intent on punishing him for a crime he did not commit, he would rather deal with them than with Miguel or the crazy preacher. He grabbed the phone and quickly dialed *911*.

"We ain't done yet!" The preacher lunged at him and grabbed his arm. A voice garbled out of the phone as it tumbled out of Zane's hand. *911, what's your emergency?*

"I'm Zane Fisher!" he shouted. "I need help!"

"Quiet!" The preacher stomped on the phone with his shiny leather shoe, squashing it like a cockroach.

"What have you done?" said the preacher. He pulled a switchblade knife out of his pocket and flipped it open. "We don't need no police round here!"

The preacher charged toward Zane with the knife held out in front of him. Zane rolled away and the man crashed to the floor. The entire church quaked. Zane bolted through the door and down the steps and into the woods.

"Get back here, son!" yelled the preacher. "You ain't saved yet!"

Zane stumbled through the woods for an hour before he stopped to rest in a palmetto thicket. The wind had picked up and the foliage around him gyrated in a rowdy moonlight dance. His heart raced and he felt thirstier, hungrier, and more exhausted than he ever had in his life. He lay back against a rotted log that was as soft as a pillow.

You have to stay awake, Zane told himself, but it was a futile command. His body and mind were sapped and he fell asleep within minutes. He dreamt of Lucia and Destiny having an argument, and then of bacon sizzling in a pan.

He woke to a cloudy, blustery morning. His eyes focused on a shiny thing beside him. He shot up and wiped the pine needles off his face.

That was not there before, he thought.

An antique covered serving platter sat before him. How it had gotten there? He wanted to know what was inside, but, at the same time, he was terrified about what he might find. He grabbed a long stick and, from a safe distance, slid the end of it under the handle and lifted the cover. His mouth watered when he saw what was inside: scrambled eggs, buttered toast, bacon, grits—all of it steaming—and, on the side, a glass filled with pulpy, fresh-squeezed orange juice.

How was this possible? Was it a dream? A drug flashback? He picked up a piece of toast, smelled it, and took a miniscule bite. It was real, and it tasted fine. In fact, it was delicious. He waited a moment to make sure he had no adverse reaction, and, satisfied that the food was not poisonous, he set about devouring it. Orange juice ran down his chin as he guzzled. The bacon disappeared in two bites. As the eggs dwindled, he noticed an image beneath them on the plate. He pushed the rest of the eggs to the side; there, painted on the ceramic, was an arrow pointing west. Things were just getting weirder.

He sat there staring at the arrow. He could look at this in two ways, he reasoned. Maybe someone was trying to help him. He hoped that was the case. But his fisherman's mind feared otherwise. What if the breakfast was bait? What if someone was trying to lure him into a trap? The implication of waking up to a hot meal in remote woods disturbed him deeply. It meant, after all, that someone had crept up to him while he slept, placed the platter beside him, and snuck off. He finally convinced himself, however, that whoever had done it could have simply killed him in his sleep if they wanted to. What did he have to lose? He finished the last dollop of grits and set off toward the west.

The wind gusts and cloud cover intensified throughout the morning and the woods grew darker as midday edged into afternoon, a clear sign that Hurricane Juan was drawing near. He trudged through towering stands of trees where nothing but pine needles and pinecones covered the ground, through dark and shady oak hammocks from which long curls of moss waved in the breeze, and, finally, to a black river ambling north. He sat on the riverbank and rested. Palmettos had sliced his legs and he splashed water on the cuts to clean them. He noticed a set of horse hoof-prints in the mud, and then he heard a stick break somewhere behind him.

He spun around and gasped, startled to see the same dark hooded figure he had seen on the road. The figure fled through the woods, the back of its robe swirling like a tail, and shot into a coppice of willow trees, disappearing among the shadows.

"Who are you?" shouted Zane, but no one replied.

He walked toward the thicket but he did not get far before something caught his eye. It was an arrow—an Indian arrow with a stone arrowhead—sitting on a log. He picked it up. The arrow pointed north, so he headed in that direction, along the riverbank. As he walked, he ran his fingers over the sharp arrowhead, which was fastened to the shaft with strands of real sinew. Someone had gone to great lengths to create an authentic replica, he thought.

Moments later, he entered a clearing strewn with stones and grass-covered mounds. As he walked farther, he saw crude lettering on the stones and realized they were grave markers. Bundles of fresh wildflowers leaned against two adjacent graves. He knelt by the nearest one and brushed away the lichen that obscured the letters. *Mela*, it read. He wiped off the next marker. *Yaraha*.

Weird names, he thought, and he continued north.

He soon came to a knoll that rose as high as the treetops. It seemed out of place among the otherwise flat terrain, but, given its height, it looked like an ideal way to get a better view of his surroundings. The ground crumbled and crunched beneath his feet as he began to scale it. He looked down. Below its thin layer of grass and soil, the hill was composed of old, sun-bleached shells. How had they gotten there? The river could not have deposited so many, even in a flood, he thought. Maybe some-one had dumped them there—but who? Commercial fishermen? Indians?

Regardless, the soft ground made the hill too difficult to climb, so he stumbled down and continued north until he came to another arrow—this one drawn in the dirt beneath a maple tree—pointing east. So, east he went, and he soon came to a trail running north through the woods. Where did it lead? Even though the last arrow pointed east, an actual trail seemed like a better option for someone lost and wandering in the wilderness, so he chose to take it.

He gazed up at the swaying trees and thick, low clouds and wondered how much time he had before the brunt of the hurri-cane would be upon him. The last place he wanted to be during a major storm was in the woods, lost. He grabbed the doubloon around his neck and rubbed it. Mid-step, he heard a shout from the woods.

"Stop!" said the voice, but as his foot came down, the ground below him collapsed and he had the terrifying sensation of falling into a pit. He hit the bottom with a thud and pain shot through his body. He tried to move, but it felt as if he were attached to the ground. A wave of dizziness swept over him when he saw the wooden spike protruding from his abdomen. Blood pumped and pooled around it like oil from a cracked cylinder.

CHAPTER TWENTY NINE

"Please do not go!" cried Mela, but Dominic grabbed his sword and made for the hut's doorway without even looking back at her and the infants.

Francisco stepped in front of the doorway to block it. "This is not the way, commander."

"Step aside, old man," said Dominic.

"You will ruin everything. You will spoil God's plan."

"There is no plan but mine." Dominic stuck the tip of his sword into Francisco's shoulder blade. The old man cried out. A trickle of blood stained his robe. "From now on, you do what *I* say."

"Dominic!" said Mela. "Stop!"

Dominic turned and looked at her. "You would just sit here and let things happen, wouldn't you? That is not my way. I am saving my boy." Then he glared at Francisco. "Move."

"If only..." said Francisco. He stepped aside and stared at the ground.

Dominic stormed through the village searching for Utina. He rushed into the chief's hut, but only Utina's battered wife sat inside. She looked at Dominic, and at the sword in his hand, and then she raised her arm and pointed west, toward the center of the village. Dominic nodded. As he left the hut, the panther in the adjoining cage snarled at him. "Soon you will run free," said Dominic.

Continuing on, he saw Francisco stumbling through the village toward the exit, holding his shoulder and cringing. "*Coward*," muttered Dominic.

He found Utina drinking cassina around the central fire with Yaba, Itori and four other warriors. They all turned. Utina shot to his feet and threw his cassina shell to the ground. He looked at Dominic with eyes full of hate. The others stood as well. The sunbaked war trophies that hung from the surrounding poles imbued the air with vileness.

First, Dominic eyed the warriors. He knew their names, their families. He had hunted and fished with them, helped them build canoes, and repair huts. He hoped they would not get in his way, especially not Itori.

Dominic then turned his gaze to Utina. The two men stared at each other for a moment, and then Dominic stepped forward. "Yati tacato," he said. *No sacrifice.*

Utina glared at the warriors. "Iqui ano." *Kill him.*

The guards approached Dominic, surrounding him on all sides. Itori stayed back, but Utina screamed at him and he advanced with the others.

Dominic looked at Itori and said, "Brother?"

Itori looked down. Dominic did not want to do it — the natives, after all, had no idea what he was capable of doing to them — but in order to save his son, he would have to take action. The positioning of the natives was almost too ideal. His mind rehearsed a swordsman's maneuver reserved for exactly such a scenario of being surrounded by enemies. Spanish soldiers would have been aware of it, but these poor natives unknowingly stood in just the right place for Dominic to slice them apart all at once by whirling around a full revolution. He had done it many times before, always with great success.

Dominic straightened his back and clenched the sword handle with both hands. He spread his feet apart. "I'm sorry," he said to Itori, but as he poised to turn, Yaba raised a small tube and blew into it. Something ejected from the other end and hit Dominic in the neck. It felt like a wasp sting. He yanked it out but, as he did, his arm felt numb. The muscles in his limbs weakened and his sword fell out of his hand and soon he could not feel his own body. He collapsed on the ground. He saw the warriors coming at him but he could not even raise his head off the dirt.

At Utina's command, the warriors lifted his limp body. Even though Dominic could not feel anything, he was still aware of his emotions — and nothing but anger coursed through him. He yearned to gouge Utina's eyes and beat him to death.

Utina shouted another command and the warriors carried Dominic out of the village and down the trail to the river. Dominic tried to speak. Release me, he thought, but his mouth refused to make the words. He was locked within his body, terrified.

As the warriors approached the edge of the river, Itori broke away from the group and paced. Dominic felt the warriors swing him back and then heave him forward. Their hands released him and he splashed into the black river. His body came to rest on the algae-covered bottom. He thought about swimming — he envisioned it, in fact, until his head throbbed — but his body would not follow any command. His lungs throbbed. He thought about the alligator and the dead boy.

Moments later, something brushed against his back and he felt a sharp pain in the skin of his arm. Suddenly he was dragged upward. When Itori wrapped his arms around him and pulled him onto the shore, Dominic realized that there was a fishhook stuck in his arm, and Itori was holding the fishing line.

"I...catch...you," said Itori, smiling.

Unable to turn his head, Dominic looked at him from the corner of his eyes. Itori laid Dominic on the muddy riverbank and ran off toward the village.

Dominic was soon able to wiggle his fingers, then move his hand and lift his entire arm. The poison that Yaba shot into him, it seemed, was wearing off. Within an hour, Dominic regained enough mobility in his legs to stand and walk. He thought about Mela and the infants. An oppressive sadness enveloped him when he realized that he could not go back to the village, not without a weapon. But he had to do something; he could not let his son die.

He stumbled onto the forbidden trail, past the gawking skulls on the posts, past the animal bone harbingers, past the abhorrent figurines hanging from trees, and stopped when he came to the Spanish helmet. Perfect. He pulled the sword out of the helmet and ran his fingers over the blade. It was smaller and lighter than his sword, but it was sharp and certainly better than some archaic spear or arrow. Next, he scooped the cobwebs out of the helmet and ran his finger over its pointed brim; the metal was sharp enough to slice skin. He donned the helmet; it fit snugly, better than his own ever had.

As he set off down the trail, Dominic savored the coldness of the metal on his scalp. He felt like himself again. It was time to make things right. It was time to conquer. He would start with the traitor.

He came to the clearing in which he and Mela were wed. It looked different in daylight — less magical, perhaps — and the image of his bride in her garland of wildflowers flashed in his mind. He stood there staring at the little oak sapling jutting from the ground. No higher than a toddler, its trunk was so thin that it swayed like a ballerina with the warm breeze gushing out of the woods. The last rain had washed away some of the ground cover and exposed the tree's upper roots. Dominic pushed a mound of dirt around its base.

"Never give up," he said, and then he continued on.

He soon came to a dilapidated shack — the rectory, he guessed — and crept inside. The air was dank and sour. "Old man?" he said, but as his eyes adjusted to the darkness, he saw no one inside. A large, yellowed bible sat open on a crooked desk. The old man's robe, with its new bloodstain, hung from a hook on the wall. A crude Madonna carved from a piece of pine sat in a recess above the doorway, her eyes and face blemished by the sap that still exuded from the wood. If he were a religious man, he might have thought she was crying.

Dominic left the rectory and found a trail behind it that led through the woods. He turned a corner and the air became cool and damp, as if an afternoon rainstorm had just passed — but none had. He pushed through dense foliage, the leaves of which dripped with condensation, and he soon smelled something fresh in the air, something pleasant. It was the scent of *agua dulce* — fresh water — but it seemed fragrant and wonderful in a way he had never before known. As he continued on, the vegetation became lush and verdant. White butterflies flitted about. A dragonfly with a prismatic blue carapace landed on his arm, tasted it, and then zipped off. The birdsong in the hollow, coupled with the rustling of wind through innumerable leaves, was almost cacophonous.

I could stay here forever, he thought.

The trail ended and he lost his breath at the splendor of what lay before him: a pool of water, wide as a galleon, clear as cold air, electrified with shades of blue more dazzling than the coralline shallows of the tropics. The water in the center of the spring welled up in undulating layers that bulged on the surface and disappeared as they spread. The rim of the pool, almost perfectly round, was bordered on all sides by a steep earthen incline swathed in ferns and flowering plants. Colossal trees created an all-encompassing canopy above, and, below, their roots reached out from the shoreline like errant veins, all vying to dip their spindly ends into the water.

Dominic stepped to the edge of the rim. He recoiled when his eyes found Francisco sitting naked and wrinkled at the waterline below. The old man was an anomaly staining the otherwise pristine dell, a whore among virgins. Francisco cupped his hand in the water and splashed his shoulder wound. Then he took another handful and sipped it.

"You selfish pig," said Dominic. The old man jumped up and grabbed his loincloth from a nearby root to cover his shriveled bits. He squinted at Dominic.

"God almighty," said the old man. "*Hernando?*"

"Pardon?"

Francisco leaned closer. "Oh, it is you. I thought for a moment you were someone I once knew. I see you found his armor."

"Come up here. Now."

Francisco hobbled up the steep embankment and Dominic pressed the tip of the sword into his neck and forced him to his knees.

"I know you are upset about your child," said Francisco, "but perhaps we can pray together for God's will to be done."

Dominic pressed the sword in harder. "No will but mine is to be done."

Francisco made the sign of the cross over his body and whispered a prayer.

"Quiet," said Dominic, his eyes on fire. "I want answers to my questions. If you try to mislead me or speak in riddles or mention God even one time, I swear I will kill you."

Francisco smiled. "As you say, commander."

"Why are you smiling?"

"Pardon me. My mind is not right."

"That has been obvious since the day I met you. Never mind. It is time for answers. First, I want you to tell me, and tell me true, who was Hernando?"

"Ah, yes. Hernando. So many memories, both good and bad. Hernando, commander, was a brave and noble Spanish soldier. He was also my brother. And, a long time ago, I took his sword — that very one in your hand — and put it through his head."

CHAPTER THIRTY

Boom. *Boom. Boom.* The sound jarred Zane's eyes open. In his waking delirium, it seemed as if he had been gobbled up by some monster and was seeing its rib cage from the inside. As the fog of deep sleep wore away and the pain in his belly sharpened his mind, he realized he was simply looking at a low ceiling lined with wooden rafters.

But whose building was it? He breathed through his nose; the mustiness he smelled, though, did nothing to help him identify his surroundings. He remembered the spike that had been sticking out of his gut and wondered how he was even still alive. In that instant before his mind had gone to black, he recalled, he did not even have time to think more than a glimmer of a thought, but the thought was this: *I end now.*

Boom. Boom. Boom. Zane sat up, wincing, and looked for the source of the noise. The room was dim and cavernous and filled with things—so many things, in fact, that they all blended into one amalgamation of clutter—but he saw no people. The walls were lined with shelves that held what had to be thousands of books, and the books that could not fit on shelves were stacked in precarious waist-high piles all over the wooden floor. Most of the books looked old and worn.

"Hello?" said Zane. The only sound that returned was another series of loud *booms.*

Zane realized he was lying on a wooden table. He swung his legs off and felt warm liquid run down his lower half as he stood. How much blood had he already lost? He was afraid to look at his wound. When he did, however, his eyes widened with surprise. Someone had bandaged him. But who? The hooded phantom? He touched the dressing; it was soaked with water, without even a trace of blood.

Zane tiptoed through an antique kitchen complete with a tree stump butcher's block, a rack of silver cutlery and cast-iron pots, a basket of fresh oranges, and a wetback stove that emitted both intense heat and the smell of roasting poultry. As a stranger creeping through someone else's domain, he thought about Mama Ethel and *Goldilocks*. A floorboard creaked beneath his feet; he paused and grabbed for the doubloon around his neck, but it was not there. Who had taken it—Miguel? Or the crazy preacher, maybe?

He spotted a doorway. Judging by the dirty floor mat and pair of boots at its threshold, the door led outside, and he hurried through it. He emerged onto a wooden porch and gazed out at what looked like a small farm covered in the stain of dusk. Scattered chickens pecked the ground. A ragged goat chewed weeds. Fruit trees of all kinds dotted the landscape. A vegetable garden flaunted the largest tomato and corn plants he had ever seen. It looked idyllic, all except for the wall of black cloud brooding over the horizon.

Boom! Boom! Zane spun around. The sound, he now realized, was coming from the back of the house. He crept to the edge of the porch and peered around. He could see the profile of a man at the far end of the house pressing a piece of plywood against a window and hammering a nail into it. *Boom! Boom!* The man wore dingy overalls with no shirt underneath and a straw hat that drooped over his face. A strange tattoo ran up his arm and across his shoulder and chest. Zane slunk back out of sight and tiptoed down the porch steps.

What should he do? He was still too shaken from his run-in with the preacher and his plunge into what was obviously a manmade booby trap to even consider seeking help from another stranger. Judging from the insane amount of books he saw in the house, this particular stranger was not exactly normal. Zane set off down the gravel driveway but he suddenly stopped—there, parked beside an old pickup, was the *U-Haul* truck. A sharp pang of fear stabbed him in the heart. He hunted for somewhere to hide and his eyes came to an immense stand of trees off to the side of the farmyard. He hurried into it.

Holding his wound, he trudged through the thick foliage and soon encountered a cool white mist like the stuff of clouds. It swirled around him and turned into droplets of water when it touched his skin. Both the mist and the greenery thickened as he pressed on and soon he could scarcely see his hand held in front of his body. When he came to the place where the trees ended, he stopped—there below him something like an immense bowl of fog swirled about in a maelstrom of wind.

A breeze parted the haze on the opposite side of the cauldron and there, approaching the edge, was the hooded figure he had seen in the forest. Zane ducked behind the nearest tree. Partially veiled by mist, the figure let the robe fall away, revealing a nude female body—lean, dark and exquisite. Plumes of black hair enshrouded her. She stepped forward and dove headfirst into the fog.

He gazed into the mist. "Hello? Lady?"

Instead of a response, a deep, guttural growl came from behind. He slowly turned. When he saw yellow eyes staring at him through the haze, his heart seized. The creature stepped into view. Zane's eyes and brain struggled to classify it. Was it an enormous bobcat? An escaped lion? And then it hit him: it was a panther. But what were the odds? Only a hundred or so Florida panthers still lived in the wild.

"Stay back," he said.

But the panther strode forward. Zane bolted. He dodged trees and leapt over fallen logs as he ran, ignoring the searing pain in his side. When he reached the outer edge of the tree line where the mist dissipated, he stopped, turned, and gazed back. He was relieved to see nothing but bushes. But then the bushes shivered and the panther pounced out of them and pinned him beneath its bulk. Zane shielded his face with his hands in anticipation for the first scratch or bite. The next thing he felt, however, was the animal's sandpaper tongue sliding across his neck and up the side of his face. The panther licked him repeatedly, like a dog happy to see its owner. He could not help but laugh at the feeling. He had forgotten he was ticklish.

"Alvar!" said a deep voice. "Let him be!"

The panther stepped off. Zane sat up and wiped the saliva off his face. The man who had been boarding up the house now stood several feet away. The hammer dangled from his hand. He stepped toward Zane, and Zane scooted away.

"Whoa," said the man. "Relax, I won't hurt you." He followed Zane's worried gaze to the hammer. "Oh, I see. Sorry." He tossed the hammer into the grass.

The panther rubbed against the man's leg like a housecat and the man stooped to pet it behind its ears. "I hope Alvar didn't scare you. He's really just a big pussycat. He's *supposed* to guard my property, but he loves to play."

The man's words carried a slight accent that Zane could not identify. "Who are you?" said Zane.

"I think a more appropriate question—you are on my property, after all—is who are you? And, perhaps more importantly, where did you get *this?*" The man held up Zane's necklace.

Zane's fingers twitched, hungry for the feel of the doubloon. "Give it back."

The man looked at Zane for a long time, and then he smiled. "We don't have to talk about this now. I think I know why you're here. Why don't you come back to the house and we'll have supper. We don't have long before the first bands hit."

"Bands?"

"Feeder bands. Outer edge of the hurricane. Radio's saying we might get a direct hit. Should be interesting." The man extended his hand. "Come on." Zane took it and, as the man helped him stand, he winced and held his wound.

"Still hurts?"

"Yeah."

"Sorry about that pit, but I have to protect my land."

"You could kill someone."

"Kill? No, not me. I aim to maim." The man pulled a knife out of his pocket and Zane froze, but the man smiled and used the knife to shave a piece of bark from a nearby tree. "Willow bark. Better than aspirin." He handed it to Zane and then headed out of the thicket. "Come on."

The panther bounded after the man and Zane followed. He looked at the bark in his hand. What did the man expect him to do with it? What if it was poisonous? He dropped it on the ground when the man was not looking. They came around the back of the house and Zane's eyes lit up with astonishment. Towering over them like a mushroom cloud was what had to be the largest oak tree in the world, ridiculous in both height and circumference.

Even stranger, dozens of animals lazed about the tree, including gopher tortoises, skunks and an opossum with babies on her back. Alvar crouched in front of the largest tortoise and pawed it; the tortoise retracted its head into its shell, making a hissing sound as it did. A squawk drew Zane's eyes upward. Dozens of birds—bald eagles, woodpeckers, owls, and a gaggle of colorful parakeets—clung to the branches.

"Carolina parakeets," said the man. "My little darlings."

"I thought those were—"

"Extinct, I know. And they would be, if it weren't for these last holdouts." The man leaned down and picked up a long indigo snake which wrapped around his arm and slithered across his shoulder. "I'll have to put all the animals in the house with us later tonight," he continued. "Hope you don't mind."

Zane looked with disgust at the snake nuzzling the man's neck. Apparently, the man expected Zane to sleep in the house with him, along with what amounted to a small zoo's worth of wild animals. What exactly was going on here? "Are they your pets?" asked Zane.

The man put the snake on the ground. "They're all wild, but I've been out here so long they've lost their fear of me. I think they sense the storm coming. They started gathering here last night. Unannounced, just like you." He smiled.

"Sir, do you have a phone?" asked Zane.

The man laughed. "I wouldn't know how to use one if I did."

"Um, okay. Well is that your pickup out there?"

"It is."

"Can I get a ride to the nearest town?"

"Sure thing. As soon as the hurricane passes."

Zane sighed.

Moments later, he was sitting on a wooden chair with his elbows resting on a wooden table that sat on a crooked wooden floor. He had never, in fact, seen so much wood in a house. It was the kind of place termites dreamed about.

"Hope you like *pollo*," said the man. He presented a steaming platter that coaxed an instant growl out of Zane's stomach. There, surrounded by potatoes, carrots, green beans, and garlic cloves, was a whole roasted chicken. The man sprinkled a handful of fresh herbs that wilted when they landed on it.

"Looks delicious," said Zane.

"Well, she should be. Chopped her head off myself two hours ago."

Zane refused to let the image of a headless chicken intrude his thoughts and instead focused on the man's knife slicing through the crispy golden skin. Pieces of juicy meat unfolded onto the platter.

"Come on, now," said the man. "Get some."

Zane took a plateful. "Thank you."

He was ravenous. He cut a piece of the chicken with the side of his fork and impaled it along with half a potato wedge.

"Wait!" said the man.

Zane stopped with his mouth open. "What?"

"You forgot the most important part of every meal."

"Washing my hands?" Zane stood up.

"No. Grace."

"Sorry about that." Zane took his seat.

The man closed his eyes and folded his hands. "Go ahead," he said.

"Sorry?"

"Go ahead and say grace."

Zane paused. "I don't really know how."

"Improvise."

Zane tried to mimic the way the man held his face and hands. "Dear God," said Zane, squinting. "We thank you for this food —"

"Don't speak for me," interrupted the man.

Zane opened his eyes to see if the man was smiling, but he was not. Zane started over. "*I* thank you for this food, dear God, and also I ask you to please…" This time, Zane interrupted himself. "Sir?"

The man looked up. "Yes?"

"I need to know something, something that's bothering me."

"What is it?"

"Do you know the man who was in that moving truck out there?"

"Unfortunately, I've known him for a long time."

"Where is he?"

"That I don't know. He took my horse last night — said something about going hunting — and I haven't seen him since. Why?"

"You mean he's still around?" Zane's breathing quickened. Sweat materialized on his forehead. He looked toward the door.

The man leaned back in his chair. "I think it's time I tell you who I am."

CHAPTER THIRTY ONE

"The story I told you," said Francisco, kneeling in the woods above the spring, "the one about how I came to La Florida with Ponce de Leon. That was not true. And I did not fall off a ship and get taken captive by the Calusa."

Dominic pressed the sword against his neck. "So you are a liar."

"We are all born with blood on our hands, are we not? I lied because the truth was a secret, one that must be kept at all costs. But now, it is time for you to know. My brother and I, you see, we joined a later expedition—Hernando as a soldier and me as a chaplain—under the leadership of a conquistador named Pánfilo de Narváez."

Dominic shuddered. "My father was on that expedition."

"I know. Álvar Cabeza de Vaca was my dear friend, and by far the most honorable man on the voyage."

"I doubt that."

"It is true. In fact, he urged Narváez to follow the coast, but Narváez's lust for gold, and for something even more tempting, drove us inland. We became lost and wandered in the wilderness for many weeks with nothing but survival as a goal. Some natives, like the Timucuans, helped us, while others were hostile. Envision it, commander. When the expedition began, we were three hundred men. When it was over, only six of us were left alive."

"More lies. Everyone knows there were only four survivors — my father, two soldiers, and a slave. They trekked all the way to Mexico."

"Yes, four survivors made it out, but my brother and I stayed behind."

"And why in God's name would you do that?"

"I was in my early fifties at the time — one of the oldest in the group — and as our expedition was passing through this region of La Florida, my heart began to fail. Narváez left me behind at Many Waters. Both your father and my brother stayed back to see me into the next world, and, just as I was about to draw my last breath, the villagers decided it was safe to reveal their secret. They said it was to help me, but, as I learned later, the Timucuans — convinced by our burnished armor and powerful weapons that we were demigods — wanted our help to protect their secret from their native enemies. Thank God they waited until Narváez had gone ahead. You see, his other goal was to find the ultimate source of power. Immortality. Natives in other regions had long spoken of a spring, hidden somewhere in the wilds of La Florida, that was blessed with restorative powers."

"Everyone knows that fairytale," said Dominic. "The fountain of youth."

"No, not the fountain of youth." Francisco gazed at the spring, its surface ignited with afternoon sunlight. "The fountain of *life* — for when the natives placed me in these cool waters and I drank its sweet nectar, I emerged completely healthy, my mind as sharp as a lance. Álvar and Hernando were astonished. We quickly realized the implications of what we had discovered and your father insisted that Narváez must never know about it, so we devised a plan. Hernando and I would stay at the village, and Álvar would rejoin the expedition. If he found his way home to Spain, he would seek council from the pope, try to gain control of the lands where the spring lay, and return on a later expedition. He brought a bottle of the water with him as proof. But he never came back. In later years, I had heard from other missionaries that he tried to convince the king to appoint him as governor of La Florida, but in the many years it had taken Álvar to reach Mexico and then Spain, the king had already granted the next expedition to De Soto, who, incidentally, met his end in these wilds just like Narváez."

Dominic kicked Francisco to the ground and spit on him. "Liar! My father never found such a thing!"

Francisco looked up at Dominic with the tranquility of a saint. "Then why is it, commander, that your father and his three closest friends were the only ones to reach Mexico alive? Don't you see? It's because they had water from the spring! My guess is they had to use it all to survive, and thus Álvar had none to bring to Spain. Denied permission to return here, he never spoke of it again, such a good and noble man as he was. You see, one sip or one submersion does not make you immortal. It only extends your life and cures your maladies. One must drink every day if one wants to halt the process of aging. A sip a day keeps the reaper away, I have always said, but I also learned that no amount of water can reverse a mortal wound."

"You learned that from slaying your brother, didn't you, you coward."

Francisco looked down. "Hernando and I lived together in this paradise for many years. But while my loyalties were with God, his remained with the crown. He found nothing peaceful about the isolation of this place. One day we heard from a native scout that the Spanish had founded a town on the coast—the inaptly named San Agustín, two days east of here—so Hernando filled a canteen from the spring, donned his armor, and set off to deliver the water as a gift to the king and hopefully earn himself governorship of a more civilized territory somewhere else."

"So you killed him."

"Am I not my brother's keeper? He would have torn the very fabric of nature by disclosing this place! The natives appointed us to guard it because they knew they could not do it forever. You see, they long ago observed that animals will not drink from the spring, none except for panthers, which are like gods to them. And for that reason, the natives—even the worst among them—will not drink from it, either. It is against the balance of nature, they say."

Dominic gazed at the spring. Despite its beauty, his heart felt nothing toward it. He was exhausted from all the emotions clashing inside, and his mind strained to make sense of the old man's wild story. The details of his father painted Álvar as a different kind of man than the one Dominic had known, and yet everything else Francisco said about the expedition echoed the few stories Dominic had heard. He ran the numbers through his head. The Narváez expedition began in 1527. If Francisco were in his fifties at that time then, by God, that would make him well over a hundred now. It seemed impossible, and yet, strangely, it all made perfect sense.

"Do you mind if I pray, commander?" said Francisco.

Dominic's eyes narrowed when he saw the rosary that now dangled from Francisco's hand. It was Pablo's rosary. The old man must have pilfered it off the beach after the shipwreck. Dominic twitched. A flood of memories tore through his mind: the roar of the hurricane, the plunge into violent waters, Juan's sandy face smiling at death, and Francisco swinging an oak log at his face. Through it all, he heard Pablo's taunts. *Your sins are unforgivable, captain! Unforgiveable!*

Francisco kissed the rosary and then gazed up at Dominic and said, "God loves even you."

Dominic's eyes bulged with rage. He lifted the sword high and, as he swung it down, he heard Francisco whisper, "Gracias," and then the old man's head bounced down the embankment and plopped into the water.

Dominic looked at the headless quivering body on the ground below him and at the red stain in the otherwise flawless spring and a debilitating combination of grief and remorse seized him and brought him to his knees. He wrapped his arms around Francisco's body and held it close, sobbing.

"*Forgive me,*" he cried out.

He wanted to kiss Francisco's cheek but that part of the old man, he realized, was at the bottom of the spring. Dominic put the sword to his own throat. He took a deep, sobbing breath and pressed the blade against his skin. But then he thought about Mela and his son. He let the headless body fall to the ground and stepped to the edge of the spring. He ripped off his helmet and threw it in the water. Then he looked at the blood-smeared sword in his hand.

"No more," he said, and he flung it toward the spring. It flailed through the air like a soul falling into hell and glinted as it sank into the dithering blueness.

He buried Francisco without his head in a shallow grave near the oak sapling and used a crude wooden cross ripped from the door of the hut as a grave marker. Then he walked down the trail and stood looking at the village wall for a long time. Did Mela think he was dead? Who would protect her and the children now that he was banished and Francisco was gone? He wanted to storm in and take them back, but he knew it was impossible without an army.

Without an army, he thought again, and an idea struck him. He looked up at the sky and used the sun to find east.

The woods off the trail were thick with creeping plants that had formed great webs of foliage. Scattered sloughs and mires impeded his way. At such a sluggish pace, he would never make it to the coast in time to save his son, and a heavy despair pressed down on him. A stick cracked off to his side; he spun around but saw only trees and bushes. "Hello?" he said, but there was no reply.

He came to a large fallen oak. Parts of it had been clawed to shreds by some animal. He stepped up onto the tree trunk and was about to step down on the other side but he stopped. There before him was a huge ball of shiny black fur. The animal spun around and rose on its hind legs and Dominic recognized the beast as a black bear. The bear sniffed the air and growled.

"Easy," said Dominic. He stepped backward off the tree trunk and heard a huffing sound. The bear came bounding over the tree and lunged at him with its claws extended and its teeth bared. Dominic fell to the ground and curled his legs up against his body and the full weight of the bear landed upon him. But it did not move. Dominic, now covered in blood, squeezed out from under the thing. He gazed at the bear and saw an arrow sticking out of its back. Itori came running up and knelt beside Dominic.

"Hurt?" said Itori.

Dominic patted his body but did not find any lacerations. "No. I am not hurt."

Itori smiled at the heap of dead bear. "Heart."

"I see that. Good aim."

Itori helped Dominic to his feet. "Where...go?"

Dominic hesitated. "To the coast."

"Itori...go."

"No."

"Itori...go. Itori...know...way."

Dominic sighed. He felt ashamed of what he had done to Francisco and even slightly afraid of what he might be capable of doing to Itori, but the wilds of La Florida harbored dangers beyond his comprehension. He could choose to be stubborn about his mission and continue alone, or he could utilize Itori's inherent knowledge of the forest and have a chance to save his son.

"Come on," said Dominic, and Itori's eyes lit up.

CHAPTER THIRTY TWO

Z ane sat speechless, having just been told the most outlandish tale he had ever heard. Did this lunatic really believe he was a Spanish conquistador named Dominic Cabeza de Vaca who had been living next to the Fountain of Youth for over four hundred years? Judging by the serious expression on the man's face, he did. Zane was terrified, and yet strangely intrigued.

"Won't you say anything?" said Dominic.

Zane tapped his fork on the plate. He still had not taken a bite. "What should I say?"

"That you believe me, or that you don't."

"You have to admit it's a pretty crazy story."

Dominic laughed. "Not to me. It's just the life that I know." He ripped a drumstick off the chicken and threw it on the floor. Zane looked down, confused.

"Alvar, eat!" said Dominic, and the panther sprang from beneath the table and seized the drumstick. Zane jumped in his chair; he had forgotten that Alvar was even there.

"Take off your bandage," said Dominic.

"What? Why?"

"Just take it off and look."

Zane peeled away the tape and lifted the gauze. Below, he found a healed scar that looked like it was already a few years old. He ran his fingers over the pink scar tissue.

"I don't expect you to believe me right away," continued Dominic. "It took me years to be fully convinced. But I am telling the truth as I know it. How does it work? That's still a mystery. Maybe there's some rare mineral in the water, something yet unknown to man that has the ability to preserve life. Or maybe there's something of the divine in it. I don't know. What I do know is that nothing decays in it. Even metal does not rust. It's a marvel, but a dangerous one. My many years on this planet have taught me that man is man throughout time…ferocious, complex, and as capable of good as he is of evil. This spring is a secret that must be protected, now more than ever."

"Then why tell me?"

"Because I think you were sent here to replace me."

"*Sent* here? By who?"

"By the one who makes the plans."

"What—God? I don't think so."

Dominic held up Zane's doubloon pendant. "Then explain this to me. Don't you see? This coin was from the wreck of my ship. *My ship!*"

"Listen, I got here because Miguel, your crazy friend—"

"He's not my friend."

"Well, whoever he is, he's a murderer. He found the rest of those coins, took me hostage, and killed at least four people like it was nothing!"

Dominic's face filled with concern. "*Killed* them?"

"In cold blood. Maybe you don't know what he's capable of, but I do, and I would be very happy if I never see him again."

A knock at the door brought Dominic to his feet. "Who is that?"

"What if it's him?" Zane scanned the room. "Where can I hide?"

The knock came again, this time as a pounding. Dominic opened a closet. "In here," he said. Zane jumped inside. Dominic shut the closet door and Zane leaned back. He felt something cold and hard against his shoulders and when he moved it made a clanking sound. A crack between the planks of the door let in a sliver of light and allowed Zane to see that the object was a polished metal breastplate, something like a knight or crusader might wear in a movie. Or a Spanish conquistador. Zane shook his head in disbelief, but he reasoned that anyone might be able to buy such a replica on the Internet if they searched hard enough.

Zane heard the front door of the house creak open. He peeked through the crack.

"Evening," said The Law. The Taxman stood behind him, his face as dark as the air, leaves swirling about him. Zane was relieved it was not Miguel. He thought about jumping out of the closet and turning himself in—ending this ordeal once and for all—but given that the two men were alone and had previously been intent on revenge, he remained silent.

"Evening," said Dominic.

"We're awfully sorry to bother you tonight, Mister—"

"Cowhead."

Drawing on the sparse amount of Spanish he had learned from Lucia, Zane realized that Cabeza de Vaca meant *head of cow* in English. He smiled.

"Right," said The Law. "Mister Cowhead. As I said, we're sorry to bother you, but an emergency call was received from that dumpy little church up the drive, and since you seem to own the land it's on—and all the land within ten miles, actually—we thought we should come down here just to double-check. The fella at that church claims it was someone pulling a prank, but, you see, those calls are recorded and what we've got on the recording is the name of a fella we're looking for. Zane Fisher. You seen any strangers round here lately?"

"No one but you," said Dominic.

"And what about that moving truck parked out there?"

"I found that old thing abandoned up on the main road. How's that saying go—finders keepers, right?"

"Not exactly. You're supposed to notify the authorities. We ran the plates. Turns out it's stolen."

"You don't say? Well, I'm not surprised. As you can imagine, people dump things out here all the time. I'll be sure to notify someone, though. Listen, I live alone out here, just like the many generations of Cowheads before me. If I catch anyone sneaking around, you can bet they'll be sorry they ever set foot on my ranch. Now, if you'll excuse me, there's a storm coming and I need to finish my preparations."

Dominic swung the door shut but The Taxman stepped forward and blocked it with his arm. "One more thing, if you don't mind, Mr. Cowhead."

Dominic stared at The Taxman, his mouth slightly ajar.

"What the hell are you looking at?" said The Taxman.

Dominic shook his head and looked away. "Sorry. I thought I saw something in your eyes. My apologies. You were saying?"

"Just one question. Do you know Miguel Orellano?"

Dominic paused. "I don't think so."

"Then why is it, Mr. Cowhead, that Mr. Orellano pays your property taxes every year, and, in fact, his family has been paying your family's taxes since this land was purchased some umpteen generations ago?"

"Oh, you must mean Miguel Ore-*yano*. In Spanish, you see, two *l*'s make a *y*. Yes, of course, I've known Miguel for most of my life. He's not in some kind of trouble, is he?"

"We are not at liberty to say," said The Taxman, and then he looked at Dominic for a long time without blinking. "You'll contact us if you see him, won't you?"

"Or if you see the Fisher kid," said The Law.

"Of course, but I must tell you—I don't have a phone."

"No, you wouldn't, would you," said The Taxman. "We'll just have to stop by again later, then, won't we." He turned and plodded down the porch steps.

The Law lingered a moment and looked up at the dark churning clouds. "Hope Juan isn't as bad as they say he is," he said.

"Excuse me?"

"The storm. It's gonna be a doozy."

The Law turned and followed The Taxman. Dominic watched them get into their car and drive off just as a sideways rain began to fall, and then he shut the door. "You can come out now," he shouted, and Zane did.

"Thanks for that," said Zane.

"We have to be careful. I think they know something." Rain crackled against the window. "It's time we brought in the animals. We can go through the back."

They approached the oak tree. There were at least twice as many animals around it as there had been before. How would they all fit in the house? It seemed crazy—as crazy as Dominic's story.

"How does a tree get so big?" Zane shouted over the bluster.

"A lot of water," said Dominic. "And a lot of love."

Dominic instructed Zane to pick up the snakes and turtles from around the tree. Dominic shepherded the larger creatures in through the door. When most of the mammals were inside, Dominic stood at the stoop and clapped his hands. All at once the birds took flight from the tree and flapped their way in. Zane ducked and almost dropped a tortoise. Dominic then gathered the chickens and, lastly, yanked the goat by a leash. But the goat jerked away, pulling the leash out of Dominic's hand and bounding into the woods.

"Suit yourself," said Dominic. "You'd probably eat all my books, anyway."

Dominic barred the door after he and Zane came inside. "It'll be a mess in here tomorrow," he said. "Not that it wasn't one already. I'll tell you what—it's amazing how easy it is to procrastinate when you have all the time in the world."

The animals quickly found various perches and dens—beneath tables, on stacks of books, along the eves of the ceiling. A small fire smoldered in the brick fireplace and, above it, an antiquated teakettle belched steam, but Zane did not recall seeing Dominic make the fire before they left. Maybe it had been there all along. Dominic pinched a clump of dried berries from a bowl on the mantel, dropped them into a conch shell, and poured hot water over them. The water turned black.

He held the shell out to Zane. "Tea?"

"No, thank you." Zane had never seen someone drink from a shell before.

"You wouldn't like it anyway." Dominic sipped. "It took me over a hundred years to acquire a taste."

Dominic sagged into a big chair beside the fireplace and lifted a baby raccoon from a stack of books, pulled a small hardcover from the stack, and put the raccoon back. He blew a cloud of dust off the book, opened it, and thumbed through the golden pages.

"The woods decay," Dominic read. "The woods decay and fall, the vapors weep their burthen to the ground…man comes and tills the field and lies beneath…and after many a summer dies the swan."

Zane scooted a rabbit off the chair across from Dominic and sat. He tilted his head sideways to read the spine of the book. *Tithonus – Alfred Tennyson – 1833*. It sounded boring.

"Me only cruel immortality consumes," continued Dominic. "I wither slowly in thine arms, here at the quiet limit of the world, a white-haired shadow roaming like a dream."

Unable to concentrate on the words, Zane studied Dominic's features. The man's hair was whitish-gray, but a few black holdouts belied the way he looked in his youth. There was something unique about him, especially his dark eyes, which possessed such depth that it was not difficult to imagine them having witnessed many lifetimes of remarkable things.

"When the steam floats up," continued Dominic, "from those dim fields about the homes of happy men that have the power to die, and grassy barrows of the happier dead…release me, and restore me to the ground."

Alvar sloped up and rubbed against Zane's knees. Zane stiffened and leaned back, hoping for the panther to leave him alone, but instead it set its paw on Zane's lap and looked at him as if it wanted something. Zane took a deep breath. He reached out with a trembling hand and stroked Alvar's head. The animal made a deep purring sound and pressed the top of its head against Zane's fingers. Zane feared that the panther might sink its fangs into him at any moment.

Dominic closed the book and recited the final lines from memory. "Thou seest all things, thou will see my grave. Thou wilt renew thy beauty morn by morn. I earth in earth forget these empty courts, and thee returning on thy silver wheels." His eyes flushed. He looked at the fire. "Do you like literature?" he asked, forlorn.

Zane thought for a moment. "I like to fish."

Dominic's smile lifted his sun-bronzed cheeks and squeezed out tears. "I was not aware the two were mutually exclusive."

"No, I guess they're not. I've just always found my peace out on the ocean."

"I can relate." Dominic swigged the last of his tea and held the conch shell to his ear. He closed his eyes and smiled. "I have not seen the sea in four centuries. Can you believe that? I was once practically tethered to her. What is she like now — the sea?"

"Well, they say there aren't as many fish as there used to be, but I still catch a few. On most days when I'm out I see a lot of trash floating around and sometimes globs of oil. And the coastline, well, it's covered with huge condos that block the sea breeze for the rest of us. But you know what? It's still beautiful."

Dominic nodded. "And mighty. Man may think he can tame her, but the ocean is one thing that will always be more powerful than him. Just look at this hurricane she spawned."

Zane leaned forward. "Speaking of *she*, I have to ask you — who's the woman in the robe?"

"Pardon?"

"She guided me through the woods. Then I saw her by the spring."

Dominic shifted in his chair. He looked uncomfortable. "Did she have long black hair?"

"Yes."

"Dark skin?"

"Yes."

Dominic rose and walked to the front window, the only one he had not boarded. He stood there looking at the deluge of rainwater streaming down the panes, at the trees jiving with the wind. He drew a deep breath and released it slowly. "It's time you hear the rest of my story."

CHAPTER THIRTY THREE

The cobblestone *avenida* piercing the town reminded Dominic of the streets he trod as a child. In the decade or so since he had last set foot in San Agustín—the only Spanish settlement in La Florida—it seemed like it had changed considerably, and not for the better.

Everything about the town, in fact, looked unnatural. The corners of the buildings were too sharp, the streets too straight, and the language spoken by the townsfolk too familiar. With the ground devoid of leaves and dirt, and most of the walls painted a sterile white, the whole place felt infertile and artificial. But as Dominic trekked farther, he realized it was not the town that had changed. It was the way he now perceived the world that was different.

The road's uneven stones caused Itori to stagger like a drunkard. "Crazy...path," said Itori, his eyes wide with terror.

Dominic realized that Itori had likely never walked on anything so solid or experienced such a foreign place. To Dominic, however, coming into San Agustín was like walking through a memory, as if a little chunk of Europe had been transported to the New World. Pockets of fresh air competed with the smells of roast pork, horse manure and spilled rum. The two-story timber and coquina buildings included a tavern, a sundry shop, a schoolhouse and a barbershop. They passed a group of Spanish ladies wearing dresses with puffy sleeves and high-necked bodices. Dominic laughed. He had become so accustomed to women going around naked that seeing them covered in lavish garments was almost bizarre.

"Women...cold?" said Itori. Dominic smiled, but when he and Itori turned the corner and found themselves in the shadow of a soldier on horseback, his smile faded. The horse snorted and Itori cowered. "Giant...devil...deer," Itori whispered.

The soldier pointed his iron lance at Itori and said, "Why aren't you working?"

Dominic stepped between Itori and the soldier. "He's mine."

"Yours?" said the soldier.

"Yes, my slave. He carries my supplies."

"And who are you?"

"I am a friend of the admiral's."

"Then why do you look like one of *them*?"

Dominic looked down at himself. Wearing a muddy deerskin shirt, what was left of his old leather trousers, and moccasins that Mela had made for him, he did indeed look like one of *them*. Dominic glanced at Itori and feigned disgust. "You compare me to this *filth*? How dare you. Have you never seen a Spanish slaver dressed in a native disguise? Waste one more second of my time and the admiral will hear about it."

The soldier eyed Dominic for a moment. "What's your name?"

"My name?"

"You have a name, don't you?"

"My name—is Captain Dominic Cabeza de Vaca."

The soldier gasped. "*Cabeza de Vaca.*" He lowered his lance and the tip of it clanked against the cobblestone, throwing off sparks. "Forgive me, sir."

"Do I know you?" asked Dominic.

"No, sir," said the soldier, "but I know you. *Everyone* knows you."

Spanish settlers stared at Dominic and Itori as the two made their way deeper into the heart of town. They soon came upon a large church. A procession flowed out of it into the street. Dominic and Itori stopped along a stone wall to let the people pass. The priest in front held a large crucifix and the four well-dressed men behind him carried a statue of *Our Lady of La Leche* on a litter covered in flowers. Each worshipper that followed had ash smudged on his or her forehead in the shape of a cross. The *Salve Regina* hymn lilted up from the procession and instigated a memory in Dominic of his father kneeling in a church, crying as he recited the same prayer.

Hail, holy Queen, Mother of Mercy, our life, our sweetness and our hope. The afternoon sun bore down on the procession and the ashen crosses mixed with sweat, melting down the faces of the people. *To thee do we cry, poor banished children of Eve.* Itori stared with wonder at the churchgoers, and Dominic studied their faces as they passed. Women he might have considered beautiful in days past now looked far too pale and plump. He saw one of them holding a rosary and his heart ached for Francisco. *To thee do we send up our sighs, mourning and weeping in this valley of tears.* Dominic spotted a familiar face. Ash obscured the man's brow and cheeks, but his eyes—as black as Dominic remembered— were unmistakable. It was his former superior, the person he had come to find. The admiral's face puckered in shock when he noticed Dominic. He stepped out of the procession. "Dominic?"

"Miguel," said Dominic.

"Good God!" Miguel grabbed Dominic by both shoulders. "I was told you were dead, that your ship was lost in a storm!"

"It was, but I survived."

"Then where have you been?"

"I was taken captive. By naturals."

"Well that explains your ridiculous attire." Miguel looked at Itori with disgust. "Is this one of them?"

"No," said Dominic. "He is my guide."

"His hair is long. He has not yet converted." Miguel then smiled at Dominic. "Come, come. Let us go to my office and reinstate you, and get you into some respectable clothes."

Dominic and Itori followed Miguel toward the waterfront where hundreds of native workers were busy constructing a massive wooden fort. Dominic could tell by the workers' circular tattoos that they were Timucuans from a different village, but otherwise their bodies looked uncharacteristically gaunt and sickly. Most striking of all, their hair had been cut short. One native lay beside a woodpile beneath a cloud of flies. It was obvious from the man's sallowness and sunken cheeks that he had been dead for hours.

"We lose a few builders every day," said Miguel. "I may need to commandeer your slave. He looks quite strong."

"He is not for the taking," said Dominic.

Miguel's brow furrowed. "No?"

As they approached the finished section of the fort, Miguel opened a door guarded by two soldiers holding lances. One of the soldiers, glistening with sweat, coughed harshly. Dominic walked through the door but Miguel put his hand in front of Itori. "He stays outside, where he belongs."

Dominic looked into Itori's eyes. Itori nodded and stepped back.

The inner chamber of the fort was dark and grim and smelled of tar and sunbaked timber. Nautical charts and town maps hung on the walls. Miguel sat in a plush, velvety chair behind a desk. Dominic looked around but saw nowhere else to sit.

"So, my old friend," said Miguel. "I am sure you are anxious to return home to Spain. I have good news for you. A ship leaves tomorrow."

Dominic glanced at the globe on Miguel's desk. "I do not want to go back to Spain."

"I hoped you would say that. I could use an extra man around here, one with your—how should I say it—drive. Now tell me, Dominic, for my records, where exactly did you wreck your ship?"

Dominic bit his lip, trying to quell his anger. "I did not wreck my ship. A hurricane did."

Miguel smiled. "I know. I just wanted to elicit some emotion from that boring old face of yours." Miguel unrolled a chart showing the coast of Florida. "Your cargo was mostly gold, was it not?"

"It was."

"Show me, here on the map, where your ship met her end."

"Why?"

Miguel's face reddened and the muscles in his neck went taut. "*Why?* Dominic, brother, that treasure belongs to the crown. We may be able to recover some of it with our native salvors." Miguel's face relaxed and he smiled. "You should see those rodents swim. Just do me this favor, and I will be at your service for anything you need."

Dominic looked at Miguel for a moment, and then he bent over and ran his finger along the chart, up past the Florida Straits, over a drawing of a sea monster, and around the curve of the southern coastline. His finger stopped just north of a small inlet labeled *Jaega*. "It was somewhere around here."

Miguel studied Dominic through squinted eyes. "Can you not tell me the *exact* location?"

"It was during a hurricane!"

"Alright, alright." Miguel drew a black circle over the area with a quill pen. "Now, tell me, what can I do for you?"

"I need your help."

"Go on."

"I want you to arrest the chief of a native village. A rebel."

"A rebel chief? Where?"

"Two day's march from here. I need a unit."

Miguel chortled. "Oh, is that all you need? Dominic, old friend, you must know that San Agustín is under constant threat from the British. We are undermanned as it is. I cannot spare a unit. I cannot even spare one man."

"You said you would do anything."

"Did I?"

Blood-red rage boiled inside Dominic, but he knew that one outburst would ruin his chances of procuring help. He thought about Mela and the twins and his anger morphed into anguish. The moon would be full in two days; even if he left San Agustín at that moment, he would have to trek nonstop to arrive at Many Waters in time to stop the sacrifice.

"You speak of looking for treasure," said Dominic. "I know the location of a treasure, one more valuable than all the gold in the world—"

"Allow me to guess. It's in the native village."

Dominic sighed. "Yes."

"Dominic, I know your tricks. You learned them all from me!"

"I implore you," said Dominic, leaning on the desk toward Miguel. "Give me some men, just for a few days."

Miguel rubbed the end of the quill pen between his fingers. "Why do you care so much about this so-called rebel chief? What benefit do you get from his capture?"

"Pardon?"

"Do not misunderstand me—I want to eradicate these rats off our land more than anyone else. But I know you, Dominic. You stand to gain something, and I want to know what. Do not forget that I taught you everything you know about the New World. I know how you think. We are alike."

Dominic glared at Miguel. "I am nothing like you."

"No? Your victims might disagree. If the king ever gave an award for the highest number of natives killed—and I have often wished he would—then you, Dominic Cabeza de Vaca, would be the clear winner. I am sure of it. Our soldiers still boast of your exploits; our priests still atone for them. So perhaps you are right, you are not like me. You are far worse."

Rage filled Dominic's face. "You made me like this!" he screamed. He knocked the globe off the desk and, as he did, his deerskin sleeve parted at the seam and revealed his tattoo. Miguel's eyes darted to it.

"Oh, I see," said Miguel, smiling. "You are a rat now. Did I not warn you about becoming their equal? I should hang you for treason." Miguel stood, put his hands on the desk, and leaned toward Dominic. "But because you were once my friend, and because I loathe all the paperwork that accompanies an execution, I will pretend that I never saw you today. You and your rodent friend will march out of town and never return. Now get out. You no longer exist."

Dominic ushered Itori down the path and glanced back at the fort. Miguel stood outside the door between the two guards, smiling. Miguel's words ricocheted through Dominic's mind. *You are a rat now. You no longer exist.* Dominic imagined running back and sticking one of Itori's arrows into Miguel's neck, but then he remembered the vow he had made after killing Francisco. For once, he intended to keep his promise.

They passed a Spanish woman and her little boy and Dominic's mind went to Mela, and to the infants. A sickening helplessness pressed down on him. Time was stealing by and he could do nothing to impede it. His son would soon be taken from him, again. He had to do something—something drastic, something radical. He saw a group of native workers slathering hot tar on a piece of timber, and then he looked at the bow slung over Itori's shoulder.

"Give me an arrow," said Dominic.

Itori looked at Dominic for a moment and then handed him an arrow. Dominic dipped the arrowhead into a barrel of tar, and then he grabbed an iron spike from a pile of rusty hardware. He could see Miguel in the distance, watching him.

Keep looking, thought Dominic. You're not the only person who taught me something.

Dominic knelt on the path and, holding the arrow close to it, hit the iron spike against the cobblestone. Sparks shot out and ignited the arrow. He handed it to Itori.

"Burn it down," said Dominic, gesturing toward the fort.

Itori nodded. He straightened his body, aimed, drew back and released. The flaming arrow made a whistling sound as it soared through the sky. Dominic watched Miguel's face twist into a look of disbelief as the arrow landed on top of the fort. The tar covering the structure burst into a towering wall of flame. Dominic could feel the heat on his face. It felt delightful. He watched Miguel and the guards scamper away.

Aaay-yeee! The native workers erupted with cheers and war cries. They danced around the burning fort and lifted their arms to the sky, rapt. Itori joined in with his own whooping shout, and then he yelled, "Burn it down! Burn it down!"

Reaching the summit of a nearby rise, Miguel put his hands on his head and rocked back and forth as he watched the fort burn, and then he turned and pointed at Dominic and Itori. "Kill them!" he screamed to the guards, his face as severe as the fire.

Dominic put his hand on Itori's shoulder. "I assume you know how to get back to the village without leaving tracks for anyone to follow."

Itori nodded. "Yes."

"We must do the opposite."

CHAPTER THIRTY FOUR

D ominic's eyes filled with tears and he stopped telling his story. Zane had been so entranced that he only now noticed the wail of the hurricane outside. Fear sank in as he listened to the gutters rattling and debris pelting the roof and gusts of wind ebbing and flowing as if some hulking beast were trying to blow down the walls. How much could the old house withstand?

Dominic wiped his eyes, looked at Zane and said, "If I could have foreseen the great evil I was bringing to the village, I would have stopped right there and given up. But saving my son was all that mattered, as if his life was worth more than anyone else's. I was a selfish man. I don't think there's any amount of penance — not four hundred years of it or even four thousand — that can ever compensate for the suffering I've caused."

"I know the feeling," said Zane.

"Do you?"

Zane tried to think of a way to change the subject. "What happened when you got back to the village?"

Dominic looked at the floor. "Pestilence. And death."

The whole house suddenly shook. Zane suspected thunder, but as the shaking continued, he realized it was someone's heavy footsteps on the porch. Both he and Dominic turned toward the door just as someone on the other side kicked it open. Wind and rainwater streamed in. The animals scurried into the darkest corners of the house. The preacher stood wet and disheveled in the doorway, looking like a drowned person pulled from a lake. His eyes locked onto Zane. "You!" he said.

Dominic sprang to his feet. "Be calm. He's a friend."

"*A friend?* He called the police!"

"You were trying to kill me!" said Zane.

The preacher stepped inside. "No! I was trying to save your soul!"

"Enough," said Dominic. He stepped toward the preacher. "Why are you here?"

The preacher's eyes blinked rapidly. "Why am I here? *Why am I here?* Can you not see? The end of days is upon us!"

"It's only a hurricane. We've been through hundreds."

"No, not this one! The signs are clear! And I saw him—"

"Who?"

"The horseman!"

Fear pressed in on Zane. "You saw someone on a horse?"

"Not just someone," said the preacher, and his voice deepened. "Behold a pale horse, and he that sat upon him, his name was Death, and hell followed with him!" The preacher's voice eased as he continued. "Can you believe it? The fourth horseman of the apocalypse, riding through these very woods! The end, my brothers, is nigh."

"I want you to leave," said Dominic.

"Leave? You would deny me refuge in a tempest?"

"I don't care where you go, but I don't want you here. We both know why."

The preacher's face flushed and inflated. "Oh, I know why. Yes I do. The love of money, my friend, is the root of all evil!"

"What are you talking about?"

The preacher pulled the doubloon out of his pocket and stuck it in Dominic's face. "I know what your ship was called. You told me! Where are the rest of these? I've been starving out here, doing your dirty work, while you sit around and horde your gold and share it with the likes of this little pagan!" He glared at Zane.

Dominic grabbed the preacher by the collar and shoved him out the door. "Get out!"

The big man tumbled down the steps and crashed into a mud puddle. "Woe to you, my friend!" he bellowed, his voice barely audible over the roaring wind. "For tonight the Lord separates the wheat from the chaff!"

Dominic slammed the door and locked it.

Zane sat wide-eyed. "Who *is* that guy?"

Dominic eased into his chair. "That guy," he said, "was the first stranger to ever stumble upon the spring after I became its protector. The civil war had just begun. He showed up one day, seething with gangrene. Said he was a confederate deserter. I pitied the poor man and used the water to heal him, but when he discovered my secret, I was faced with a decision. Let him stay, or silence him forever."

"You mean kill him?"

"I was tempted. But, as I said, I made an oath to never kill another person, with my own hands at least. I have kept that oath, and I will continue to. But as for that man, I did not have to kill him. I found a use for him. You see, although *my* killing days were over, I knew that as the population of La Florida grew, more people would start finding the spring. Yes, his methods are a little disturbing — he insists on baptizing his victims before he dispatches them — but he's prevented the secret from getting out on numerous occasions. In exchange for his services, I provide him with water from the spring and plenty of food. Unfortunately, though, I think the loneliness of eternity is eating away at his mind, as you can see."

Zane had a look of disgust on his face. "You let him *kill* people if they find the spring?"

"What else am I supposed to do? I am not proud of it. And I have, on several occasions, insisted that he let certain ones go free. But imagine if this thing got into the wrong hands. The entire balance of the world would be destroyed. Think about it. Knowing he is destined to die, man still fears that his actions might one day be judged. Give him immortality, on the other hand, and he will have nothing left to fear."

Zane felt exhausted from the many directions his mind was being pulled. He rubbed his eyes. "I need to lie down."

"Of course. I have a room prepared for you."

Dominic led him down a long hallway. They passed an open door and Dominic motioned toward it. "That is where I sleep, in case you need anything."

They came upon another door, this one shut tight. "What's in there?" said Zane.

"It's private."

"Okay."

"I mean it."

"I said okay."

Dominic led Zane to a small, damp room decorated with a hodgepodge of antiques and curiosities. A bedpan sat on a wicker chair. A deerskin rug lay in the middle of the floor. A carved wooden paddle hung on the wall. Zane collapsed onto the four-poster bed and gazed at the frilly hand-knitted canopy above.

I have to get out of here, he thought. But no part of his body willed to move. He felt his motivation drain away. He watched the walls tremble and listened to the wind rustling outside but he was too exhausted to worry about the storm anymore. Sleep took him within minutes.

He dreamt about the part of Lucia's body that he cherished the most—her smile. Perched on the edge of his skiff, her hair whipping all around, she reached out to touch a porpoise as it surfed the bow wake and when her fingers met its slick, shining skin her mouth opened in the most vibrant smile Zane had ever seen and that was how he always wanted to remember her—not splayed out on a gurney with paramedics peeling off her clothes and strangers looking at parts of her body even he had not yet seen and the loud god-awful sirens jarring the gossipers out of bed and the flashing lights turning the inlet parking lot into a nightclub in which no one wanted to dance.

The beat of hooves jolted Zane awake. It took him a moment to remember where he was and to recall why such a sound should even concern him, but his mind ignited and he jumped off the bed. He put his ear to the boarded-up window. Despite the roar of the storm outside, he could hear the clacking of a horse.

It's him, he thought. Miguel.

The room felt cold. He shivered. He hurried out of the room.

"Dominic?" he whispered as he walked down the dim hallway. "*Dominic?*"

No one answered. Zane stopped when he came to the door that Dominic had forbidden him to open. It was ajar. He stood there looking at it for a moment. Then he put his ear against it and listened. Despite the wind heaving outside, he could hear someone whistling a sad melody.

"Hello?" he said. "Dominic?"

The whistling stopped. Zane pushed on the door and the hinges creaked as it opened. All the air left his lungs when he saw a shadowy figure standing in the corner of the dark room. It was the woman. She wore the robe, but the hood was lowered and Zane could see her long hair and dark eyes. She put her index finger over her mouth as if it to say *shhh*.

"Who are you?" said Zane.

"Get out of there!" Zane spun around and saw Dominic approaching from the other end of the hallway.

"The door was open," said Zane.

Dominic seemed confused. "Open?"

"Yes, and the lady…" Zane spun back to the room, his finger ready to point at her, but she was gone. "Where'd she go?"

Dominic reached the doorway and looked inside. "Where did *who* go?"

Zane rubbed his brow. "The woman, the one I saw by the spring, she was in here!"

Dominic put his hand on Zane's shoulder. "Are you sure?"

"I'm positive!" Zane scanned the dark room. A wooden owl carving sat on the windowsill. A panther sculpture, and some kind of bone, lay on an antique dresser.

"It's okay. I believe you."

"You do?"

Dominic nodded. "I need to tell you what happened when I got back to the village."

A chilling scream—shrill and high-pitched—came from somewhere outside. Dominic turned toward the back door with a look of terror on his face. "Good God," he said, and he bolted to the door and unbarred it.

Zane followed. "Wait! I heard a horse—"

Dominic flung the door open and stepped into the full tumult of the hurricane. His shirt flapped on his body and his hair thrashed. Zane stepped outside, too, and the driving rain pummeled his body and numbed his skin. Dominic put his hand on his forehead to shield his eyes from the rain. He squinted. His jaw dropped open.

"He knows you're here," said Dominic.

Zane followed his gaze and was overcome with nausea. There, hanging from a rope tied to the oak tree and twitching as it spun in the wind, was the goat, its stomach cut open and its entrails piled on the ground like a plateful of spaghetti. Tiny round puddles were scattered about in the mud. Dominic knelt and splashed the water out of one of the puddles. The shape was clear—it was a horseshoe track.

Dominic grabbed Zane's arm. "Come inside! Now!"

Chapter Thirty Five

H ope and fear filled Dominic when he heard drums throbbing through the forest like a low heartbeat. The landscape became increasingly familiar as he and Itori trudged west. They soon came to the little brook where Dominic had killed his first deer and where he had touched Mela for the first time. He and Itori leapt across and paused to listen for the Spaniards. With their clanking armor and hacking coughs and loud curses, it was easy to tell that the soldiers were keeping pace.

As the light faded, Dominic feared that the moon might rise out of the woods at any moment. Would they reach Many Waters in time? He made sure to put all of his weight into each step in order to leave deep and noticeable tracks.

Dominic and Itori soon reached the entrance to the village. They stopped and waited. The drumbeats from within the walls were jarring and Dominic could hear Yaba's distinctive shrieking. His anger seethed. He yearned to storm into the village and save his family, but he knew he had to be patient.

Moments later, Miguel emerged from the woods on horseback, followed by ten armored soldiers carrying lances and swords. Miguel looked at Dominic and mouthed the word "morir." *Die.*

Dominic took a deep breath and looked at Itori. "Ready?"

Itori nodded, and they headed into the village side by side. Two native watchmen sitting along the inner part of the entryway jumped up. One of them ran into the village, shouting. The other stepped in front of Dominic and put his hand up.

"Hani," said the guard. *Stop.*

Dominic slugged him in the face. The native fell back against the wall and rumpled to the ground.

"Pardon me," said Dominic.

He and Itori approached the center of the village where a towering fire raged. Around it, natives romped to the pulse of drums. When the watchman attracted their attention with his screaming and pointing, however, the drums abated and the people stopped. Utina, standing on a platform with a shark tooth knife in his hand, turned his baneful gaze to Dominic. His eyes flickered in the firelight.

Yaba, standing beside Utina, also turned to look at Dominic. The old shaman's face wrinkled up in a sinister smile and his chest quavered as if laughing. Red paint covered his skin and he wore a gaudy eagle feather headdress. He held something small and squirming in front of his body. Dominic heard a sharp wail—his heart dropped. It was his infant son in Yaba's hands. He looked around and saw Mela tied to one of the seven columns, her tears spilling onto little Isa who lay sleeping in a papoose slung across her stomach. Mela's eyes met Dominic's.

Save him, she seemed to say.

Utina shouted something and pointed in the direction of the village wall.

Here comes my army, thought Dominic, but when he turned to look, orange light bathed his face. At first he did not recognize the bulbous glowing thing climbing over the village wall, but when he heard the drumbeats resume and the natives cheer, he realized that he was looking at the moon, vivid and glorious and wicked in its fullness.

Timucuan warriors—the same ones who had thrown him into the river—surrounded Dominic. One of them grabbed Itori by the hair and forced him to his knees. Itori cried out and the warrior kicked him to the dirt.

"Give us the rebels!" shouted Miguel. The natives all turned toward the entryway just in time to see Miguel entering the village on his horse, surrounded by his soldiers. The drumbeats went silent again.

Dominic jumped up and pointed at Utina and Yaba. "They are the rebels! They are performing a sacrifice!"

Miguel jerked the reigns and his horse trotted toward Dominic and Itori. The surrounding natives cowered, staring at the horse in fear and wonder.

"Their rituals are of no concern to me," said Miguel. "I came for you and your rodent friend. Do you know how defenseless you've left the king's interests? *Do you?*"

Dominic put his hands together to beg. "Kill me. I do not care. But do not be so stupid as to leave this place without ridding your land of those evil men up there."

"The only evil man I see here is you." Miguel looked at Dominic for a moment, and then he turned to his soldiers. "Bind these two criminals, and then kill the chief and that bird-man and whoever else stands in your way."

"Thank you," said Dominic.

Miguel spit on him. "I am not doing it for you."

A soldier pulled Dominic's arms behind his back and another did the same to Itori. The rest approached Utina and Yaba. Utina shouted something and all at once the Timucuan warriors surrounded the Spanish soldiers. The soldiers wielded their lances but the warriors lunged and a struggle ensued. Dominic jolted back and used his weight to knock down the soldier who was tying his hands. His eyes found Yaba scurrying off the platform with the baby under one arm.

"Stop!" screamed Dominic. Yaba spun around with a knife in his hand. He held the knife to the baby's tiny chest and pushed it in. Blood formed around it.

Dominic heard a whirring sound and then a *thwack* and Yaba's hand stiffened and the knife fell to the ground. Dominic looked into Yaba's dazed eyes. The old shaman's head tilted back and his mouth gaped open to reveal an arrowhead; an arrow had pierced the back of his head, straight into his throat. Dominic lunged forward and ripped the infant out of Yaba's arms. Yaba buckled to the ground.

Dominic looked for the source of the arrow and found Itori standing in the distance, holding his bow with a look of satisfaction amid the melee of clashing soldiers and natives. Itori never saw or heard Miguel coming up behind him and when Dominic shouted it was too late—the lance was already sticking out of Itori's chest. Itori looked at Dominic, and at the baby in Dominic's hands, and his mouth quavered.

Brother, Itori seemed to say.

Dominic nodded. *Brother*.

Miguel ripped out the lance and Itori collapsed. Miguel focused next on Dominic. Smiling wickedly, he flipped the reigns. Dominic grabbed Yaba's knife and hurried to Mela.

"My love," he said, and he used the knife to sever the twine that bound her.

"What have they done?" she said, plucking Yaraha from Dominic's arms. The wound in the baby's chest was deep. Thin, watery blood streamed out. She touched his tiny mouth and gasped when she pulled her hand away—her fingertip was bright red.

"Quickly," said Dominic. "Take him to the spring."

"You know I cannot. The balance—"

Dominic grabbed Mela by her shoulders. "He is half native, but he is also half mine. Do as I say. Take him there. Wash him."

Mela looked at Dominic, and then at the whimpering baby in her arms. Her lips parted to say something but she stopped.

"Go!" shouted Dominic, and she hurried off.

Dominic heard Miguel's horse bray. He whipped around, expecting to be slain, but instead he saw a group of native warriors scale the horse and rip Miguel off of it.

"Release me!" screamed Miguel, but they threw him down and stomped on him.

Dominic looked around and realized that none of the Spanish soldiers were left standing. Native warriors surrounded him and closed in. He dropped the knife and extended his hands, arms crossed at the wrist. He had done all he could to save his son. As much as he hated to think it, the rest was in God's hands.

The worst part of that night and the following day was not the insatiable mosquitos or the biting gnats or the temperature that fluctuated from cold to sweltering; it was being tied next to Miguel that tortured Dominic the most. They sat bound to the columns in the village center. Five armed warriors kept watch.

Utina prepared an altar in front of them and placed his ceremonial club on it. Dominic knew that it would be used to execute him and he doubted he would live to see the next day. There was simply no way out. For the first time in many years, he thought a simple prayer. *Forgive me.*

Miguel, it seemed, was also pondering the hereafter. His face covered in blood and soil, he smiled at Dominic. "I imagine the demons in hell are preparing a banquet for us at this very moment. We shall soon meet the great deceiver himself!" He laughed.

The first sign of a problem in the village came that afternoon when one of the native guards collapsed. Dominic had watched the man throughout the day. It started with watery eyes and coughing, and then the man broke into a sweat. His knees buckled and he hit the dirt with a thud. The other natives stood over him and poked him, and then they dragged him away to a hut.

Within hours, the other native guards succumbed to the same mysterious ailment, as did their replacements. Dominic scanned the village. Men, women and children lay about the ground, trembling and crying out. Utina, coughing, stumbled out of his hut. The chief's eyes were puffy and red, and his body gleamed with sweat. He lurched up to Dominic and knelt in front of him.

"*Iqui na,*" said Utina, but Dominic did not understand.

Utina pulled a knife from his waist belt and sliced the twine that bound Dominic, and then he held the blade up to Dominic's neck. Dominic froze.

"When you get to hell," sneered Miguel, "hold the gates open for me."

Utina made a stabbing motion toward Dominic's neck and Dominic closed his eyes. Nothing came, though—no gouging blow, no pain—and he opened his eyes, confused. Utina spun the knife around and offered it handle-first to Dominic. At once

Dominic understood. Utina wanted to be put out of his misery. He was too much of a coward to do it himself.

Dominic took the knife. He stood and threw it as far as he could. Utina collapsed to the ground, sobbing.

"Suffer," said Dominic. "Suffer well."

Dominic looked around the village. No one was standing. Some of the natives writhed on the ground but most were not even breathing. An intense sadness overtook him. Was his family suffering, too? He turned toward the village entrance.

"You cannot leave me here!" said Miguel, struggling to break free. "I will die!"

Dominic turned. He had never seen the admiral so grimy and pitiful. Dominic sighed, and then he stooped and untied Miguel.

"Go back to San Agustín," said Dominic, "and never come back."

Miguel stumbled out of the village. Dominic followed. He watched Miguel disappear into the woods, and then he hurried down the forbidden trail. When he came to Francisco's grave and saw the fresh wildflowers strewn on it, sorrow swept through him. He headed toward the spring and found Mela sitting on the bank, singing to the two infants as they suckled her breasts. She looked up, beaming.

Dominic picked up the boy. He looked as healthy as ever, the wound on his chest now nothing more than a faint scar.

"I am sorry," said Dominic.

"Why?" asked Mela.

He gazed into the azure waters. "I killed Francisco."

"I know."

"You do?"

Mela smiled placidly. "It was part of the plan."

"What are you talking about?" He sat on the ground beside her.

"Have you not pieced it together?"

"Pieced what together?"

Mela touched his face. "They chose you, Dominic. Francisco had been praying for someone to come and replace him for years.

He was ready to go. And then the hurricane brought you right to him. They knew they had the right man."

"Why?"

"Because you are selfish and you fear death. And they could see the fire in your eyes."

Dominic rubbed his forehead. "What about Yaba's predictions? They have all come true."

"Yes, but he made some of it happen himself, like baiting the alligator."

"To silence the boy and protect Utina?"

"Utina did not kill my father. Nor did Yaba."

"Then who did?"

She hesitated. "After Francisco used the water to heal him, my father made me promise two things. He asked me to become your wife. And he asked me to send him back...back to the beauty."

Dominic's face twisted in shock. "*You* killed Ona?"

"He never wanted Francisco to bring him back." She sobbed. "It was the most difficult thing I have ever had to do."

Dominic put his arm around her and pulled her close. "What about marrying me?"

"I wanted to do that." She smiled through her tears.

"That baby should be dead." Miguel's voice startled them.

They spun around. Mela gasped. Dominic stood and glared at Miguel.

"Be calm," said Miguel. "There's been enough death for one day, don't you think?" He looked around at the spring, his eyes wild with wonder. "So, the rumors are true!"

"I told you to go away."

"I started to, but then I remembered your tale of a treasure, and, I have to admit, curiosity got the best of me. I must say, if this is what I think this is, I am thoroughly impressed."

"What do you want?"

Miguel smiled. "I want to make a deal."

CHAPTER THIRTY SIX

The wind outside came like throbs of pain that would surge and abate and then surge again. Zane and Dominic stood in the living room, gazing out at the storm through the front window, searching the inkiness for any sign of Miguel. Water trickled from leaks in the roof. A raccoon lapped at a dribble.

"Making a deal with Miguel," said Dominic, "was like making a pact with the devil. I knew that. But all I cared about was protecting my family. The agreement we made seemed simple enough. I would live by the spring to guard it, and he would go back to the coast and carry on with his work. I supplied him with water whenever he ran out. Over the years, I have heard, he has amassed enormous wealth, but it's never been enough for him."

"What about the village?" asked Zane. "Didn't the disease affect you?"

"It was nothing but a fever," said Dominic. "My genetics, I guess, gave me immunity, and our children, being half-European, were also spared. Mela would have died from it like the rest of them, but she was saved, I think, when she got the water on herself while healing our son."

"And you lived together near the spring?"

Dominic sighed. "We did, for some time. But not long enough. No matter how much I begged her, Mela refused to swim or drink the water, and I finally just had to accept it. We never talked about it. There was nothing to say. She had made her decision and I

265

could not convince her otherwise. As the years flashed by, we just took on our roles according to her stage in life. I stayed the same, but soon her hair began to gray. She became like a mother to me. Time hurried on. Her body arced like a hook, her hair thinned to something like a white mist, and her eyes became so foggy that one day she could no longer see. But she never lost her happiness, never once complained. She would sit by the water and sing her native songs and tell me stories of her younger days, as if she forgot I was there for most of them. And then one day I found her out there leaning against that old oak tree—our tree—with her hands folded across her lap and her frail little heart pattering no longer." Tears welled in Dominic's eyes. "It all happened so fast."

A white glow shone through the window. Dominic and Zane looked out to see the police cruiser pull up, its windshield wipers going at full speed, its headlights illuminating the deluge. The car doors flung open and The Law and The Taxman jumped out and ran to the porch. They pounded on the door.

"Mister Cowhead!" said The Law. "Let us in!"

Dominic went to the door. "It's not safe here!" he shouted. "Come back after the storm."

"It cannot wait. We have to talk to you now."

"About what?"

"About the blood we found in that abandoned *U-Haul*. Open up."

Dominic unlocked the door and put his hand on the doorknob, but the glow in the window went dark.

"The headlights went off," said Zane.

"What the hell?" The Law said outside.

Two gunshots rang out, followed by a reverberating thud. Zane recognized the sound as that of a body falling on the front porch. There was another gunshot, and then the voice of The Taxman yelling "Drop it!" and then a series of louder gunshots that sounded like they came from right behind the door and then another thud and then nothing but the grumble of distant thunder and the spray of rain on the walls.

Dominic pressed his ear to the door. Zane did the same and heard a raspy whisper outside. "Help me," it said.

"What do we do?" said Zane.

Dominic turned the door handle. "We help."

Wind rushed in as Dominic opened the door. Zane peered out. Spent bullet casings littered the porch. Two bodies — The Law and The Taxman — lay side by side. Part of The Law's head was pulp and his shirt and skin were peeled back around a large hole in his chest. The Taxman, however, was still moving; his chest rose and fell in slight, jerky spasms. The bullet hole below his right shoulder gurgled each time he breathed. His glassy eyes wandered to Dominic and Zane. "I don't want to die," he whispered.

Dominic loomed over the man. "He doesn't have long."

"Can you help him?" said Zane.

Dominic gazed into the darkness. "I can carry him to the spring."

"What about Miguel?"

"I can't let an innocent man die."

Zane took a deep breath. "I'll help you."

"No. It's too dangerous."

"You can't do it alone."

Dominic looked at Zane for a moment. "Come on."

Zane and Dominic each took an arm over their shoulders and hoisted The Taxman. As they stumbled down the porch steps, the man winced. "Where the hell are you taking me?" he hissed.

"Quiet," said Dominic.

The rain softened into a fine, swirling mist and by the time they reached the spring it had fully abated, as had the wind. Zane looked up, surprised to see the stars more vivid than he had seen them in years. "Is the storm over?"

Dominic glanced up. "No. We're in the eye. We probably have ten or twenty minutes before it picks up again."

A large tree had fallen into the spring, its upturned roots reaching out of the ground like a deformed hand. The bank was littered with broken branches, shredded greenery and flower petals that had been stripped by the wind. Dominic and Zane carried The Taxman down the steep embankment and laid him in the water. He gasped. His body tensed. His lips parted and he pulled in a short breath.

Dominic leaned down and whispered something in his ear; The Taxman nodded once, glanced at Zane, and then nodded again.

"My church, she's blowin away!" The accent was unmistakable. Dominic and Zane gazed up to see the preacher looming at the top of the embankment.

"I told you to leave," said Dominic.

"I did, but then he found me," said the preacher.

"Who?"

"The horseman." The preacher's eyes jerked to the side and there, stealing out of the gloom, came Miguel on a horse. Miguel glared down at Dominic and Zane, his eyes dark and menacing and his hair as disheveled as the wind-ravaged foliage around him.

"Odd night for a swim, don't you think?" he said. He jumped off the horse and held his gun to the preacher's head.

The preacher trembled. "Please don't, sir."

"*Tranquilo, mi amigo gordo.* As long as our friends here cooperate, that little brain of yours will stay in your big fat *cabeza* where it belongs."

"What do you want?" said Dominic.

Miguel smiled. "To make a deal."

"I'll never make another deal with you. I don't want you coming here anymore."

"Oh? You'd cut me off just like that? This is *my* spring."

"The kid told me about the murders. There was to be no more killing unless it was to protect the secret. We both agreed."

"Oh, and tell me, Mr. Cowhead, how well have you been protecting the secret? Do you think I don't know about the others? How did you decide which ones should die, and which ones to spare? You pretend like you're some changed man, but deep down you're as much a killer as I am." Miguel aimed the gun at Dominic.

Dominic trembled. "Do it."

Miguel did. In the darkness Zane saw the red-hot bullet zip through the air and hit Dominic square in the chest. Dominic fell back into the spring and sank out of view. Miguel aimed the gun at Zane.

"Where did you hide my coins?" said Miguel. "Tell me, and I will let you go."

Zane had no choice. "They're on the beach. I buried them, in that sea turtle nest."

Miguel seemed to ponder it for a moment, and then he smiled. "Smart boy. Shame you have to die now."

"You said you'd let me go!"

"Did I?"

Miguel pulled the trigger. *Click.* He pulled it again. *Click.* He threw down the gun. "Guess we have to do this the old-fashioned way."

Miguel headed down the embankment. Zane stepped backward. "You don't have to."

"Oh, but I do." Miguel grabbed Zane by the neck and thrust his face into the water. Zane reached back and tried to pull Miguel's hand off his neck, but Miguel was too strong. In his panic, Zane inhaled water, coughed, and inhaled again. Numbness spread through his body and there came a harsh buzzing in his ears, as if his head was infested with cicadas. But he also felt a surprising peace and clarity.

How ironic, he thought. I'm going to drown in the fountain of youth.

But then Miguel's hand suddenly released him.

Zane pushed himself out of the water and crawled along the bank, gasping and coughing. He looked up. Miguel stood motionless, gazing out at a Spanish conquistador standing waist-deep in the spring, the waters around him teeming with starlight. It was Dominic, wearing an armor helmet and holding a sword, his eyes on fire.

"It is time to rid the world of your stench," said Dominic, and, with the furor of a beast, he charged Miguel. They tumbled onto the bank and rolled on the ground. Dominic lifted the sword high with one hand and aimed the tip at Miguel's head and brought it down with great force but Miguel dodged it and the sword stabbed deep into the soil. Miguel grabbed Dominic's face and squeezed it. Dominic pulled the sword out again and pressed the blade against Miguel's neck.

"What about your vow?" said Miguel.

Dominic stared into Miguel's eyes with tempestuous anger. "I will break it for you."

"Then you will lose your soul..." said Miguel. The preacher's boot smacked into Dominic's face and the helmet rolled off Dominic's head, stopping at Zane's feet. Miguel, now brandishing the sword, towered over Dominic. "...as well as your life."

Miguel thrust the blade deep into Dominic's chest. Dominic's body stiffened and arched off the ground, and then it fell limp.

"Sorry, boss," said the preacher, looking down at Dominic. "I got a better-paying job."

Miguel slapped the preacher on the back. "That you did, my plump assassin. Now, please finish our work."

The preacher pulled a switchblade out of his pocket and stepped toward Zane. In the deepest range of his voice, he said, "The Lord sent thee on the way, and said, go, and kill the sinners!"

Zane backed away. "What about thou shalt not kill?"

The preacher smiled. "Power was given to him over the earth, to kill with sword, with famine, and with death, and with the beasts of the world!"

The big man thrust his knife at Zane. Zane ducked and came up holding the conquistador helmet. He swung it at the preacher and felt the brim of it slide across the big man's neck. The preacher stood there dazed, and then he let out a little cough. Blood gurgled out of his mouth and, at the same time, out of the gaping incision on the front of his neck. His eyes rolled back and he dropped to his knees, and then he fell onto his side, and blood came surging out like a torrent.

"Oh, well," said Miguel. "I probably would have had to do that anyway. Who could afford to feed him?"

Miguel approached with the sword. Zane backed away until his shoulders pushed up against the trunk of the fallen tree. "Please, I'm young."

"So what? Does it really matter if I kill you now or you die in fifty years?" Miguel put the tip of the sword against Zane's forehead and brought it down lightly across his face until it came to his neck. "Do you know how many wars I've fought in? Name any major battle in the last few centuries and I was probably there on the front line, reveling in the chaos, basking in the bloodshed. The men I fought with and against are now dust, so I can say with certainty that your life is nothing but a spark — here today and gone tomorrow — and when I'm still fighting a few centuries from now, I won't even remember what you looked like."

A dark, robed figure appeared behind Miguel. Its arm rose up and jabbed the preacher's switchblade knife into Miguel's shoulder. Miguel screamed and spun around and slammed his fist into the hood. The figure crashed to the ground and lay motionless.

"You filthy rodent!" shouted Miguel. He reached back and pulled the knife out of his shoulder and threw it in the water, and then he turned again to Zane. With two hands he lifted the sword above his head. Zane cowered. Miguel hesitated, however, when a deep growl emanated from the edge of the bank above. Miguel slowly turned his head. He shuddered. Two yellow eyes glowed in the darkness. The panther stepped into view.

"Get outta here," said Miguel.

The panther's nostrils twitched. Its gaze fell upon Miguel's bloody shoulder wound. Zane recalled the last words Mama Ethel had said to him. *The cat's gotta eat if he smells any meat.* He looked at Miguel and said, "You're the meat."

Miguel kept his eyes locked on the panther. "What did you just say?"

"Eat, Alvar!" yelled Zane. "Eat!"

The panther sprang off the ledge. Its mouth clamped down on Miguel's shoulder and its claws ripped into his sides and together man and animal tumbled down. Miguel's screams and the panther's snarls melded into one horrible yowl until all that remained were the sounds of crunching bones and a tongue licking wet flesh.

Zane backed away and stooped beside Dominic. Dominic was still breathing, but his breaths were labored and heavy, and the wound in his chest spurted blood like a little geyser. Zane grabbed Dominic's shoulders and pulled him toward the spring.

"No," said Dominic. "No water."

Zane stopped and let go. "Why not?"

"The balance." Dominic coughed. "Here, this is yours." Dominic opened his hand, revealing Zane's doubloon necklace.

Zane reached for the doubloon but stopped. "That belongs to you," he said, and he closed Dominic's hand around it.

Dominic coughed again. "Will you hear the rest of my confession?"

"What do you mean *the rest*?"

"I told you most of it in the house." Dominic smiled, which looked like it hurt. "But there's one more thing."

"Okay."

Dominic drew a deep, raspy breath. "Time has helped me find peace with most people. And it's helped me find peace with the man upstairs. But there's one person I haven't forgiven, someone I've been at war with all my life."

"Who?"

Dominic's gaze fell toward the spring. "Myself." His hand delved into his shirt and pulled out the end of an old rosary that hung around his neck. He pinched one of the beads. "But tonight," he whispered, "I surrender," and his whisper stretched into a soft breath which was his last.

Zane sat there staring at Dominic for a long time, confused by what he saw. Was it real, or a trick of light? He tilted his head and moved closer. Sure enough, Dominic's mouth was curved up in a tranquil smile.

Movement caught Zane's eye and he turned to see the robed figure stirring on the ground. He crept over and pulled back the hood. It was the mysterious woman, her eyes closed and her lower lip bleeding.

"Mela?" he said. "Are you Mela?"

"No." She opened her eyes. "I'm Isa. Mela was my mother."

CHAPTER THIRTY SEVEN

The Taxman sat on the front porch rubbing his fingers over his healed bullet wound. He shook his head and creased his brow, his expression wavering between astonishment and fright. Zane and Isa sat nearby, side by side on the door jam, staring out at the high gray clouds moving like a glacial river across the sky—the last wisp of the hurricane.

"So," said Zane, "how old are you really?"

Isa smiled. "You're not supposed to ask a woman her age."

"Well, what about your brother?"

"Yaraha and I were adults when my mother died, and my father gave us a choice. We could stop aging, or we could go the way of nature. I chose to stay with my father. My brother, though—he was more like our mother. He never went near the spring, and one day, just after his eightieth birthday, he had a heart attack and died."

"I'm sorry."

"Don't be. That was hundreds of years ago."

The thought of being alive for so long sent fear into Zane. "What's it like to live forever?"

Isa looked into his eyes. "It's lonely." Then she gazed down. "I carry within me the last blood of the Timucuans, and my other half comes from those who decimated them. Every day I can feel them fighting inside of me. I'm their last battlefield." She looked at Zane again, this time with tears in her eyes. "That's what it's like."

273

Zane sighed. "It'll be hard for me to get used to living away from the ocean."

"It won't."

"What do you mean?"

"You don't have to stay here."

"But your dad said I was sent here, sent here to guard the spring."

"That's what he believed at first. So did I. He asked me to stay hidden until we knew for sure. But then we realized that you are too good, that you don't have the fire in your eyes." Isa smiled and touched Zane's hand. "That's not a bad thing."

"Then who will guard it? You?"

Isa shook her head. "No, not me. Now that my father is gone, I will leave soon. I want to experience a normal life. I want to die like everyone else."

"Then who?"

The Taxman stood. "Me."

Zane's face went stark with shock. "You?"

The Taxman nodded. "That's what Mr. Cowhead whispered to me down by the water. And I can't deny that this spring, whatever the hell is in it, saved my goddamn life. If this thing got out into the world… take it from someone who has seen the worst in people, it would be a very bad thing."

"What am I supposed to do?" said Zane. "I'm a fugitive."

"I can take care of that with one phone call," said The Taxman. "Kid, I have to tell you something. I didn't give a damn about catching you or bringing Miguel Orellano to justice. I wanted that gold for myself."

Zane felt a flush of anger, but he could see from the sadness on the man's face that regret had torn him up. The Taxman sat down on the porch steps and gazed at the clouds. "People died because of me." He buried his head in his hands.

....

A meld of elation and sadness whirled around in Zane as he drove Dominic's sputtering old pickup truck down the road. Isa

274

had tossed him the keys and asked him to promise that he would come back for a visit. He would think about it, he told her.

He took his foot off the accelerator as he passed *Café Risque*. He smiled when he saw Destiny's old *Buick* in the parking lot. He recalled lying on its roof and staring at the universe and missing every chance to kiss her. Maybe it just wasn't meant to be. He thought about Lucia. No one could ever replace her. He stepped on the gas pedal.

Traffic swelled as he pulled into Gainesville. He found the *Spinner* and saw his father's SUV parked in front of it. He hurried inside and searched the crowd until he saw his father sitting at a table with some woman, but his father did not see him. Skip took a sip from a glass of ice water and said something to the woman. When the woman smiled and shifted her hair, Zane's mouth dropped open. *Mom?*

Zane wasn't sure what shocked him the most—the fact that Skip and Samantha were sitting within fists' reach of each other, or that Skip was not guzzling something hard. Samantha pulled Skip's glass of ice water toward her and took a sip—out of the same glass. Zane slunk away and fled through the exit.

Shands Hospital was one of the most imposing buildings in town, and as Zane parked and looked up at it, nausea swirled in his stomach. He put his hand on the truck's door handle but hesitated. His eyes came to a plastic water bottle in the cup holder. Someone had scribbled on it with a marker. *For Zane*, it read, and then below that, *For Ever*. He stared at the bottle for a long time.

The air inside the hospital lobby felt uncomfortably cold. Zane walked up to the receptionist. "Can I get the room number of a patient?"

"Certainly," said the receptionist. "Why do you look familiar?"

"I've been here before."

"Thought so. What's the patient's name?"

"Leather Heath—" Zane blushed. "Sorry, I mean Heather Reynolds."

The receptionist typed, paused, and nodded. "Heather Reynolds. Hospice. Room 413."

Zane tapped the floor of the elevator with his foot as it carried him to the fourth floor. He found room 413 and peaked through the open door. Leather Heather, gaunt and gray without her wig, lay in a hospital bed watching *Jeopardy* on the television.

"Who is George Thorogood?" she said, her voice a frail hiss.

"Who is Bruce Springsteen?" said a *Jeopardy* contestant.

"Oh, sorry," said Alex Trebek. "The correct answer—who is George Thorogood."

"Dumbass," said Leather Heather.

Zane smiled. She hadn't changed a bit.

"Excuse me," said a voice. Zane spun around to see a female orderly pushing a food cart.

"It's time for Ms. Reynolds' dinner," said the orderly.

"Can I bring it to her?" asked Zane. "I'm visiting."

"Fine by me. I think you're the first visitor she's ever had."

The orderly handed him a covered tray and continued down the hallway. Zane watched her go, and then he set the tray on the ground, uncovered it, and pulled the water bottle out of his pocket. He poured a few ounces into the mashed potatoes and stirred them, and then he drank half the milk and filled the glass back up with spring water.

"Dinnertime!" he said as he strode into Leather Heather's room.

Without taking her eyes off the TV, Heather pointed at her bedside table. "It's about time," she said.

Zane nodded. "You're right. It is."

He pushed away a cluster of pill bottles to make room for the food tray, and one of the bottles tipped over. *OxyContin*, it read. He looked at it for a long time, and then he put the tray down.

"Be sure to drink your milk," he said.

"Who are you, my mommy?" she said, still not looking at him. "What is infinity?"

"Sorry?"

"What is infinity is correct," said Alex Trebek. "That puts you in the lead."

Zane smiled and crept out of the room. He looked back one last time and watched Heather sip the milk. "Good girl."

Zane took the stairs to the fifth floor. His breathing quickened as he walked down the familiar hallway, and when he heard the awful mechanical sound of the breathing machine, his heart battered against his chest and his palms went clammy. Suddenly it came into view — Room 519. He put his hand on the doorknob and turned it. Taking a deep breath, he walked inside.

No matter how many times he had gone inside that room, he always lost his breath when he saw his love reposed like a sleeping princess in her dungeon full of monitors and medical equipment. A clear tube protruded from Lucia's mouth and her chest swelled with each *phumph* of the ventilator. Her hair looked like it had been recently brushed, and a bouquet of fresh lilies sat in a vase beside the bed. Their fragrance was intense and nauseating — Lucia's mother always brought lilies when she visited the hospital.

Zane touched Lucia's face. "It's me, Lu. Zane."

She gave no reaction, but he was not expecting one. In the years since she had gone into the coma, he had never even seen her flinch. He always hoped, however, that she could hear him — that his words somehow infiltrated whatever dark emptiness she had fallen into.

"I miss you so much," said Zane. His eyes welled with tears. "Forgive me." He grabbed hold of the breathing tube and ripped it out of her mouth. An alarm blared from one of the monitors. Lucia's chest sank like a deflating balloon.

A burly male nurse burst into the room and glared at Zane. "What are you doing?"

Zane held the water bottle to Lucia's mouth. "It's okay." He tipped the bottle and sent the water cascading down her throat. The nurse lunged forward and batted the bottle out of Zane's hand.

"You'll kill her!" said the nurse. He pulled Zane away and together they crashed into the monitors and apparatuses, sending all of them — including the breathing machine — crashing to the floor. Pieces scattered everywhere.

A white-haired doctor and the female orderly ran into the room. The orderly attended to the breathing machine, frantically trying to reassemble it, while the doctor checked Lucia's pulse. He looked at Zane and yelled, "Who the hell are you?"

"Please talk nice," said Lucia.

Everyone looked toward the voice. The doctor's jaw quivered. "Lucia?"

The orderly dropped part of the breathing machine, but no one turned to investigate the crash. The nurse, focused on the miracle, released his grip on Zane.

"Why's everyone staring at me?" said Lucia, her eyes dreary, as if just waking from a nap. "What's going on?"

Zane approached her. "You were in a coma."

"How?"

"Because of me."

She paused for a moment, and then something clicked. She took his hand in hers. "How long was I out?"

"Five years."

"*Five years?*" Her eyebrows furrowed into that cute, serious look she always got when something puzzled her. "That's a long time."

"I know," said Zane.

"I think I dreamt about you."

"Good dreams or bad?"

"Good."

Zane squeezed her hand. "Lu, I know you just woke up, but I have to ask you a question."

"Okay."

"There's something I want us to do together in a few months."

"What is it?"

"Have you ever seen baby sea turtles hatch?"

Lucia smiled. "No, never in my life."

ABOUT THE AUTHOR

Sean Bloomfield is a third-generation Floridian and former fishing guide. He grew up on Florida's Space Coast and studied creative writing and filmmaking at *The University of Tampa*. His prose and films have won numerous awards. Working as a documentary filmmaker has helped him travel the world, and Sean has spent a substantial part of his life in such distant places as Bosnia-Herzegovina, New Zealand, Fiji, Brazil, Costa Rica, Croatia and Rwanda. Now living back in his native Florida, Sean loves the ocean and spends most of his free time either on or below the water.

CRAVING MORE?

V isit **www.seanbloomfield.com** to connect with the author, discuss the book, order more copies, and learn about the secrets and symbolism in *The Sound of Many Waters*. Was the novel based on fact? Will there be a sequel? Come and find out. Plus, answer three questions about the book for a chance to win a real Spanish treasure coin that was found in a shipwreck off the coast of Florida.

Made in the USA
Columbia, SC
21 December 2019